Julia Drum has worked in theatre, broadcasting and management training. More recently, she has coached and supervised other coaches, supporting people in the public sector, as well as in private organisations. She is married and has a son and daughter and three grandchildren. This is her first novel.

To my family, both nuclear and extended

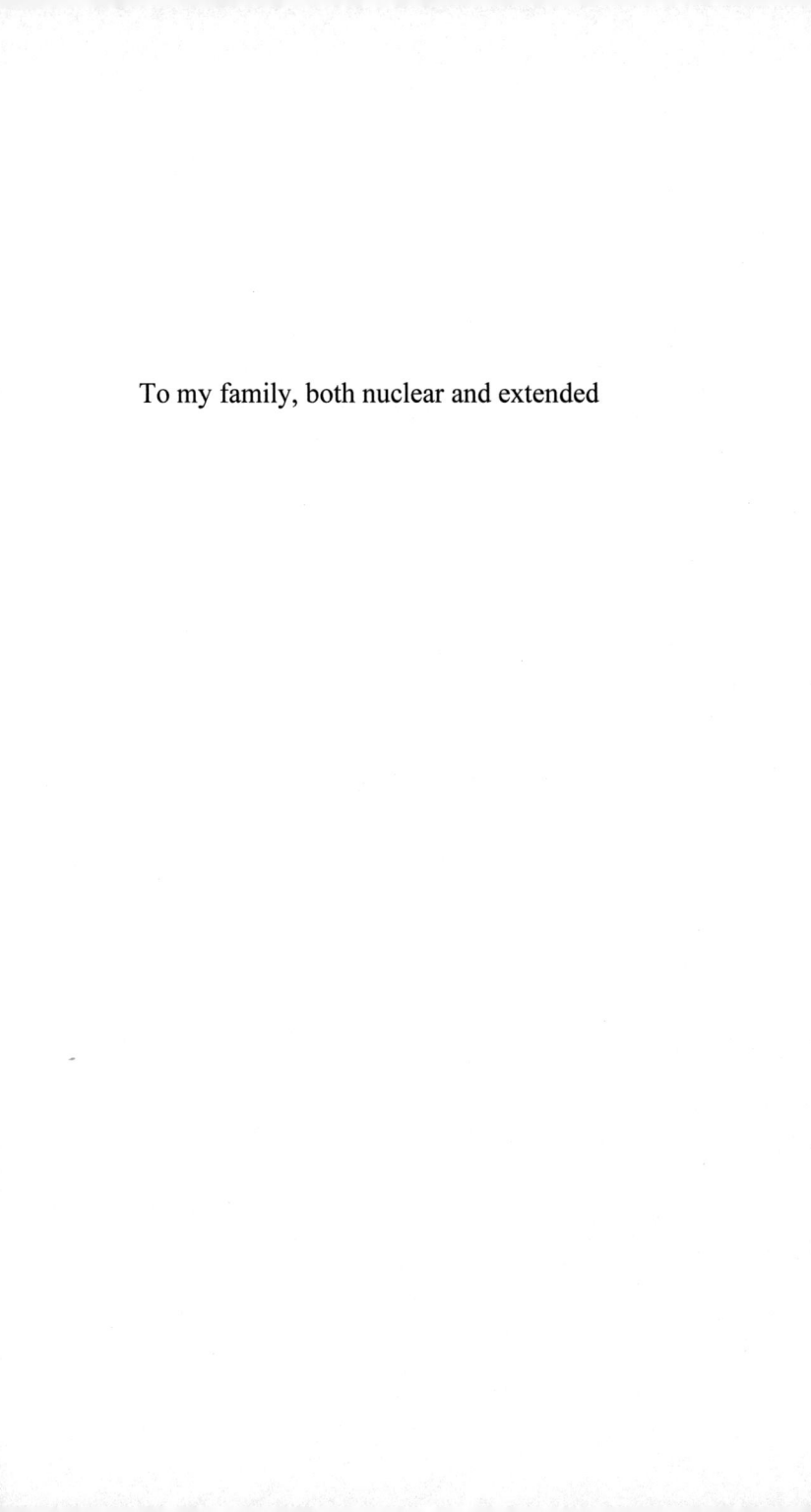

Julia Drum

SPRINGWELL

AUSTIN MACAULEY PUBLISHERS™
LONDON · CAMBRIDGE · NEW YORK · SHARJAH

Copyright © Julia Drum (2019)

The right of Julia Drum to be identified as author of this work has been asserted by her in accordance with section 77 and 78 of the Copyright, Designs and Patents Act 1988.

All rights reserved. No part of this publication may be reproduced, stored in a retrieval system, or transmitted in any form or by any means, electronic, mechanical, photocopying, recording, or otherwise, without the prior permission of the publishers.

Any person who commits any unauthorised act in relation to this publication may be liable to criminal prosecution and civil claims for damages.

A CIP catalogue record for this title is available from the British Library.

ISBN 9781788788595 (Paperback)
ISBN 9781788788601 (E-Book)

www.austinmacauley.com

First Published (2019)
Austin Macauley Publishers Ltd
25 Canada Square
Canary Wharf
London
E14 5LQ

Many thanks are due to friends and relatives who unwittingly inspired or shared information leading to the people, places and situations in this work of fiction.

Special thanks go to Sally Cakebread, Jacky Hyams and other friends who chivvied me 'to get on with it' and demonstrated their faith in my ability as a storyteller.

Thanks, too, to the addictive effect of sports shown on television, which gave me the time to write while my husband and son were engrossed in watching Formula One, athletics, football and rugby.

I also appreciated the praise and insightful comments from Hilary Johnson and colleagues when I submitted an early draft. Their suggestions about structure and reducing the number of characters stimulated a major rethink.

Thank you especially to the team at Austin Macauley, who, apart from adapting my book to their publishing style, left the story unaltered.

Part 1

Chapter 1

Today is the day my lover died. I will never know whether he still recognised me. We lived, together yet apart, in an elegant house built in the late 18th century amidst 34 acres of land, Springwell. One day, an unexpected visitor arrived to be with him in his last hours. I can, at last, share my story with someone who will understand and for whom it may be important.

As we sit here in the grounds, let me tell you about my birth and early life.

My name is Christine Rose Preece. My parents had lived on the first floor of a shared house in Tooting, South West London. My father, Alfie, had been killed on active service in 1943. He had been on a week's leave during February that year and only reluctantly returned to his regiment in Chatham, where he'd been trained as a welder. From there, he and his fellow Military Engineers travelled to France to help assemble bridges replacing those blown up by the Germans. He and my mother had spent those precious passionate few days making up for lost time during their war-induced separation, and in the process created a baby.

The other occupants of the house were Mrs Aldrich and her husband. They lived on the ground floor and grew vegetables in the rear garden. Lately, they had acquired a few chickens who provided us all with the occasional egg, supplementing our meagre rations. Mrs Aldrich had also started growing flowers over the Anderson shelter at the end of the garden. Mr William Aldrich, known by everyone as Billy, was acting as a Fire Warden for the offices at the end of our street. Being too old for active service he had volunteered to sit on roof tops at night sharing a tin helmet with two other wardens, (resisting the temptation to smoke his Woodbines) in order to give warning of any fires from bomb strikes or watching out for other unusual happenings in the surrounding area. He had often spotted looters rummaging through bombed homes and had identified some of them to the police.

Suddenly, the siren! Another air raid. The ascending moan crescendoed until it found its sustained note. It was November, Rose Preece had been having contractions for several hours. She was standing in the kitchen, holding onto the cooker during a painful contraction. A kettle was starting to boil on the back burner. The siren continued. She squatted down.

"Come on Mrs P; get into the shelter," Billy called up the stairs as he grabbed his tin hat and gas mask on his way to his roof top shift.

All he heard in reply was a scream, followed by another.

"I've got to get the others," Billy said to his wife. "Go and bring her down."

"I think she must have started," said Mrs Aldrich above the urgent sound of the siren.

"Go and get her!"

"If you see the midwife, tell her to come quickly."

"If I see her."

Mrs Aldrich ran upstairs as fast as her thick legs could manage, and was just in time to see my mother start pushing me out.

"You're doing well, keep pushing, the midwife will be here soon."

She turned off the boiling kettle, and squatted down and saw the crown of a hair-covered head starting to emerge.

"I can't, I can't."

"Yes, you can, you're nearly there; a couple more pushes and…"

A pause while primeval noises emerged from my mother's mouth and Mrs Aldrich led the baby's slippery body onto the floor between Rose's legs.

"It's fine, well done, it's a girl."

Hoisting herself up heavily, Mrs Aldrich found a pair of scissors, poured some hot water from the kettle on them over the nearby sink, and cut the cord.

She quickly wrapped the baby in a drying up towel.

"Get up, get up, we've got to get to the shelter."

"I can't, I just can't."

"Give yourself a minute, and we'll get you there."

"Take the baby, take the baby," screamed my mother as nearby explosions shook the house. "Take her, take her."

Mrs Aldrich ran with the baby and reached the Anderson shelter. She could hardly make herself heard above the noise of bombs exploding nearby.

"Is the midwife here?" she shouted. "It's Mrs P from upstairs."

"Oh my Lord," said a woman sitting with her 3-year-old son in the shelter. "Give it to me," and she took the baby, and started sobbing. "You go and get Rose."

Mrs Aldrich ran back to find Mrs P in the hall delivering the placenta.

"Come on, come on; no time for that," and tried to pull her towards the door. The bleeding was heavy and the new mother fainted. Mrs Aldrich ran out to get help and just then the house was hit.

Mrs Aldrich staggered to her feet, dizzy, covered in dust and blood, but alive.

There was no sign of Rose under the rubble in the hallway.

Chapter 2

I grew up knowing that Mrs Aldrich had saved my life. She became a surrogate grandmother when I was taken to live with my Auntie Vi. Violet Walker was 18 years old. She worked as a Nippy at Lyons Corner House in the Strand. She'd had ambitions to be a dancer, and had trained at a local Ballet School on Saturdays until the war intervened. Her elegance and beautiful deportment had got her the job. The Nippies had a reputation to maintain and her supervisor there had hopes that Violet would work her way up to manage one of the floors. My mother, Rose Walker, was 5 years older than Violet and had trained as a seamstress, taking after her mother and helping her with alterations for Oxford Street stores and occasional dressmaking for women in Tooting. When she married her childhood sweetheart, Alfred Preece, she had been 18 and expecting a child. Sadly, Rose miscarried a month after the wedding, and then Alfie had been called up.

Violet greeted the baby's arrival with a confusing mixture of emotions. She'd lost her beloved sister and she knew little about looking after a baby. She loved her job, particularly the glamorous soldiers and airmen who frequented the Corner House when they were on leave. She had hopes that one of them might turn out to be Mr Right. But Mrs Aldrich's arrival when the All Clear sounded would put a stop to that.

"Look," said Mrs Aldrich, "I know it's not ideal, but you are her family."

"But when she's screaming, what do I do? I don't even know how to change a nappy."

"I've made some arrangements; I hope you won't mind, but in the shelter there was a woman whose baby was stillborn 2 weeks ago. She still has milk. I've asked her if she could feed the baby, and she did while we were in there waiting for the All Clear."

"Then give her to her."

"No, it's not right. She must be with her family."

"Have you told our mum?"

"Not yet."

"She'll be back shortly. She was collecting some alterations from a place near Oxford Street. How am I going to tell her about Rose? She adored her."

"Well, I'm sure she'll adore the baby too."

Mrs Walker ran in.

"I heard about the bombing. Is Rosie alright? I can't get anyone to tell me."

Mrs Aldrich told Violet to put the kettle on.

"We don't think so. She was in the hall when the bomb struck; they're trying to get at her now."

"Her baby's due next week. I was so looking forward to being a grandmother."

"You are a grandmother!"

Gwen burst into tears.

"Oh my Christ! Oh my Christ! I'm sorry to swear, but oh my Christ! And where's the baby; what was it? Is it alright? Where did it go?"

"It was a girl. I don't know what it weighed but it was born around the time the siren went off. I was with her."

"Oh poor Rosie, first her miscarriage, then her husband, now this!" She sat down, sobbing. Violet brought a tray with cups of tea.

"Sorry we don't have any biscuits."

"Biscuits, biscuits! How can you think about biscuits at a time like this!"

Violet sat down with her mother, both of them sobbing and hugging each other.

Mrs Aldrich told Gwen about the woman in the shelter and when they had calmed down slightly, she led them across the other side of the Rec to where Rose had lived.

In the developing darkness they had to navigate some deep shell holes, broken glass and timber and pass by some smoking ruins. Then they saw the house. They clung to each other in horror.

As they arrived, Billy and some other wardens were clearing the rubble.

"Found her, found her," Billy shouted. The others came over, and neighbours rushed to help where they could. First a hand appeared, then a body. Rose's head was partially smashed, her clothes dishevelled and bloody. They pulled her out, and someone took off his coat and covered her. The men all removed their hats and a shocked silence descended.

Mrs Walker fell to the ground, Violet's arms around her.

"Mrs Walker, Mrs Walker!" a young woman's voice called. "Here's the baby, your granddaughter," and she showed my grandmother the bundle still wrapped in a tea towel but with a baby's blanket over the top.

"I can't bear it; my Rosie gone."

"Give her to me," said Violet, taking the baby and looking slightly horrified at the pink creature still covered in a slimy substance from the birth.

"She needs to be cuddled and fed again."

"I can't do that," retorted Violet.

"If it's alright, I can. What do you want me to do?"

"We can't think about that now. It's such a shock – my sister gone."

A WVS woman, in a green uniform, who had been handing out hot teas to the people clearing the rubble came over with three mugs of tea.

"Look, why not let this lady look after the baby until you sort yourselves out. She's got a little boy so she knows what to do. She lives local so you can see the baby when you want to. That'll give you time. Anyway, the Council will want to know what's to be done with her, and…"

"Yes," said Violet, "That'll give us time."

And so it was that I was looked after by Mrs Jennings as a wet-nurse for 5 months with daily visits from either my aunt or grandma. Little Toby loved the baby, but Mr Jennings wasn't too keen on the arrangement, although he agreed for his wife's sake if it helped her get over the loss of their little girl. However, when Ivy Jennings became pregnant again, he insisted that the baby, now named Christine Rose went back to her real family.

The Council had approved the arrangement and Christine Rose was formally adopted jointly by her Aunt Violet and maternal grandmother. This arrangement was unusual but members of the Adoption Committee knew that Mrs Walker was 'getting on a bit', and as one of the officials had put it, "A bit forgetful," and that Aunt Violet would be doing most of the caring.

Mrs Aldrich later told me that I was named Christine, because everyone was thanking Christ that I had survived, and Rose after my mother.

***

Grandma Walker continued doing alterations for some of the big stores in Oxford Street, which was a feast or famine occupation relying on the fluctuating demands of war-time shoppers and the increasing need for make do and mend when fabrics became scarce. However, good as her skills were, she started to forget some of her clients' instructions, and by 1950 had had a stroke and was confined to a ward in the local Tooting Hospital. She died 3 years later. We visited her each weekend, but she ceased to recognise my aunt, calling for Rose every time we visited, so eventually I went alone.

"Hello, Rose, my dear," she would say.

At such a young age I didn't like to contradict her, but I used to say, under my breath, "I'm your Chrissie, not Rose."

Violet had given up her job as a Nippy. She told me later that she felt cheated and resentful at first, but when she took me there occasionally for a meal and we had to go through a new self-service system, she said she was quite relieved really, as she would have hated to just stand behind a counter adding up what people had bought.

My playmates were Toby Jennings, who I treated almost like a brother, and his baby brother, John, who was born in 1944, again during an air-raid, but in a hospital that was untouched by the bombing.

On my late father's side of the family was Grandad Preece. His wife, Marjorie, had died a few years after their only son, my father, had been killed.

"She just wasted away; nothing dramatic. Woke up one morning, made a cup of tea; took it up to her. Opened the curtains. Thought she was asleep, but no. Dead. Couldn't live without the boy. Hoped your arrival would help her, but…nothing could help."

They'd retired to Eastbourne just before the war.

"Not moving out just because of some Jerries," he had told his friends. He had refused to move from his flat in Marine Parade, even when the town was decimated by bombs.

Auntie Vi and I, and occasionally the Jennings boys, spent some time there each summer. The downside was that the experience was rather smelly, Grandad tended to wear the same clothes day after day, and the fishing boats disgorged their catch nearly opposite, so when the weather was hot, the smell caught in our throats. But he and Auntie Vi just about tolerated each other.

"She's a prickly one, that Vi. Sharp nose, sharp tongue! Not like Rose. Gentleness itself. They were so in love, her and Alfie. Such a short time together." He would shake his head sadly, go into the living room and take down their wedding photo and gaze at it for ages.

However, he enjoyed having the boys there. He missed his only son, and it gave him an opportunity to relive the stories he'd told Alfie, and to play some of the games that boys of that age liked. He even rowed us out in a little boat so we could try to catch fish ourselves.

However, the best part of our holidays were Uncle Bertie's shows every morning at the bandstand where Auntie Vi used to leave us while she went to do the shopping taking all our ration books.

"Come on up," called out Uncle Bertie. "Time for our talent show."

"Go on, Chrissie," said Toby pulling me out of my chair.

"Only if you go too," I said, my stomach suddenly churning.

"What can I do?" replied Toby.

"Sing one of those songs, you know, one of those marching songs Dad sings," said John.

"OK, if Chrissie comes too."

"What am I going to do?"

"One of your funny little dances," said Toby.

So we climbed the steps to the stage and stood in a queue of other children.

When it came to my turn, I swallowed hard and breathed deeply, walked to the centre of the stage and started dancing a hornpipe that Auntie Vi had taught me. The pianist quickly picked out a nautical tune to accompany me and I felt a smile working its way across my face. The audience applauded. I turned and bowed feeling emboldened by their appreciation.

"Any more where that came from," said Uncle Bertie who had come to stand beside me.

"A butterfly dance," I whispered.

"And now for a butterfly dance," Uncle Bertie declaimed. A pause. At last the pianist found some suitable music and I danced around the stage flapping my arms as if I had wings and occasionally stopping as if I had landed on a flower. I gave a deep curtsey and the pianist played a final chord. Again, applause. I was getting to enjoy this. Uncle Bertie thanked me and turned to ask Toby his name.

"I present Mr Toby, who is going to sing for us." Toby had already told the pianist what he would sing, so she played a military introduction and Toby sang *It's a Long Way to Tipperary* in his treble voice. John marched up and down the stage in time to the music, and at the end they both bowed and smiled as they received their applause.

After the talent competition (a ginger haired girl who could dance on pointes won and received an I-Spy book about the seashore from a man dressed up as a Red Indian), Uncle Bertie did a magic show. Then a Punch and Judy stand was brought forward and we mimicked the Professor's voice as Punch set about his cruelty. We shouted, "Don't hit the baby," as if we too had swazzles in our mouths, and, "It's behind you," when the crocodile came creeping up. There was often a concert at the bandstand too, where the older folk used to listen to the band or a concert pianist, and conduct discreetly with their hands. All along the Promenade were carpets of flowers. Grandad Preece knew the names of them all: African marigolds, red and white geraniums, and petunias, which gave rise to us all singing: "*I'm a Lonely Little Petun*ia in an onion patch," as we walked along the Prom. How we relished the fresh air! After all the smog that shrouded London and caused us to cough up horrid yellowy-black phlegm and blow unmentionable nastiness into our cotton hankies, we had fresh air and sea-breezes, as well as the whooshing sound of shingle being churned up by the waves. We loved watching the elegant people going in and out of the Grand Hotel, and sometimes the boys and I used to go out on light summer nights to see them arriving in their evening dress to go dancing.

We had trips out to Beachy Head: "Don't you dare go near the edge you lot," shouted Grandad as we ran about and tested who was the bravest by standing as close as we could without slipping down onto the jagged rocks and the sea below.

At bedtime when the boys shared a put-u-up and I lay top to toe with Auntie Vi in a single bed, we told each other ghost stories inspired by the scary sound of Moaning Minnie, the light boat.

Chapter 3

One morning Grandad returned from making a phone call from the box at the end of Marine Parade.

"Fancy coming for a trip to the countryside?" he said as we were finishing off our breakfast.

"Where? Where to?" we all shouted, apart from Auntie Vi who stopped doing the washing up, and turned to Grandad.

"Can you manage without me? I've got lots to do."

"No problem. We'll hop on a bus and be back in time for tea. Do you want our ration books?"

"No, we've got enough for tonight, and anyway I need a bit of time to myself. I'll whip up some sandwiches."

So off we went, Toby, John and me, giving Grandad a hard time catching up with us.

It was a glorious day, hardly a breeze wafting in from the sea, and it gradually got hotter as we went inland on the Green Southdown bus. Luckily it wasn't too crowded so our singing of *One Man Went to Mow* didn't disturb the other passengers. In fact a couple of them joined in.

We arrived at a little village and bought some pop from the local shop. Then we walked jauntily along country lanes, picking a few early blackberries as we went and in the process smearing the juice on our faces as we ate the bitter fruit.

"Now, now, you lot. Look smart; we're going to see the man I batted for, so tidy up."

"Grandad, did you play cricket?" I asked, suddenly finding myself blushing when Toby kicked me and said, "Don't be silly. He was a batman, weren't you Mr Preece?"

"Ah, the Great War. The one that was going to end all wars. What a bloody business that was."

"Grandad, you swore!" My shock at this language brought me back to myself.

"No, sweetheart, I mean it was bloody, like blood. But enough of that. I'm going to have a long chinwag while you play in the garden and have your picnic."

After what felt like ages we turned a corner and walked up a track finally coming to a set of tall grey stone pillars with large globes on top. One of the pillars declared "Springwell" in lichen smudged writing. Then, just inside what should have been wrought-iron gates, but were now military-looking barriers, was a sentry-box. Grandad stated his business and the barrier was raised. Toby took the opportunity to ask if he could lower it.

"Let me, let me," said John.

"You're not big enough," said Toby, but the guard let them both have a go.

"Quick march, you lot!" said Grandad. So we marched briskly along the long tree-lined drive.

"Wow!" we all gasped as the most beautiful house I'd ever seen came into view. Grandad went up some stone steps and disappeared inside, while we were sent off to play in the back garden. Only it wasn't just a garden; it was a huge expanse of lawn sloping down from a pair of curved stone staircases. At the bottom of the slope were trees, and to the right was a lake glinting in the sunshine. We ran the fastest we could and collapsed by the lake.

What a welcome it was to take off our shoes and sandals and to wriggle our toes in the cool, silky water. After watching the dragonflies and trying to catch little frogs that hopped from one water lily pad to another, Toby started looking for something.

"What's going on?" I asked.

"Trying to find something; jam jar or something. See if we can get some minnows or even frogs."

"Well, I'm going for a tinkle." And off I went in search of a nearby bush where I could squat down unobserved. I'd just pulled up my pants, almost catching my sash in the elastic, when,

"Hello, there," called a voice from behind one of the trees sheltering the lake.

A soldier in khaki uniform emerged.

"What are you up to then?" he said in a posh voice.

"Just visiting with Grandad," I said, emerging fully dressed from my makeshift loo.

"Is he a soldier?"

"He fought in the Great War. He's a batman," piped up Toby. "He's gone to see an officer he served with."

"Well, well, well."

"Who lives here?" I asked.

"We come here for training. It's like a college, or school. You go to school, I should think, so it's a bit like that. We've got a talk about the First World War now. Look!"

He pointed to the slope leading up to the great house. There were at least twenty soldiers walking and running up to the mansion, and more in the distance looking like beetles scurrying towards some tasty morsel.

"Off I go too. Bye!" And off he went.

Soon the grassy hill was empty.

"Let's see what's going on," said Toby. "I'm a commando, so creep with me."

We followed at a distance and crawled up the slope; then we ducked down as we climbed the steps. We crept nearer, and peered through one of the huge windows and saw soldiers sitting on fold-up chairs all looking towards a large military gentleman with a big moustache. He was pointing a long stick at various places on a huge map stuck to a sort of easel. Then Grandad stood up and said something. The next thing we knew he'd spotted us and was waving his arms, and some of the soldiers turned to the window. We fled, almost tripping over each other as we leapt down the steps and ran back to the lake.

"So much for being invisible commandos," I said, as we all giggled and fell about laughing as we put on our sandals and found a bench where we ate our sandwiches and drank our Cherryade.

After using the empty bottle unsuccessfully to catch the little creatures in the water and playing hide and seek around the lake, we saw all the soldiers coming out, lighting up cigarettes and smoking pipes, and leaning against the stone ballustrades. So we started to make our way back to the steps.

"You rascals," laughed Grandad Preece as he emerged with the moustachioed military gentleman.

"We were being commandos," said John.

"Not very successfully, I noticed."

"Have you had a good time?" asked the gentleman.

"You're a brigadier, aren't you?" spotted Toby who had learned about the different insignia from Grandad and had spotted the crown and three pips. I scrunched up my toes and ran the insole of my sandal up my left shin, ostensibly scratching a midge bite, but in fact reflecting my jealousy. How come Toby knew so much more about military things than me; it always made me feel small and left out of conversations.

"Yes, well done lad," the brigadier beamed at Toby. Then he turned to Grandad, "Thank you for taking part. Your view-point was valuable, and they enjoyed and learned from it."

"Well, thank you for inviting me, sir. It was a privilege." He saluted, and off we all went.

However, on the return bus Grandad was quiet. He looked deep in thought, and when we started to sing again, said quietly, "Not now, not now."

By the time we reached Marine Parade, the burning smell of a hot summer's day had disappeared and instead dark clouds had formed and seemed to be pressing down on our heads.

"There's going to be a storm soon," Auntie Vi said. "Make sure you stay inside."

And sure enough we heard thunder rumbling in the distance as we changed into our slippers and Auntie Vi ordered us off to bed.

"What, no supper?" Grandad asked with surprise.

"No time to make any, what with the washing and tidying up after you lot."

"Right, my little commandos. Fish and chips."

"Let me come!"

"And me!"

"And me!" we shouted.

We threw ourselves at him, and with a sly look at Auntie Vi he pleaded, "Come on, Vi; they've been really good keeping themselves out of the way today. It must have been boring for them waiting for me."

"Please, please, please," we squealed in unison.

"Alright, as it's our last evening here. But mind you get back before the storm."

"Tomorrow! I didn't know we were going so soon. Why can't we stay longer?" I queried. "It's not fair."

"Now, now. Auntie Vi has to get back to work." He turned away from us, but we heard him say, "But you could have waited till the weekend, Vi, couldn't you?"

"Out you go. Get those blooming fish and chips and don't get wet, I've enough to do without dirt and wet clothes messing up the place."

So we put our sandals on again while Grandad got some money out of a metal box on the kitchen mantelpiece, and we half ran and half skipped along a narrow twitten into a back street to the nearest fish and chip shop as the thunder grew closer.

As we came out of the steamy shop, the heavens opened.

"Auntie Vi won't like this!" I said.

We covered our heads with the newspaper-wrapped parcels of fish and chips.

Lightning lit up the buildings leading down to the sea. Then an almighty *CRASH* as the thunder blasted, even before we'd had time to count how far or near it would be.

"Run as fast as you can," shouted Grandad as he padded along behind us carrying John.

"She won't like this," he muttered under his breath, "sharp nose, sharp tongue."

Sure enough she didn't. I don't think I'd ever heard a woman swear before. Even Grandad was shocked.

"Not in front of the children, Vi. You weren't brought up in the gutter, was you?"

I helped to wipe over the floor; anything to make peace, and even Toby fetched towels so we could dry our hair. We ate our fish and chips in silence dressed in our pyjamas.

The following day we took the train back to London, leaving Grandad to his memories.

Chapter 4

One morning in April, I forget which year, Auntie Vi and I had just had our breakfast in the sunny kitchen of Grandma Walker's house. It was a Sunday. We had our traditional egg and bacon, and Auntie Vi and I had our usual argument about going to Church. Since Grandma had gone into hospital, we seemed to row more and more, especially when she pulled my hair painfully tight as she was plaiting my mousy coloured hair.

"You're hurting! Stop it!"

"You ungrateful little…" and she'd give me a slap round my ear.

"I can't bear Sundays. You're always so cross and it's so boring," I moaned. "Can't play out, no shops open, can't do anything. Boring, boring, boring!"

"Well, it's the only entertainment you'll get today, that's for sure. Go and put your coat on. And yes, we are going to Church."

I went upstairs moaning to the cat about how I always had to do what I was told, when suddenly there was an almighty rumble, followed by a crashing sound. I ran downstairs to see what had happened. Auntie Vi was covered in dust. The kitchen ceiling had collapsed. She wasn't hurt, just rooted to the spot in amazement.

"Come on, come on, Auntie, Vi. Get out of the house."

I must have been 7 or 8, but took charge automatically.

I sat Auntie Vi on the front garden wall and ran next door with Tabby tucked under my arm. The neighbours had heard the crash and were already on their way to see what had happened.

"Bomb damage. Obviously. Come inside and have a cuppa. What a shock for you both!"

I took Auntie Vi into their kitchen. Their house was detached so wasn't affected by the collapse of ours, but even so they were anxious whether theirs might be structurally unsound too. Mr

Turner, I think his name was, went to the phone box to call someone and within 10 minutes a fire engine had arrived. They checked it was safe for us to go back in, and suggested we collect some things and that we stay elsewhere until the surveyors could assess the damage.

We went to Granny Aldrich's old house, which had been superficially renovated since the bombing when I was born. She made up beds for us in the living room, as there was another family living upstairs.

So much for my boring Sunday.

When I went to school the next day, I was the centre of attention.

"'Chrissie-no-mum', how exciting. Was there a bomb? Did you get hurt? Where are you living? Was your cat alright?"

"Yes, the cat's alright. I took it to Granny's with me. I don't think her cat's very pleased."

"She's not your real granny, is she?" asked a girl called Margaret who we called Maggie.

"No, but she's old. I can't call her Mrs Aldrich for ever."

Toby 'Jug' came over with his brother. "Wow! I wish our house would fall down then we could go into a prefab with an indoor lavvy."

I hadn't thought of that. Prefabs were exciting. All mod cons and some of them had little gardens. I knew Granny Aldrich was waiting for one as her house was due for redevelopment.

We went into our classrooms and I tried to concentrate on my lessons, even though I was distracted by the excitement of the previous day.

We all had nicknames then. I suppose 'Granny' was a nickname for Mrs Aldrich. Toby was 'Jug' or 'Juggins' after the ornaments many of our families had on the mantelpiece. Some names were cruel, but said casually, like mine. There were other children who had descriptive nicknames, such as 'Johnny-no-dad' who had lost his father in the war, and 'Pattie Pickle' who couldn't tie her shoe-laces properly and kept tripping over them. Others were just shortenings of their names, such as Maggie, Angie, Pete, Wally and Joe.

The only time I felt uncomfortable about my nickname was on November 11th.

I don't remember being told about my mother, but she was a presence at home. Auntie Vi had a picture of her and my dad on their wedding day, as did Grandad Preece. I had a picture of her too, but she was rarely spoken of. Too painful. However, at school a teacher might accidentally say, "Give this note to your mother. Oh, I'm sorry, to your aunt." But this kind of slip-up happened to several children. "I'll tell your dad what you've been up to!" for example.

"But I don't have a dad," a child would reply, sometimes quite defiantly, if they'd been particularly naughty.

On each November 11th morning on school days there was a special assembly. The whole school had to keep the two minute silence at eleven o'clock.

All the children who had lost someone in the war had to sit near the front. Some of the older ones actually remembered their fathers, and it was usually fathers, who had been killed, and their sobbing was uncontrollable. I cried too, caught up in the general sadness of the occasion. When the rest of the school had filed out, we, the bereaved, were given a short homily on how the brave heroes and heroines had died for their country and we must be proud of their sacrifice. Then we were led back to our classrooms.

In those days nearly everyone would observe the two minute silence: buses stopped, men in the street took off their hats. The country would come to a stand-still.

***

A year or so later, Auntie Vi, Granny Aldrich and the Jennings family were rehoused. It was an exciting time. For the first time Toby and John had an inside bathroom and a separate toilet. They lived next door to us. Granny Aldrich was our neighbour too and delighted in having a smart kitchen and a place of her own.

"I wish my Billy was still with us. He would have loved this. Still, the heart attack. Shock for me, but quick for him."

Each Prefab had two bedrooms and a living room. The floors were a uniform brown, some plastic-like substance that had been poured onto the concrete floor. In the summer we were sometimes too hot, and in the winter, too cold. However, the luxury of having homes of our own made up for the inconvenience. We were near Tooting Bec Common so Toby, John and I spent many hours playing in the fields, but our main playgrounds were still the scarred remains of shops, offices and houses.

"Get a jam jar, we're going fishing," called out Toby one morning after a night of heavy rain. We ran to the nearest bomb site and sat at the edge of a crater dangling our lengths of string into the water, or dipping our jam jars into the oily water and scooping up debris, and sometimes a small water creature.

"Got one," John shouted.

"Let's see, let's see."

"It's a water boatman," identified Toby. "Brilliant. Let's take it home."

Most of the craters contained a mixture of pieces of wire, concrete, glass, sections of mosaic from dairies and shops, scraps of clothing, cardboard and cigarette packets. One day we'd been 'exploring' and came across a bomb site with rosebay willow herb growing profusely. "Let's collect some to take home for salad," I said. So we started picking at the stalks and leaves. The boys got bored so they wandered off to the centre of the site.

"Come on, Chrissie," they called. "Look what we've got." They had found a large piece of metal sticking out of the ground. I went over and saw what I thought was a giant fish with flippers.

Suddenly Toby shouted, "Get away, get the police. It's a bomb!"

John and I rushed across the twisted metal and broken bits of concrete and out of the site to find someone. John spotted a policeman on his bike a few streets away and ran, shouting. He leapt into the middle of the road to stop him.

"Woah, young man, you nearly knocked me of my bike."

"Sir, sir, we've found a bomb."

"Having a game are we?"

So I put on my sensible voice and told him, "We really think it is. It's got fins too."

He suddenly took us seriously. "A UXB? Whereabouts?"

"Round the corner there, in the bomb site." We both pointed.

He blew his whistle to summon other officers and then jumped on his bike and rode to where we'd indicated. Another policeman joined him as our Bobby was checking that it really was a bomb.

"Phone the bomb squad," he said to his mate.

We were told to stay out of the site. We, and a gathering crowd, stood round the edge watching him tentatively pulling some twisted metal away.

"Go home, you lot," the other policeman told us as he chalked 'Keep Out' on a dark slab of metal.

"No, we want to see what's happening," said Toby.

"I've called the Bomb Disposal Squad. They'll clear the whole area, so hop it. Where do you live?"

So Toby told him, and he wrote the address in his notebook.

We all walked reluctantly away, looking over our shoulders occasionally to find out if the bomb squad had arrived.

After what seemed ages, we heard a bell ringing, and then some men dressed in their bomb disposal uniforms arrived in the back of an army lorry.

A man called out on a loud-hailer: "Evacuate the area, evacuate the area." Several policemen and servicemen started knocking on people's houses telling them to go to the local church hall. "If you've got a shelter still, go in there," one of them said.

How exciting it all was. But unfortunately we were sent away and decided to go back home.

"You're late back," said Auntie Vi.

"There was a bomb."

"No, really?" she said disbelievingly.

"I promise, really," I responded.

Then Toby piped up, "Yes and I found it."

"We called the police," I said.

And John said, "Both of us, I found him."

"No, you didn't, I did."

"I got him off his bike."

"Suppose so, but I showed him where it was."

"Stop it. Why can't you just tell me without arguing? What's happening now?"

"The bomb squad are there and people have been evacuated."

"I expect it'll be on the news," said Auntie Vi. But it wasn't. It was obviously such a common occurrence that it didn't warrant a news item.

However, the next day as I was finishing my breakfast glass of milk before school Mr Jennings popped in.

"A policeman came to the door this morning."

"Not in trouble again, your Toby," Auntie Vi commented, as Toby had already had a clip round the ear from our local Bobby for scrumping apples, been caned at school for smoking and once had appeared in front of a magistrate for stealing sweets from a shop.

"No, quite the opposite. Praise for calling the police so quickly."

I came into the hall.

"I was there too, so was John, we all found it."

"Well, the police are pleased with you all, then, but Toby's the oldest so that's why they mentioned him."

"Unfair," I said, and stormed back to the living room.

"Being difficult, is she?"

"Yes, ungrateful little beast, after all I've given up for her."

"I know, I know. You've done your best."

And Mr Jennings went off to work.

I'd overheard what they'd said. I don't think he realised that Auntie Vi took it out on me: her lost ballet career, her time as a Nippy, looking after her mother, and bringing me up had all taken their toll.

Chapter 5

"Let me have it, let me," I screamed at John who had taken the creamy top of the milk for his fruit salad.

Auntie Vi had been giving John and me our tea after school. There was always an argument about who should have the creamy top of the pasteurised milk.

"I can't wait till we go to Eastbourne again. All the milk there is creamy," said John.

"Gold, gold top. Grandad looks after us. Always gold!" I sneered.

"Go and stay there again, then you won't have to fight about it," Auntie Vi retorted. Sometimes when Mr and Mrs Jennings were going out in the evening Auntie Vi took Toby, John and me in for tea. Normally she didn't mind, but on this particular day she was expecting a gentleman friend to call.

"I want you all out of the house by 6 o'clock," she said.
"When's Toby coming back?"

"Doing his paper round," said John.

"When does he get back?"

"About quarter to," replied John.

"We might catch the pictures if we're lucky," I said. "Will you give us some money?" I asked expecting a negative response.

"Well as it's Saturday tomorrow, and you're too old for Saturday Morning Pictures now, I suppose so." She took out her purse from behind a cushion on the settee and gave me some coins.

"That should be enough."

I was eleven, Toby, nearly 14 and John 10. Roger Bannister had recently completed a mile in four minutes, and every day on the way home from school we tried to match his performance. Consequently we were always hot and sweaty when we arrived, even though we'd splashed ourselves with water from the horse-troughs we'd passed on our way home.

"You'll have to change your clothes; you stink," complained Auntie Vi.

So I went and put on my spare clothes, which doubled as my Sunday best: a dress, jacket, socks and shoes, and John went back to his Prefab to change.

Toby finished his paper round and came to Auntie Vi's to see what was going on.

"A film. Auntie Vi says we can."

"And she's given us the money," piped up John.

So we went with Toby to see an adventure film set in Africa. Very exciting, but I didn't like the smell of smoke everywhere in the cinema. It even made the screen cloudy. I was quite relieved to get out into the cool of the evening.

When I came back, Toby and John left me and went next door to where their parents had just returned.

I marched in to tell Auntie Vi about the film. I couldn't see her. Then I heard sounds coming from her bedroom. Not snoring, more like grunting. I thought better of walking in as she hated me going into her room, so I went into mine and put on a record. *How Much is That Doggie in the Window* was all I could find, so I sang along to it for a while.

Then I put myself to bed and as I was reading one of my books, *Ballet Shoes*, I heard someone creep out of the Prefab, closing the door with a click.

Next morning I asked Auntie Vi who it was.

"Oh, just a friend; anyway, none of your business."

So Auntie Vi did have a life apart from me, I thought.

***

I woke up one morning to find Auntie Vi holding a brown envelope.

"You've passed, you've passed, you clever little thing. Fancy that a Grammar school girl! I can't believe it. First one in our family. Just shows how well I've brought you up. Shame your Grandma isn't here to see it. Mind you she was well out of it. Wouldn't have registered."

"Let me look, let me see."

I was so excited. I didn't think I'd do well in the arithmetic paper, but I knew my general knowledge and English were good as I read such a lot and increased my vocabulary from Granny A's *Reader's Digest*. Auntie Vi's "curiosity killed the cat" comments often put me off asking questions. It annoyed her that I wanted to know everything about everything. Studying was an escape for me. However, she was obviously proud of me, and took vicarious credit for me passing.

"Let's go and tell Granny Aldrich." We both danced round the living room and I quickly threw my slippers into a corner and slipped into my outdoor shoes.

"Granny A, Granny A," I called out as we approached her porch.

"I've passed, I've passed."

"My word, what a commotion. Let's have a look at you. My goodness what a big head you've got; full of brains!"

We all laughed, and I thought this was the happiest I'd been for ages. I loved studying and had looked with envy at the Grammar School students walking home swinging their satchels from their arms, or carrying them on their backs.

"I must go and find out about Maggie. I hope she's passed too."

So I ran down our road, crossed over the main road and turned into a street of terraced houses. I ran up the garden path and rang the bell for longer than normal.

"Where's the fire?" said her dad. "You seem excited."

I waved my brown envelope at him.

"Where's Maggie? How did she get on?"

"I passed, I passed," she squeaked as she rushed towards me. We compared letters and went out into the back garden to do a victory lap of honour round the flower beds.

"Come on you two, you'll be late for school at this rate," her mum called out from the upstairs back bedroom, "And Dad's got to get to work."

"Take us by car today, Daddy," said Maggie. "Please, please, please."

So we got into his car which smelled deliciously of leather and arrived in style at our Primary School's gate.

Most of the children in my class had received their results. About a third of us had passed, but Mr Dawson, our teacher, congratulated all of us on our hard work, and told us that whichever school we'd be going to we would make him proud, he was sure.

When I returned home, Auntie Vi was still working at her job in the local haberdashers, so I went round to the Jennings'. Mrs Jennings was in. I liked to pop in and see her when she didn't have the boys around. We had a special bond, which we never spoke of, but we both felt really close, and she gave me more affection than Auntie Vi generally did when there was no one else at home. She was sitting in the garden looking after little Sandra, who'd arrived unexpectedly four years previously. Mr Jennings had been annoyed at first: "Another mouth to feed," he'd said, as his wife had only just established herself back in the local shoe shop when she'd discovered she was pregnant, and the extra money had been welcome. However, both she and her husband were overjoyed that the baby was a girl as they had sad memories of their stillborn daughter. After Toby making some crude jokes about how babies were made and how they came out (which none of us could believe was true, although it was), the boys had taken the new arrival to their hearts, veering from being over-protective on the one hand to annoyance at the baby's crying on the other. Mrs Jennings missed her job, but occasionally helped out on Saturdays if they were short-handed. Then Mr Jennings would look after the children if he wasn't too busy at the garage. Or she'd take Sandra round to her sister's house which was on the way to the shop. Mrs Jennings particularly enjoyed placing children's feet under the X-Ray machine and making sure that their Start-Rite shoes fitted properly. "With a little bit of room for growth" was her refrain in the rhythm of "with my little stick of Blackpool rock". She'd fitted almost all the shoes for the children in my class.

"Guess what," I said.

"Ooh, I can't imagine. Your cat's had kittens?"

"No, I passed my eleven plus."

"Well done," she said, showing surprise, even though I'm sure Auntie Vi must have bragged about it to her. She gave me a big hug, and so did Sandra. "You're very clever," said the little one.

"That's going to change your life, going to Grammar School," said Mrs Jennings.

"I'm really excited. I love school. I love finding out new things."

"I'm going to school soon," said Sandra.

"You'll enjoy it, I'm sure," I responded.

"Wish our Toby was a bit more like you, reading and studying and things," confided Mrs Jennings.

"But he knows such a lot about nature and animals and can build things. He made that go-cart at Easter. It was brilliant."

"Yes, he'll be fine. He's not into reading though. Can't remember when he last had a book in his hands. But he'll be good at mending things. Work in the garage like his dad maybe. Do his City and Guilds and set up on his own one day, I hope."

"That is much more useful than just reading books," I said and we laughed.

"It's what you do with all that reading that matters," Mrs Jennings said. "I just hope he doesn't get in with a bad lot. He's already been in trouble a few times."

"I'm sure he'll be alright," but secretly I wondered. He'd started making friends with some older Teddy Boys, and I wondered if he was going to join a gang. I found them really frightening the way they hung around near the Dance Hall in the evenings tossing their flick knives from one hand to another, and making rude remarks to passers-by. As far as I could tell it was all done for show, but I'd heard that some gangs were violent.

The summer of my eleven plus I couldn't wait for the holidays to be over, even though I was enjoying myself in Eastbourne. Grandad Preece was particularly ebullient. He had won money on the horses. He used to bet with a bookie's runner who operated under cover of a window cleaning business. Usually he lost or just about covered his outlay by backing horses each way, but this time he'd got a 50/1 winner. We had ice cream each day, and went for trips to places like Pevensey Castle and even a show at Devonshire Park Theatre. We read together in the evenings, Charles Dickens, and even some Shakespeare. He was determined to help me prepare for the new level of education I was about to experience and was pleased to have the opportunity without the irritation of Auntie Vi or the energetic Jennings boys around.

The big day came. I put on the second-hand uniform which Auntie Vi and I had bought from a sale at the school. I walked round to Maggie's house and we both caught the bus to our new school. It was only five stops away.

"Near enough for you to walk, and save some money," Auntie Vi had said, but Maggie and I wanted to go by bus as it felt more grown-up.

"We've got our own playground even," said Maggie. For the first year we were segregated from the main one, but still managed to mix with many of the older children. There were clubs to attend with pupils from across the school. We were expected to learn the names of all the prefects, and, most particularly, of the Head Girl and Head Boy. Imagine my surprise when I joined the school choir and had, on one side, the Head Girl, and Clemmie, the local pharmacist's daughter who was 14, on the other. Both were really friendly and helpful, particularly as my sight-reading was pretty non-existent and I kept losing my place in *The Christmas Oratorio* which was my first exposure to Bach.

Clemmie was very precise in the way she spoke, having done elocution for several years. She corrected my pronunciation, but praised my deportment and even copied it. Auntie Vi had seen that I stood up straight and moved gracefully by giving me rudimentary ballet lessons. Maggie became jealous of my involvement with an older girl and for a few years we both mixed with different friends. Academically we were separated too: she was in the French group and I was in the Spanish group for languages; she was in the top maths group and I was in the second to bottom, but coping well.

However, in 1958 our school had organised for our year to go and see *West Side Story*. It was a Christmas treat and related to our study of *Romeo and Juliet*. I happened to sit next to Maggie.

"I'm in love," she said. "George Chakiris. He's gorgeous."

"I want to dance like that! But, so sad. What a terrible ending." We had both cried at the tragic outcome and for days afterwards the last phrase of the music haunted me. I had never heard or seen anything before that brought up such strong emotion in me. The only musical I could compare it with was *The Pajama Game* which I'd seen when I was 10 or 11. I could still remember some of the numbers, but the story of workers against bosses and the complications of factory romance had none of the raw passion and tragedy of *West Side Story*. Maggie and I would go to each other's homes and play the record for hour after hour. I persuaded Auntie Vi to go and see it too and she went with the Jennings family in the following New Year. She, Maggie, John and I would dance to the music. Little Sandra tried to dance with our help, but her callipers restricted her movement. She'd caught polio in 1956, probably in the local swimming pool which had since been closed.

"I'm going to work in the theatre," John announced one day. "I must be part of all that, I just must."

Unfortunately, I had to leave school at the end of the school year as I was fifteen. Auntie Vi had been struggling for years financially what with paying the rent and feeding and clothing a growing teenager. Almost each week she'd take an article of jewellery down the road to 'uncles', and then when she got her wages, would retrieve it from the pawn shop if she had enough money to buy it back plus interest. As I'd become an adolescent, our relationship had become more and more stormy.

"What is it that makes you so special?" she often asked, when all I was doing was asking for some treat, or money to buy some fabric to run up a dress. "After all I've done for you!" was a regular comment when I disagreed with her, or went off in a huff. But in retrospect I think these were the typical reactions to a moody girl who was frustrated by the limitations of money and stimulation as well as Auntie Vi's wish to be seen as respectable, and, possibly, marriageable.

She arranged for me to work in the same haberdashers as her, standing behind the long drapers counter, measuring out lace, curtain trimmings and ribbons. Opening the wall of glass-fronted drawers in the cabinet behind me to bring out handkerchiefs, gloves, cards of buttons, Coates and Sylko thread, needles and pins, sewing machine bobbins and even articles of underwear made me feel as though I was of importance in our community. Best of all was when mothers came to order Cash's name tapes for their children. Suddenly I knew a vast array of people by name.

"Oh, Mrs Webb, have you thought of this particular colour. Mrs Shaw, we have some remnants, if you're interested."

A fascination for me was the pneumatic tube system for collecting the money and delivering the change. The carrier jar had a swivel lid and I felt really important putting the money and bill into the jar, engaging the customer in conversation, or serving the next, while we waited for the change.

I gradually realised how much she'd sacrificed for me and tried to make it up to her, in spite of her often showing her impatience and resentment towards me. I even bought tickets for the Festival Ballet with an early wage packet so she could see her favourite ballerina, Alicia Markova, before she retired from dancing.

Auntie Vi worked in the section with me, but I noticed she was taking longer and longer for her lunch hours, leaving me alone with the manageress.

"She's gone to see that bank clerk again, I reckon," she confided in me. And sure enough when I returned from my shorthand/typing evening class one Thursday, she told me that she and Herbert Armstrong were engaged.

Their wedding was an intimate affair: Auntie Vi, Grandad Preece (who gave her away), me, Granny Aldrich, who was a witness, Herbie himself, Mr and Mrs Armstrong, his Auntie Ethel, Uncle Bert (another witness) and sister Monica.

His parents were concerned that the bride was "at least five years older than Herbert". But they were charming with me, really interested in my studying, and Mr Armstrong said he'd put me in touch with a nice temping agency in Oxford Street when I was ready. We went upstairs in a local pub for a meal, and Grandad lent them his flat for their week long honeymoon. He stayed with me.

"They won't want you around much longer," he said.

"I don't really want to stay," I replied. "I find her really annoying."

"It's because you're a grown up now. No good having two women in the same kitchen," he joked. "And I know she can be a bit awkward at times. She's had to put up with you too," he laughed.

"Do you think they'll have children," I asked.

"I doubt it. She's young enough, but she told me she'd brought up one young'un, and didn't want to repeat the exercise."

"So I've put her off?"

"Not your fault. But she did have to change her life considerably, and I doubt if she'll want to change it again."

So I determined to finish my night classes as soon as possible, get into the world of secretarial work and find somewhere else to live.

Part 2

Chapter 6

"My word it's cold," said Clemmie as we slithered our way through snowy streets to the corner of Carlton Terrace and Waterloo Place where we'd left her car.

"You don't remember '47 do you? Freezing. Not much fuel to keep us warm either."

"Not really. Just Auntie Vi telling me off every time I left a door open. Oh yes, and helping to put up the winter curtains, or rather pretending they were the fur of some animal, a bear, I think, and rolling about in them. God, I must have been irritating."

"Still are!" She laughed. "I remember how cold it was in the classroom, and smelly with the paraffin heater giving off the most horrible fumes, and falling over in the playground cos the boys had made a slide which froze over and…" she stopped in her tracks.

"Oh no! Just look at that." The snow had drifted over the Morris Minor's front bumper.

"We can shift that, easy," I said hopefully.

So we got to work. By the time we'd cleared the snow our woollen gloves were soaked through.

"Need any help, girls," said a voice approaching along Carlton Terrace.

"Not sure yet," Clemmie called out. She opened the door and tried to start the engine. I watched her as she made three failed attempts.

"Take the starter handle, Chrissie, and give it a crank."

"I'll help you with that," said the voice which, now that I could see him, emerged from a handsome, military type.

I bent down and inserted the handle and gave it a crank.

"You need to do it a bit harder than that," he said.

He covered my hands with his leather gloved hands and together we turned it. Once. Nothing. Second time, yes, the engine started.

We both stood up.

"Thanks. Didn't know it was so hard."

"Cigarette?" he said.

"Yes, OK." So he tipped one out from a silver cigarette case. As he lit it my hand instinctively covered his, steadying the flame.

"Do you rescue maidens in distress often," I said, coughing on the strong tobacco.

"Only when they're as pretty as you."

"Oh, come on!"

"Well, it's not many girls come out on an evening like this."

"We went to a matinee; off home now."

"What did you see?"

"*One for the Pot*."

"One of Brian Rix's farces, was it? Who was in it?"

"Come on Chrissie. Got to get back." Clemmie called from within the car.

"Brian Rix himself. Very funny. Just the thing for this type of weather."

"Off you go then. Mustn't keep you."

As Clemmie turned the car our Good Samaritan stood by the pavement and raised his hat and waved us on our way.

"You are a one," said Clemmie.

"Why?"

"Picking up strange men."

"Nothing strange about him. Good to have a helping hand."

"Army, do you think?"

"No idea." But I was already wondering about him. Tall, good looking, polite, well-spoken. "Rather dishy," I accidentally said aloud.

"Chrissie! You won't see him again."

"More's the pity," I muttered.

Chapter 7

When I was 17, I had gained enough confidence to offer myself for a temping secretarial job. The agency in Oxford Street that Auntie Vi's in-laws had introduced me to had been impressed that I'd studied at night school, looked smart and spoke well (thanks to my friend Clemmie constantly picking me up on my lazy speech). My first was a three-week stint in the office of an Oxford Street store. I felt very grown up in my navy suit and thick tights hiding my increasingly hairy legs, about which I hadn't the courage to ask Clemmie, but knew I should. Auntie Vi would have given me a sermon about vanity had I asked her so I hadn't confided in her any of my teenage anxieties. Periods! She never mentioned the word. Maggie helped me there as she'd started a few months before me, but one day I opened my underwear drawer and Auntie Vi had discretely put a pack of Kotex pads and a belt beside my knicker pile. Nothing had been said, by either of us, but I did feel the beginnings of a womanly bond between us. Now I regretted the modesty we had in our relationship. How did she keep her legs looking smooth and hairless? I'd seen her wearing fine denier stockings and I yearned to wear tan or even nude tights with my short skirts. Luckily, I was in the staff ladies room one afternoon and found a girl from the office shaving her legs with a man's razor. Within a few days I'd copied her, and graduated to the tights of my dreams.

The following assignment made me uncomfortable about my increasing attractiveness to the opposite sex. I was working in a construction company's office and was one of only three girls, or rather young women as we liked to be called. My boss, a big rotund man accosted me in the stationery cupboard, and tried to grope my breasts. I quickly shoved him out of the way, left the office and went straight to the agency where I was told,

"You shouldn't lead men on. Look at you in your short skirts, not leaving anything to the imagination."

I'd lost money too as I'd walked out.

I refused to change my fashion style, but they obviously valued my work skills as my next placement was with a famous soft drinks company near Marble Arch. I loved the Regency building and started to read up about the style of architecture. I also enjoyed going into the park for my lunchtime sandwiches, but the work was boring: typing up invoice after invoice. Perhaps the agency was punishing me.

After three months of these short assignments, usually during secretaries' illnesses or holidays, I found myself at a publishing company in Bloomsbury, off Tavistock Square. I hadn't been to this part of London before so, determined to make a good impression, I arrived too early having over-estimated the journey time. There was a man sitting on the step of the converted Georgian house, reading a copy of Peace News.

"You come to work here?" He looked in his late 20s, maybe even early thirties. He was dressed all in black, wearing a beret and smoking a foreign cigarette. He stood up from the front step and shook my hand. *Quite a beatnik*, I thought. I nodded.

"I'm the new temp. Christine."

"I'm Oliver, Oliver Mooney. I'm one of their writers."

"What's that you've been reading?" We sat down side by side on the stone steps.

"I'm really interested in non-violent action. I went on a demo last Easter. You know, ban the bomb. It's my purpose in life."

I thought he was very profound. It surprised me that someone would start talking to a stranger about something so serious, and the furrows on his brow certainly implied thoughtfulness. A few minutes later a tall dark-haired woman wearing a smart tweed suit arrived.

"Morning, Miss Eversley," Oliver called out as he stood up. "This is our temp. She's come to help out."

"I certainly hope you're better than the last one. Her spelling was atrocious as was her time-keeping. Come on in." She unlocked the door and we walked from the hall into a ground floor room with a small switchboard and two desks facing the windows, each with Imperial typewriters.

"This is where you'll be working. Oh, Oliver, would you be a dear and make Miss, er, sorry I didn't get your name."

"Christine," said Oliver before I could reply.

"Yes, make Christine some tea; I might as well have one too."

"The agency in Oxford Street sent me. I've got my references here," I offered as she walked me up some stairs to an airy office overlooking the street.

Miss Eversley read through the references and looked me up and down.

"You seem to have worked hard to do your secretarial training. Do you enjoy studying?"

"Yes, I am really interested in lots of things."

"Such as?"

"Oh, I liked the law element at night school, and history at school. Particularly history, oh, and architecture a bit. I like ballet too, my aunt trained as a dancer once, and, well, I get interested in lots of things."

"Politics?"

"Well, I think the Government takes care of that, but, well, I haven't really had to think about it much yet."

"We all need to take an interest, whether or not we are old enough to vote. I see you're still 17. Time to start thinking about what issues are important to you. But I mustn't start lecturing. Let me tell you about this lovely publishing business." And she proceeded to tell me about Mr Blackwood and Mr Green who had been to university together and decided there was an opportunity to publish educational books. They started with books to help infants to read. That's when Miss Eversley had started. She explained that they engaged freelance writers and illustrators and she showed me the room where they could sit and work at the back of the building overlooking a small garden. They generally came in during the final stages of their work, during the preparations for going to press. My role would be to type up their manuscripts, correct their spelling and punctuation if necessary, and also to receive dictation from Miss Eversley and prepare her letters ready for signature. She emphasised that there would be other duties at times, but for me to get acquainted with the business as a whole first. Another girl, Gladys, would be answering the phone and putting through the calls to Miss

Eversley and Mr Blackwood as well as doing secretarial duties for him. A Mr Oxenford did the accounts, coming in mainly on Thursdays to make up our wages but he also got involved in the contracts for the freelancers and paid the bills monthly for the printers and stationers. Apparently Mr Green had had a serious accident and didn't often come in, but he was still an important partner. My engagement was for one month.

However, towards the end of the month, Miss Eversley had asked if I would like to be a permanent junior in the company. I had been delighted. I loved the work. Although the pay was average, I found it a stimulating environment with so much to interest me. They all treated me as a valuable member of their team and I felt I was contributing to children's education too which was a bonus.

Oliver was one of the freelance writers. He wrote about whatever was requested. One year the main subject was English Grammar. Another six months he might be adapting fairy stories into reading books suitable for 5-year-olds in their first year at school. He lived with his mother in a typical suburban house, but with an amazing sloping garden terraced on three levels. The Christmas Eve of 1961 we had all been invited there for an office party. It was a mild winter so we spent some time in the surprise sunshine examining the skeletal greengage trees, raspberry canes and blackcurrant bushes that were Mrs Mooney's pride and joy. The lowest level of the garden was a dedicated vegetable patch with a garden shed made from the remains of an Anderson shelter.

The seven of us had feasted on Mrs Mooney's devils on horseback, pineapple and cheese on cocktail sticks and a variety of salads served with baked potatoes in their jackets followed by iced Christmas cake. We drank a warm punch which made me feel a bit squiffy after only one glass, but everyone else had several so the party became quite raucous, and there was a bit of teasing directed towards Oliver.

"Not found a girl yet?"

"No, too busy with my writing."

"Oh come on, you can't live here going on 30. Time to get a move on and get wed," was the gist of these jibes.

Oliver took it all in good spirit, but I felt he was getting tired of the banter, so I asked where he did his writing, and he showed me the 'Library'. It was the small third bedroom overlooking the front porch. It was crammed floor to ceiling with shelves filled with reference books on one wall, anthologies of poems and stories and fiction on the other. His desk faced the bow window in front of which was a large sill, heaving with books and literary magazines many of them with slips of paper marking what must have been useful pages of information. On the desk was a heavy Imperial typewriter with a half filled piece of typing paper in the carriage.

"A present from Mother: a Model 6," said Oliver.

"Do you expect me to be impressed?"

"Of course. It's the latest!"

"Didn't know you were fashion conscious."

He playfully tapped me on the nose and smiled.

"You are funny, Chrissie."

"Come on down you two; time for some carols," someone shouted.

Mrs Mooney was sat at the piano. She was a short woman, dumpy and jolly, with the remnants of a soft Irish accent. She seemed to disappear into the leather piano stool and I wondered how she could reach the pedals. She was a proficient piano player. Her Winifred Atwell interpretations could grace any local pub, and her accompaniments to solemn hymns supported the choir at the local Catholic Church when the organist had other engagements. So, with Mr Blackwood singing Bass, Oliver and Mr Oxenford both straining to sing Tenor, albeit somewhat out of their natural range, Miss Eversley on Alto, and me and Gladys as Sopranos, occasionally rising into descant, we covered *O Come all ye Faithful, While Shepherds Watched, Silent Night* and the *Holly and the Ivy*, followed by the *Hallelujah* Chorus. Mr Blackwood then started the speeches of appreciation for such a lovely evening, and we waved goodbye calling out "Happy Christmas".

On the drive along the A3 from New Malden Mr Blackwood confided he was worried that Oliver was "one of those..." sharply rebuked by Mr Oxenford. "Rubbish, I've seen him chatting up a girl, and he quite fancies you, doesn't he?" he said, turning his head to where Miss Eversley, Gladys and I were squashed into the back.

"Who, me?" I said. "Well we get on alright."

"He's flirted with me a bit," said Gladys.

"Now, now, we can't have that in our office," joked Mr Blackwood.

"What about me?" said Miss Eversley. "I'm not too old for that sort of thing, you know."

We all laughed as Miss Eversley seemed to me to be ancient, but she was actually only in her early 40s, her hopes of marriage dashed when her fiancé was killed in the war. I'd gathered from Gladys that she'd been a teacher but found being with the children she might never have, too distressing, or that was the rumour. Then I was dropped at a station and started my trip home to Northfields, complicated by the fact that Mr Blackwood had assumed I was still living on the Northern Line, and had confused Clapham Junction with Clapham North. In fact, by the end of my first year I had saved enough to move out of my aunt's home. After her marriage, I'd felt in the way as Grandad had prophesized. And, apart from feeling in the way, I had become more independent and wanted digs of my own. Clemmie had moved to West London when she'd got married and encouraged me to find lodgings near her.

Chapter 8

"Anyone going near Piccadilly on their way home?" Mr Blackwood called out across the office.

"I could, if you like."

"I thought you're on the Northern Line, aren't you?"

"No, moved to Northfields. On the 'Dilly or District now."

"Ooh! Coming up in the world are we?" teased Gladys.

"My aunt got married so I thought I'd get out of her hair."

"Yes, she won't want you around now," she retorted.

"It's not quite like that…"

"Anyway, girls, I've got a manuscript to go back to Mr James. His Club's just off Piccadilly so could you drop it off, Christine? The Messenger's gone home early, his wife's ill."

"Anything serious?"

"It often is with her since she had rheumatic fever. She has flare ups."

"Poor thing. Shall I go now?"

"Get you home early for a change."

"Thanks."

So I took the manuscript, delivered it to the Receptionist at Mr James's Club in Pall Mall and walked up towards Piccadilly.

Bump! "I'm so sorry," I blurted out.

"That's alright…" A moment while the man looked carefully at me and raised his hat in greeting. "I recognise you… er… 'Kitty'?"

"Christine, actually." Suddenly I knew it was the man who'd helped me and Clemmie start her car when I was struggling with the starter handle during the snow earlier that year.

"I shall call you Kitty, you look as though you should be Kitty. I'm Andrew."

"Oh, Kitty?"

"It could be a nickname for Christine, don't you think?"

"Could be, I suppose."

Actually I felt flattered that suddenly I had a special nickname. And that he'd remembered me. I had certainly remembered him, in my dreams and occasionally in dull moments at work.

"Fancy a cigarette?"

"Why not." I looked up at his face while he lit my cigarette, noticing his slightly squashed nose and grey eyes. The cigarette was really strong and unfiltered leaving bits of tobacco in my mouth which I tried to remove as delicately as I could. As he put the blue packet away, I spotted the word 'Gitanes' on it together with a picture of a gypsy playing a tambourine made to look rather like smoke.

"I don't know these," I observed.

"French, actually."

"I've never been there, France."

"Oh, you must go. I travel a bit for my work. But London's what I know best."

We stayed chatting outside Trumpers where he'd been for a haircut, mainly about how lovely this part of London was, and he pointed out some of the different architectural styles around us.

"Well, nice to pass the time of day with you," I said. "Must be off."

"Meeting your boyfriend?"

"No, haven't got one of those yet," I laughed.

"Give me your phone number."

So I did.

"Bet you won't call."

"You cheeky thing! Bet I will."

"Thanks for the ciggie."

***

We went our separate ways, he walking west along Jermyn Street and me going east towards Piccadilly Circus Station. However, I spotted a phone box in a little alleyway near a church. I just had to tell Clemmie. Luckily she was at home.

"Guess who I've just bumped into."

"The Queen?"

"No, don't be silly. I met the man who helped us with the starter handle."

"No!"

"He actually recognised me."

"Well, I'm not surprised after the way you looked at each other."

"Get away!"

"No, I mean it. There was something going on there. What did he say?"

"Just good to see me, something about architecture…"

"Sounds deep."

"Just chatter while we had a ciggie: a French one."

"Très chic."

"No, it didn't make me."

"Make you what?"

"Sick."

Clemmie laughed. "I forgot you didn't learn French."

"Anyway, he took my phone number."

"So, he took your phone number, ah ha!"

"Do you think he'll phone?"

"Well, if he said he would. He did look sort of military. Efficient type."

"I do hope so."

"Don't raise your hopes too high. Probably married with kids."

"No, I don't think so. The way he looked at me, I think he was…. Oh no. My money's running out. Talk to you again… Oh those wretched pips."

Faintly: a "put some more in…" came from Clemmie.

Too late. I couldn't find any change. The phone cut off.

Chapter 9

The following evening my landlady, Mrs Wendover called up the stairs just after I'd returned to my room having experienced one of her mid-week supper dishes. "Phone call for you dear."

"Thanks," I said, thinking it was probably Clemmie asking me about my meeting the previous day.

"I'm as good as my promise," said a man's voice. "You've lost your bet!"

"Oh," I said, not sure how to react. "So I have."

"Do you fancy having tea with me tomorrow?"

"I can't, I'm working."

"What time do you get off?"

"Five, usually, unless there's something urgent."

"Well, meet me outside Fortnum's at 5.30. There'll still be time to have some tea."

"Ooh, Fortnum's. That's a bit smart."

"Well, we can be smart too. How about it?"

"Sounds lovely." My mind suddenly rushed through my meagre wardrobe wondering what to wear. "Is it very smart?"

"You don't need evening dress," he laughed. "Just come in your work clothes; you don't wear overalls do you?" Again he laughed.

"What sort of work do you think I do?"

"Not in a factory, certainly. Something elegant I shouldn't wonder."

I was flattered.

"Well, I'm a……personal assistant in a publishing house," I said, elevating my status a few notches.

"I knew it was something elegant."

We both laughed.

"Don't be long," said Mrs Wendover. "I need the phone."

"Got to go now. See you tomorrow, Friday."

I returned to my room and looked at my work suit. It needed a good brushing after wearing it for most of the week. I wondered if I should wear a dress instead. I took out the smarter of my two winter dresses: three-quarter length sleeves, round neck with a small Peter Pan collar, nipped in waist and skirt that touched the knees. It was navy blue wool with a tweedy pattern. I hadn't worn it for work before, but it looked appropriate enough for both a secretary and a personal assistant. The only issue was that it was slightly longer than my coat. But I could wear my raincoat. So that was sorted.

I went out to phone Clemmie at the phone box.

"Watch out," she said. "This could be the beginning of something dangerous. It's not like you've been properly introduced, or anything."

"It's only tea, Clemmie."

"Well, watch out."

Much as I loved Clemmie, I did resent her over-protective attitude towards me. Ever since we'd been in the choir together at school she'd vetted my various potential boyfriends, warning me off some of them: "He only wants one thing, that one," she'd say. I knew she was right because on Saturdays she helped out in her father's chemist shop. When boys from our school came in for rubber johnnies, she used to call her father to serve them, and disappear into the dispensing area at the back of the shop until they'd gone. Hence, she built up a profile of which boys were safe to go out with, and which were only after one thing. When she became head girl she became even more controlling of my movements. I suppose she looked out for me because Auntie Vi had found me too challenging during adolescence to control me at all, and her resentment had made itself felt, emotionally and physically. As Clemmie was 4 years older than me, she took on a big sister role, which I appreciated most of the time. Now that she was a married woman, and married to a doctor (however, junior) she had absorbed the manner of a doctor's wife, giving unasked for advice whenever prompted by the situation. I did value her friendship and always listened, but often did completely the opposite. However, two suggestions I obeyed were to get qualified as a secretary, and to find lodgings in Clemmie's part of London.

At work on Friday I was greeted by Oliver. "You look smart today. Going for another job?"

I certainly hadn't meant to give that impression.

"No, meeting someone after work," I replied as I hung my mac on the coat stand.

"He must be special for you to spruce up so smart."

"No, just a friend, but we are going to Fortnum's for tea."

"Ooh, that's a bit upmarket, isn't it?"

"Not my idea. Just meeting outside probably."

"Come on you two," called Miss Eversley. "Get a move on. Mr Blackwood's got Mr Green coming in today and wants to show him that we're all working efficiently."

So we settled down, Oliver in his office, or rather the office where the freelance authors tried to get some peace and quiet while they were preparing their manuscripts for printing, and I joined Gladys who was already busy at her typewriter.

Just after lunch, my usual sardine, pepper and vinegar sandwiches, washed down with a cup of sweet tea, Mr Green appeared leaning heavily on his stick. He was still a partner in the firm he had set up with Mr Blackwood, but increasing bad health meant he only came in once or twice a month to check that everything was functioning as he liked, and to have a meeting with Mr Blackwood about any changes that might be necessary. An earlier modification, according to Miss Eversley, had been when the school leaving age was raised to 15 in 1947 and they increased the proportion of school text books compared with other books that they published. Gladys and I wondered whether this was a routine meeting or if it had a special agenda.

Since starting with Blackwood and Green I had progressed from clerical duties to secretary. Gladys worked mainly for Mr Blackwood and I worked mainly for Miss Eversley, but also helped the freelance writers.

Mr Green was always very polite to us girls. He asked after our families and were we enjoying our work being "in the front line of educating and informing our readers". It was very much the same speech each time.

"Yes, Mr Green; thank you Mr Green; so good to see you here, Mr Green," we would chorus.

I started to wonder whether I would be able to leave on time today, but Mr Blackwood came out of his office and said we'd all done very well, and he let us go home early.

"Fancy a coffee or something, you two," said Oliver as he came out of the freelancer's room. "Oh no, you can't, can you," he said to me, "You've got an assignation."

"Hardly that Oliver," I retorted.

"Just me, then," said Gladys, "Just a quick one, I'm off to the flicks after work."

So I visited the toilet on the ground floor (the Partners had their own on the first floor) and checked that I looked smart.

"Are you going to Russell Square station?" Miss Eversley said as I came out of the toilet.

"Yes, I'm going that way."

"I just wanted to have a quiet word."

"Nothing awful?" I said.

"No, not at all."

So we walked across the central garden and across the road to the station.

"Mr Green and Mr Blackwood are ever so pleased with you, you know."

"Oh, thank you. I do love working here."

"Yes, they think you could take on a bit more responsibility."

"What sort?" I wondered as I was already busy, and sometimes found it difficult to finish my work within the 9 to 5 hours.

"Helping do some proof-reading with the authors, for example."

"Oh and discover what those funny squiggles are that appear in the margins."

"It's not as complicated as it looks; I've got a little booklet you can have a look at over the weekend." And she passed me a slim volume, which I quickly skimmed through.

"Not as much a challenge as shorthand, and you can have this by your side to remind you," she said.

"Oh, I recognise this one, and that," I said as I spotted the squiggle for delete and one for paragraph. "I think I know some of these already."

"And, you'll have a pay rise – you're on, what now?"

"5 guineas a week."

"Well, we might get it up to £5.15 shillings."

"Oh, thank you. My rent has just gone up, and the tube fares cost a bit."

"We were all impressed that you came in during the tube strike. Very conscientious. Gladys didn't manage it, and it was noted."

"Well, I was lucky that the buses were still running, and I got up extra early to make sure I did."

"So you didn't lose a day's pay."

"No, I couldn't risk that."

"Well you're a bright young thing, so keep it up," she remarked as we stood outside the station. "Off home now?"

"No, meeting a friend."

"Well, enjoy your weekend."

"Thanks, I shall."

What a very adult conversation that was, I thought. And I felt I was walking on air with her compliments, so by the time I met Andrew I was fairly bouncing along the street. He was outside the shop, looking at the window display. He must have caught sight of me in the reflection. He turned and raised his hat.

"So you got away."

"Yes, we were let out early."

"Sounds like a caged animal, or a child at school."

"Well, they're quite strict." So I babbled on about where I worked and described some of the people there as he ushered me through the store into the tea room. I was aware of a delicious smell of freshly baked cakes.

"And they obviously appreciate you," he managed to chip in.

"Oh yes, and they're going to let me do proof-reading starting next week."

"So being a personal secretary is more than just typing and shorthand."

"Well, I did exaggerate a bit, I'm really a shorthand typist."

"But with potential."

"Yes, they seem to think so."

A waitress came to our table and asked for our order. Andrew ordered for us both.

"A selection of cakes and…" turning to me, "What sort of tea do you want?"

"You choose," I said, only having had PG Tips and Lyons Red Label before.

"If I can't have Boh tea, I like Darjeeling, it's light, from India or Orange Pekoe Tips, much stronger, from Ceylon."

"I didn't realise there's so much to choose from." I said, looking at the extensive list on the menu. "Darjeeling for me," I said to the waitress.

"Some people treat tea badly, but here they really know the different types. After all they were the early importers."

And he proceeded to tell me about the value set on tea in the 18th century, about the locks on tea chests and the traditional shell-shaped spoons for dispensing it.

"My aunt has one of those," I said, "It lives in the tea-caddy which has got pictures of a Chinese Emperor and some elegant Chinese ladies on it. But what was that Boo tea you mentioned."

He laughed. "Boh tea. When I lived in Malaya we had delicious tea from a plantation high up in the hills. Called Boh. B – O – H."

"What were you doing there?"

"It was part of my National Service, helping get rid of the rebels who were decimating the British and Malay owned rubber plantations, amongst other things."

"Oh, the Emergency. I saw a Newsreel about it. Didn't it finish recently?"

"Yes, a couple of years ago."

"All due to you."

"Hardly, I was only there for part of my eighteen months, but then they called on me again after a short break."

"It seems a long way away. I'm not even sure if it's further than India."

"Yes, much further. And very different. It's mainly jungle and humidity. Not the most pleasant climate, but it's amazing how quickly we adapted. Of course, we had ceiling fans in our offices, and the shutters on the window were designed to give some through draft."

"Offices, you said. So you didn't fight."

"Well, my sort of fighting was to find out information, verify it, and pass it through to the fighting forces; psychological fighting, rather than physical."

By this time our bone china plates, cups and saucers were in place and a cake stand appeared on the centre of the table. Our tea was poured through a silver strainer. There were slices of lemon on a saucer and a jug of milk. "I've always put milk in first." I commented.

"Try it without, it might surprise you."

I did, and it was delicious. However, I put in a little milk after a few sips, more out of habit than because of the taste.

Andrew continued talking about tea, its Chinese origin, the spread of tea plantations through Malaya to Ceylon, and on to India. It seems his family were something to do with the tea trade a long time ago.

"My goodness," I said, "You can trace your family all that way back."

"Yes, how about you. How far back do you know about?"

So I told him about my dramatic birth and how I lived with my Auntie Vi (but I called her Auntie Violet – it sounded better). I mentioned my dead father, and my grandma who had helped bring me up for a few years until her mind went. I spoke about Grandad Preece in Eastbourne.

"Oh, I know Eastbourne quite well," he said. So we went on to reminisce about the places we had both visited.

Our conversation continued after our tea when we stood outside Fortnum's for a while before Andrew said, "I'll walk you to your train. Which line are you on?"

"Piccadilly, to Northfields, and you?"

"Off to Victoria."

So we walked together towards Green Park Station chatting about meeting up again soon.

"What ho, Finchie" came a voice from the corner of Old Bond Street and Piccadilly.

"Oh! Chalky, fancy seeing you!" replied Andrew as this tall military type came to our side of the road having leaped across the busy thoroughfare narrowly missing being hit by a number 9 bus.

"Taking risks as always," commented Andrew.

"You too, I see," said Chalky, looking me up and down. "Pretty little thing."

"Miss Preece, meet Rupert Stratton-White, otherwise known as Chalky."

"Hello," I said offering a gloved hand which Chalky was too excited to take.

"Off, you go, Miss Preece. See you, er at the office," Andrew stammered.

"Goodbye then. Usual time?" I said, colluding in his deception.

"Yes, of course," said Andrew.

"Secretary, then," said Chalky.

"Yes, and a very good one too," I overheard as I walked towards Green Park Station. "Now what are you up to, Chalky?"

"Oh, this and that. Fancy a bite at my club....?" Then the traffic drowned out their voices as I waited at the traffic lights at the St. James's Street crossing.

After that, I could only think of Andrew as Finchie.

***

At our next teatime meeting I asked about Chalky.

"He was a year above me at school, then met up at Army training down in Sussex."

"He certainly made assumptions."

"He's always jumping to conclusions, but just the man you need if you're in trouble. He was over in Malaya too."

"I thought you covered up really well."

"But what was I covering up? The fact that I've rather taken to you?"

"Oh, have you, indeed," I commented, feeling the heat of a blush spread up my neck.

"Yes, definitely."

"Well, what are you going to do about it?" I said cheekily.

"I think you are a very naughty girl."

"Want to find out?" I said, my boldness surprising me.

"What about your many boyfriends?"

"I told you, I haven't got one."

"Well you might have one now," he said, running his foot up my calf.

Then our tea and cakes arrived, and the conversation turned to how my proof-reading was coming on.

We kept giving each other secret knowing smiles although we were keeping up a respectable conversation.

My heart was beating faster than I'd ever experienced.

As I was finishing a moist piece of Madeira cake, he suddenly said,

"When."

"When what?" I spluttered shooting a few crumbs across the tablecloth.

"When are you going to meet me again, but not just for tea."

"Oh, my goodness, you really mean it? Um, well, how about next Tuesday?"

"Tuesday's fine. I'll meet you outside Fortnum's."

"And then what?"

"Wait and see," he teased.

Chapter 10

I could hardly sleep at all that weekend. I was excited, and somewhat nervous. *Why had I led him on so? Was this going to be like the disappointing fumbles I'd experienced with a few teenage boys after we'd been dancing at St. Anne's Crypt, in Soho, where we jived to the latest pop songs? Would he be disappointed in my body, my small bosoms? Did I know what to do? What would I wear, or not wear?*

I had a long walk in Walpole Park on the Sunday and stopped to look at the grey herons beside the pond. I became calmer. Life felt better than it ever had before. I was actually going to be Andrew's girlfriend. A proper grown up girlfriend.

Tuesday came. I left the chaos of my room where I'd been rummaging through my wardrobe, changing my mind about whether to wear this dress or that skirt and jacket. My chest of drawers had disclosed lots of greying white underwear, so I'd opted for a black bra and almost matching knickers, a simple suspender belt and my favourite nude-coloured stockings: I'd only recently got round to wearing tights, but they were woollen and not very attractive; also I wasn't yet comfortable about getting them on and off gracefully.

During the morning at the office my emotions distracted me somewhat, but I double checked my work regularly, just in case I'd been careless and made the necessary corrections. At least I remembered to make the teas at about 11.00. I took one to Oliver who was concentrating hard on his work, so we didn't chat as we usually did. Miss Eversley almost bumped into me as I came out of the freelancers' room, and said, "I'll take mine, thanks," and, "How are the publisher's marks going?"

"You were right, they're much easier to learn than shorthand. Thanks for having faith in me."

"You're a bright girl, you could do a lot to better your position, you know."

"What do you mean?"

"Evening classes."

"Oh, I had a few years at night school doing my secretarial course."

"No, I mean, choose a subject, foreign language or, have you got A Levels?"

"No, I left school too early; just took my GCEs in the 5th Form."

"Well then. English would be a good one. Or History. Try the City Lit they do everything there."

"Thank you," I said. "That might be an idea, I'll think about it."

Miss Eversley could easily have treated as an inferior, like she treated Gladys, but I always felt she looked on me as a budding professional, someone worth taking notice of, nurturing me.

So I went to Mr Blackwood's office feeling buoyant. Not only was I meeting Andrew, or rather, 'Finchie', but I was being appreciated at work.

In my self-absorption I forgot to knock. I pushed open the door and found Mr Blackwood with Gladys on his knee obviously engaged in taking down something more than shorthand.

"Oops, I'm so sorry," I stammered, putting down his tea cup quickly on a shelf and retreated blushing into the corridor.

I went back to my desk and started work again.

"Don't be jealous," Gladys said as she came into the room, smoothing her skirt. "Just a bit of fun."

I didn't know what to say, so I just smiled sheepishly and carried on with my work. I was surprised at Mr Blackwood, more than Gladys. He had a lovely wife and two children. Whatever got into him! Or perhaps Gladys was the one to blame. But who was I to talk. I was off to meet my new boyfriend this evening, and who could tell where that would lead to.

***

After work, I hurried to Fortnum's which was becoming 'our shop'. As usual 'Finchie' was admiring the window displays and turned to greet me as he spotted me in the reflection.

"Hello, Finchie," I said.

"Ooh, getting familiar now are we?"

"You don't mind, do you?"

"No, it's what my close friends call me – and we're going to be close, I shouldn't wonder."

He took me by the elbow and led me, not into the store, but to the corner of Duke Street St. James's. We walked down the street towards Pall Mall but stopped outside an art bookshop. We turned left up a couple of steps to a set of doors leading to some flats above the shop. There was a creaky lift, but as someone was inside it on their way up, we took the stairs. On the third floor Finchie took out a set of keys and ushered me into a small apartment. I walked, slightly out of breath from the climb and the anticipation, into the tiny hall and from there entered a living cum dining room beyond.

"Is this where you live?"

"No, just overnight sometimes; my pied a terre."

I wasn't quite sure what he meant by pied a terre, but realised it was his London pad, and that he must have a home elsewhere too. I put my coat, hat and scarf on one of the hooks on the back of the door, joining his, and crossed the room. The gas fire was already lit sending an orange glow into the room. Its quiet hissing was calming and a familiar sound, similar to the one in my lodgings. The small dining table was next to the heavily curtained window. I drew back one of the curtains and saw a garden below where some yellow crocuses were poking their heads between the hardened mounds of greying snow obscuring much of the grass. Turning into the room with my back to the window there was a hatch opening from a small kitchenette on my right. Facing me beyond the table was a leather Chesterfield settee with a matching armchair. I went to sit down. Andrew came towards me.

"Would you like a drink," he said turning to a cabinet near the serving hatch.

"Just some tea please," I responded, slightly breathlessly.

So he went into the kitchen and filled the kettle and put it on the gas stove.

"You are a little darling, Kitty," he said as he peered through the hatch.

"Not so little, Finchie." I stood up. "Look, I'm nearly as tall as you."

"Yes, in your heels **and** standing on tip-toe."

"Come and measure," I said.

He was about 6 feet tall. I was 5 foot 5, slim with a long body and what I thought were short legs.

We stood back-to-back for a few moments and I savoured the feel of his body against mine.

"I think you're cheating!"

"No I'm not." But of course, I had. I'd stood on tip-toes but still wasn't as tall as him.

He returned to the kitchen, made our tea and slid the cups and saucers through the hatch. He'd even bought some cakes: chocolate eclairs and mille feuilles. My favourites. We carried them to the table.

"Come on, Kitty, take off those shoes and we'll see who's tall now."

I padded over to the window standing as stretched up as I could in my stockinged feet. I turned to look out of the window.

"That's the London Library and the East India Club and their gardens," said Andrew, snuggling up close to me and kissing me on my neck. I felt his arms go round my waist and he hugged me close to him. I felt the warmth of his body. I sank into his embrace.

"Ooh, that's nice," I said, as he turned me towards him and bent his head down to kiss me on the lips. He led me away from the window, moving us both towards the bedroom.

"Perfectly proportioned," he murmured as he placed me on the bed, removed his jacket and tie, and kicked the bedroom door closed.

***

On the way home on the tube, I felt that everyone was looking at me. Was it obvious that at last I had lost my virginity? Actually had proper grown-up sex. I felt myself blushing. Then I couldn't stop myself smiling. I was careful not to make eye contact with any of the people in the crowded carriage as we journeyed beyond Earl's Court, shedding commuters, until by Northfields there were only a few people left. I hugged myself as I walked from the station to my digs.

"Have you eaten?" called up Mrs Wendover as she heard me mounting the stairs.

"Yes, thanks," I lied, too excited to eat, and content with the cakes we had eaten after my whole body had been explored and adored.

"I'll come down for some milk later."

In my room I looked at myself in the mirror. Did I look different? No, just my eyes were very bright and I kept grinning at myself. What a secret I had. I put a record on my Dansette, bought at the end of my first year with Blackwood and Green: The Beatles, *Love Me Do*.

The next morning I was still on a high.

"Someone's happy, today," said Oliver. I'd obviously been singing while I made the morning tea.

"Yes, definitely."

"Anything exciting. Come on tell, tell."

"Well," I started, then thought better of confiding my secret to a work-mate, especially a man.

"Just happy really. It's a lovely day. There isn't so much snow, I almost feel that spring is coming. Can't a girl just be happy for no reason?"

"There's always a reason. Only asking."

"Come on you two lovebirds," called out Miss Eversley as she passed the kitchen.

"We're only friends," I called after her.

"I know, I know. Just get to work, Christine. Oliver's got a deadline; can't afford to be distracted."

Oliver laughed. "Actually, the copy's ready; just needs proof-reading."

"I'll do it, if you like," I offered.

So we sat down in the freelancers' room and set about the proof-reading. Oliver read aloud, and I put publisher's marks in the margins on my copy.

"Any pictures in this one?" I asked.

"Not many. A centre spread and a few photos near the end."

"Oh, a dull book then."

"Rubbish. It's an exciting journey round England's Cathedrals."

"You need a couple of plans then, of the insides."

"That's what I thought but Mr Blackwood thought it would bring the target age down."

"For Secondaries then."

"Yes, Religious Education."

"I still think some plans would help."

"Let's get Miss Eversley to intercede."

"You make a list of what floor plans you need and I'll type it up."

"Thanks. You're a pal, Chrissie."

"All part of the service," I said.

Chapter 11

The sickness hit me first. Unfortunately, Green Park Station received my initial donation. In the crowded compartment I suddenly felt clammy and stood up to get near the door. I had difficulty in holding it in. I leapt from the over-heated train onto the platform just before depositing a neat pile of part-digested porridge on the floor by a litter bin.

"You all right dear?" said an elderly woman.

"Something I ate," I said, "or just the heat."

A West Indian platform attendant hastened to the spot. "Don't worry," he said as he threw a bucket of sand over the offending pile.

"I'm so sorry."

"You OK?"

"I'm fine, just hot."

"Sit down here for a while, dear."

"I'm OK I'll just get the next train."

"Is it what I think it is?" said the elderly woman who had hovered behind me.

"I don't know."

"It will pass," she said.

I took off my gloves to wipe my mouth with the hankie she offered me. She glanced down at my hands.

"Oh!" she paused. "Definitely something you ate, or the heat – ah, here's my train." And off she went.

I thanked the station worker and got into the nearest carriage too, noticing briefly that the elderly woman had moved to the far end of the carriage.

I continued my journey to work feeling rather clammy and nauseous, but under control.

"You look a bit washed out," said Oliver.

"Yes, been sick, something I ate. I'll be OK."

"I'll get you a cup of tea. Sugar?"

"Yes, 2. Thanks."

I managed to get through the day, concentrating on the mundane tasks, such as filling the Roneo machine with ink or responding to requests for paper clips from the stationery cupboard. These activities were interspersed by typing up various writers' near-illegible hand-writing that somehow turned into fascinating stories or facts about subjects I knew little about.

The following day was Saturday. An opportunity for a lie-in before cleaning my room and picking up some shopping prior to meeting my friend Maggie for the theatre.

But again, the nausea. Someone was using the shared bathroom, but the separate toilet was free. I went in, opened the small window above the lavatory and sat down, hoping the nausea would pass. But no, I continued to feel really queasy. Perhaps a walk in the fresh air would help.

It was that time of year when shops and offices felt over-heated as centralised heating systems came on anticipating cold autumn weather. But the weather was mild, mid-October, with leaves changing colour and unexpected warm days making clothing decisions challenging. I went out without a coat, just a thick jumper and skirt.

I walked to our local Martin's newsagent and bought *The Times*. Miss Eversley had suggested *The Times* leader was a good way of 'stimulating the intellect', and I hoped that by concentrating on an editorial I could move my mind from my stomach to my brain. I sat on a bench in Lammas Park and started to read.

However, my nausea continued and reluctantly I returned to my digs.

"You look a bit peaky," said Mrs Wendover who owned the house. She was dressed in her cleaning outfit: flowery overall and headscarf styled from her 1940s' hay day. She was using some red polish on the step. The pungent smell turned my stomach and I threw up over a fuchsia in a small triangular bed to the right of the front door.

"Oh dear, good thing I've got my bucket here – must have been waiting for you to do that," she said as she threw a pail of grimy water over the flower bed. "Let's hope it's not morning sickness," she laughed.

"No, just something I ate."

"Now, now; no casting aspersions on my cooking."

"Of course not; must have been a dodgy sandwich yesterday lunchtime."

"Let's hope so."

"I put your bill under your door."

"Thanks, I'll settle up when I come down later."

After I'd rinsed my mouth out at the small basin in my room, I lay down. My mind started whirling. *Could it be? Surely not? We'd been so careful. Oh my God! Suppose it was. What would I do? No, it can't be. When was my last period? But I'd never thought to keep a note of them; perhaps June, perhaps July. I hadn't seen him the whole of August. Oh, no!*

With this dialogue going on in my head I dozed fitfully for the rest of the afternoon.

I was supposed to be meeting Maggie to have a pre-theatre meal at the Stockpot in Panton Street. I was in two minds about going. However, by 4 o'clock I felt fine and was actually looking forward to the distraction.

On the way downstairs, I bumped into Mrs W.

"Feeling better, dear?" she asked, as I settled up my bill.

"Absolutely fine, thanks."

"Going anywhere nice?"

"Theatre, I hope, if the queue isn't too long, and a meal in town."

"So you'll be quite late, then I'll leave the kitchen door for you. Where're you eating?"

"Probably at the Stockpot near the Strand."

"Won't be as good as here," she laughed, "but makes a change, doesn't it?"

She only provided evening meals Monday to Friday assuming that we young things would be off out at the weekends, which we usually were, and I was looking forward to a change from her limited menu. I was generally out seeing Finchie on Tuesdays and Thursdays being what he called his 'sunk asset' so I didn't experience the repetitive menu as much as the three other lodgers.

When I met Maggie outside the Stockpot, she immediately commented

"You look terrific."

"I don't feel it, I threw up today – and yesterday morning."

Her expression changed. "My sainted aunt!"

"What?" I said.

"Oh … my … God."

"No! It can't be."

"Oh … my God," she repeated. "Could it be?"

"I suppose it's just possible, but no!"

"You'd better get checked up."

"I don't think I need to – I bet it's something I ate. Dodgy sardine sandwiches or something."

"Better to know sooner rather than later."

"I don't want to think about it. I want to enjoy my evening."

"Well, if you need to, er, you know, I've got a friend who knows someone."

I interrupted. "Look, I'm sure it isn't. I don't want to talk about it."

"OK, OK."

So we ordered our meal. All I could manage was some soup and a cup of tea.

Afterwards we walked the whole length of the Strand to the Strand Theatre to see Frankie Howard in *A Funny Thing Happened on the Way to the Forum*. The play was fun and took my mind off the niggling worries I was starting to acknowledge might have some truth in them.

The following week I went for my Tuesday 'sunk asset' after work. I had been sick each morning and recognised that perhaps it wasn't something I'd eaten. I walked down Duke Street St. James's feeling anxious about telling Andrew what I suspected. I was slightly early and popped into the bookshop beneath the flat.

"A gentleman left this for you, miss." The shopkeeper handed me an envelope.

"Not today, Kitty. Work event. See you Thursday instead."

"Thanks."

"Not bad news, I hope," the shopkeeper said, reading my disappointed expression.

"Not really, just inconvenient. Thanks for…"

"It's a pleasure, I'm used to being a poste restante!"

The evening was warm and still light so I walked back up to Piccadilly and crossed over into Dover Street hoping to spend some time at the ICA seeing some exhibition or another. The pictures distracted me from my anxiety. Feeling restored I walked back to Green Park Station, bought an evening paper from the crippled ex-serviceman calling "Star, News and Standard" and returned to Northfields.

***

"Sorry about Tuesday, Kitty, but you got my message?"
I burst into tears.
"You didn't miss me that much did you?"
"Oh, Finchie – I'm in such a state. I don't know what to do."
"What's up? Lost your job?"
"N… no," I started to stammer.
"Come and have a drink; that'll cheer you up."
"N…n…no." I burst into another flood of tears. "I think I'm pregnant."

He sat down drawing me onto his lap.
"Are you sure? I've been so careful."
"Well I've been sick in the mornings since last Friday, and I haven't had my, you know…period thing since July."
"You didn't tell me."
"Well, it's not something you tell a man, is it?"
"Not normally, I suppose. But we do know about these things."
"What am I going to do, Finchie?"
"Let's have a cup of tea, and think about it." He went into the small kitchen and after a while passed 2 cups and saucers through the hatch.
"Sugar's on the table."
I continued to well up with tears.
"Look, I know a really good doctor. He's just off Harley Street. I can get you an appointment. And I'll pay if you need to…"
"That really frightens me. I might talk to Clemmie, she's married to a doctor. She'll know what to do."
"Well, my offer is there. It takes 2 to make a baby, so let me help."
"My God! A baby. I hadn't thought of it quite like that."

We spent the rest of the evening talking through various scenarios. I could see he was concerned and somewhat distracted by my news. He walked with me to Piccadilly Station and actually kissed me goodbye on the cheek. In public. Something he'd never done before.

"Take care," he said as he passed me through the barrier to the escalator, where I disappeared from his view.

At Northfields Station I phoned Clemmie.

"Sorry it's so late, but I need to talk to you."

"It's after 10.00. Can it wait till tomorrow?"

"OK, see you after work tomorrow. Whereabouts?"

"Come here. James is on nights at the hospital starting tomorrow, so we can have a good chinwag."

"See you around 6.30?"

"I'll make something to eat – or go to the fish and chip shop on your way here."

"I'll do that. Thanks."

Chapter 12

After work on Friday I collected the fish and chips and walked over to her house, breathing heavily with apprehension as to what her reaction might be.

"How many months gone are you?" she asked sternly after I'd blurted out my news.

"Three or four, I think."

"And no sickness before last week?"

"Actually, I have been feeling different, under the weather really, for a while. What am I going to do?"

"Get rid of it!" said Clemmie ever practical. "You won't get lodgings with a baby, you'll lose your job. It's not worth it."

"I just hate that idea, but what's the alternative?"

"Have the baby and get it adopted."

"I'm scared, Clemmie. Why do we always have to suffer for enjoying ourselves?"

"I did warn you."

"Yes, but do I ever listen?"

"Not often. What does Finchie say?"

"He knows a doctor who can, you know, and he'll pay."

"Well, take him up on his offer; it's his fault for not using a johnny."

"But he did. That's what I can't understand. I couldn't get a cap fitted cos I'm not married, so it was up to him."

"Ask him to marry you then."

"A shotgun wedding."

"Why not. You're obviously crazy about him."

That got me thinking. I had my suspicions that he might already be married but I'd pushed those half-conscious thoughts to the far recesses of my mind.

Why was he only available on most Tuesdays and Thursdays but never at weekends? He didn't normally show affection in the street, but I'd assumed that was his posh upbringing. I'd caught a glimpse of him once when I'd walked past the Opera House on my way back from an evening class at the City Lit. He'd had his arm draped over the shoulder of an elegant woman wearing a long fur coat. I'd been too scared to mention it to him in case it spoiled the magic of our 'sunk assets'. Oh! How stupid I was. Cinq a sept. That's what the French call their bits on the side, their mistresses, their totty. I decided to confront him next time we met.

***

I stormed up the stairs, stamping on each tread.

"You're married, aren't you?"

"What's brought this on, Kitty, you haven't even come in the door."

"That's why, when I said I was pregnant, you didn't say 'Let's get married, darling.'"

"Well, actually…do you want the truth, brutal and straight."

"Yes, you mean… toff." (I couldn't think of a stronger word, and however angry I felt, I didn't want to lower myself by using a stevedore's language).

He half laughed at the odd expression, but quickly settled his face to reflect the seriousness of the situation.

"Well, Kitty. Yes, I am married…no don't interrupt. Happily married, but we both often work in separate countries and don't see each other all that often."

"So you don't love me. It was all just pretend. You exploited me, a common little girl from south of the river. Just using me for your pleasure."

"No, no. I do love you. Why didn't I tell you? I didn't want you to stop seeing me. You have made me so happy. And I don't think you're a 'common little girl from sarf of the river'," he imitated. "I think you are adorable, intelligent and…"

"You can't love two people."

"How do you think parents love each other and each of their children?"

"Now you're thinking of me as a child!"

"Calm down. No, I think of you as a lovely woman who has made my life richer and happier."

"You're just soft soaping me."

And I sat down on the Chesterfield and cried. He put his arms round me.

"Listen sweetheart, we'll fix something up."

"I'm not having an abortion; it's too dangerous, and anyway it's illegal."

"There's a clinic in the countryside where you could have the baby. I know several Debs who've been there…"

"All with your babies."

"Don't be ridiculous. You are the only one; it's a surprise for me too, you know. I can sort it out and pay, so don't worry on that score. I could even say I was your cousin, if you like. They are very discrete and kindly."

"Clemmie says I'll be kicked out of my lodgings, and I'll lose my job."

"I doubt it. People are becoming more enlightened now. The war saw to that."

"Well soon I'll be huge and I won't be able to disguise it. What then? And what about my work?"

"I can't predict how they'll react. Even married women often have to give up their jobs whether they are pregnant or not, so you need to find out if they'll want to keep you on."

"I wonder if I can talk to Miss Eversley about it."

"Well you've spoken fondly of her. Why don't you tell her the situation and see if she can help."

"She'll be so disappointed in me. She thinks I have potential. Obviously only the potential to get myself up the duff!"

That made him laugh, and by the end of the evening we were both laughing and imagining the various scenarios when I told Miss Eversley.

"I've got to tell my aunt too. She won't be too happy."

"Give people more credit. You never know who's been carrying a similar secret around for years."

I decided to tell Auntie Vi when I went to Sunday lunch the next weekend.

***

She slapped me round the face.
"You little slut. How dare you."

"Don't be like that! I didn't mean it to happen."

"That's what they all say. 'It can't happen to me, I did it standing up! It can't happen to me I had a bath afterwards.' Oh you stupid, stupid girl."

"Well it's done now, and I'm going to have the baby and get it adopted."

"And in the meantime, lose your job, lose your lodgings. Don't think you can stay here, cos you can't. What would people think?"

"Thanks for nothing. I didn't have to tell you. I thought you might help me. I'm off."

I decided to go straight round to see Granny Aldrich as she lived nearby.

"What's that red mark on your face?" she said when she'd opened the door. "And you've been crying. Come in. Tell me all about it."

So we sat in her cosy sitting room nursing mugs of tea while I told her the whole story.

"What a shame he can't marry you. Bit above your station, but he sounded just right for you."

"Well, my fault for not finding out before I got involved."

"Just put it down to experience. I heard about lots of these situations in the war. Young men coming back from the Front and finding their girl friend or wife had had a baby. Some men coped well with it – you never know what they'd got up to themselves. Others, no. Beat their wives up, even deserted them."

"You are so understanding," I remarked.

"I've seen it all, dear. Nothing shocks me now. I am in my 80s, you know, so I've been around a long time."

So I went back to Northfields, my face still blotchy from Auntie Vi's slap, and from crying, but at least I'd got someone who understood.

***

I worked out I was about 4 months pregnant. I looked in the mirror each day to check that I didn't look like it, but gradually I'd had to take out my waistband and was worried that soon I'd had to go into smocks.

The sickness was passing, but I was getting anxious about the next stage.

Clemmie's husband James was really helpful. He explained everything about pregnancy and the process of labour. I couldn't believe that part of me still thought the baby would come out through my belly-button when that wasn't the way it had got in! We had a laugh about it. Clemmie said she found it terrible that single women couldn't get any form of contraception unless they had a letter saying they were formally engaged. We had a moan about Hire Purchase too. The fact that James had to sign forms when she was the one who had chosen the cooker, the fridge, the table and chairs and the settee that were on the never-never.

Gradually I began to enjoy being pregnant. It was my little secret. Until one day when I was working and I suddenly felt a movement inside me.

***

"What's got into you, Chrissie, you nearly knocked all those papers off the desk," said Gladys.

"Just cramp," I said, not wishing to let her into my secret. I'd been wearing looser and looser clothes, thanking heaven the weather was cold, so I could be wrapped up and not reveal my changing shape. I decided that it was time to talk to Miss Eversley.

The next time she came into the room I asked if I could have a word with her, in her office.

"Of course, dear."

We went upstairs together. I was determined not to cry or be pathetic in front of her.

"Come in and sit down."

"I have some terrible news. Not terrible, um, difficult news to tell you."

"Oh dear. What is it?"

"I'm pregnant, expecting a baby."

"My word, I am surprised. Can I ask if anyone here's involved?"

"No, certainly not, no one here. I'm very professional at work, but truly sorry I've let you down."

"Don't even think about that. These things happen. So, how far gone are you?"

"I've been told it'll be mid-February."

"I must say you've hid it well."

"One of the advantages of having a long body, I think, and it being cold, so I can cover up."

"Does anyone else know?"

"Only my friends and family?"

"I mean, here, Gladys, for example."

"No, definitely not Gladys."

"Leave it with me. By the way, how are you going to manage with a baby?"

"I've decided to have it adopted."

"No chance the father can marry you?"

"Unfortunately, he's married. I didn't know until recently."

"The cad!"

"No, I should have thought to find out before getting involved."

"Well, it takes two."

"I haven't told Oliver. I haven't seen him for a month or so."

"He's doing some work for the School Broadcasting Council, something to do with Teachers Notes, I think, to accompany BBC programmes. He'll be back in the spring."

"I might tell him."

"I don't know what reaction you'll get from him. He's very fond of you."

"I'm fond of him too. He's taught me a lot, and made me see the world in a different way."

"Well, good luck. In the meantime I'll have a think about what we can do here."

"I don't want anyone else to know. I suppose I'll have to leave." I started to feel tearful.

"Don't jump to conclusions. Let me have a think."

"Thank you for being so understanding." I returned to my desk and fended off questions from Gladys with, "Oh, just talking about my next project," which was true.

For a few days the following month I totally forgot my own troubles. I was walking to Russell Square station one Friday evening having stayed late to finish some urgent work when I heard a commotion in the street.

"I can't believe it," shouted a young black woman. "Kennedy's been shot! What will happen to us now?"

People rushed to the newsvendor outside the station. He'd been told the news by a station worker who'd been listening to the radio, but it wasn't in the editions of the evening papers. It was true; it was reported on the BBC. Kennedy had been shot in Dallas, Texas.

Then a young man came out of a nearby shop. "He's dead. He's dead." Several of us crowded into the tobacconist's to listen to the radio report.

A strange silence filled the air. The street outside had become frozen in time as the tobacconist turned up the volume so as many people as possible could hear the news.

Kennedy had become a hero to so many people. He'd averted a terrible conflict with Cuba, he was slowly appreciating the need for civil rights legislation, he was a central figure, together with his glamorous wife, in world news coverage. He'd even had "Happy Birthday" sung to him by Marilyn Monroe. He was a sexy international figure. And now he was dead.

My journey back to Granny A's was dreamlike. People on the tube were talking to each other about the horrific news. It was as though the whole of London was in shock. What must it have been like for the Americans? When I reached Church Street, Granny A already had the news on. We both sat there amazed that someone could shoot a President. Not just any president, but one who seemed to be doing so much good. I was starting to see things from a different perspective. The world was not just about me and my anxiety about how my pregnancy might affect my future, it was about other people. At last I could understand why Oliver cared so much about the different causes he supported.

Of course, by the time I went back to work on the Monday I had read reams of information in the newspapers, and seen too many sequences of the moment he'd been shot, the distress of Jackie Kennedy, the drunken eulogy given by George Brown, who'd apparently known Kennedy well, the unusual investiture of LBJ by a woman, which worried some people, but she was the appropriate person, in spite of some of the opinions expressed, and the assassination of Lee Harvey Oswald.

***

I continued to see Finchie, who was even becoming excited about the baby.

"Kitty's having a kitten," he joked. But he still didn't come out with me in public, not even for a sandwich in St. James's Square.

"I still can't get over the fact that I didn't realise you were married." Anger still welled up in me, mixed with embarrassment at my own naivety.

"I should have told you. Thought you'd never get involved with me, I suppose."

"You must have got married very young."

"I did. Adolescent passion. Seduced by the daughter in the French family I'd gone to stay with. Exchange visit, to bring my French up to scratch for my exams."

"So that's what inspired you to go to the Sorbonne, not an English university."

"I was married by then. She comes over sometimes."

"Will you tell her about me?"

"I doubt it. But the French seem quite sanguine about affaires. They are discreet though."

"Obviously that's where you got your taste for 'a bit on the side'."

"You mean more to me than that! I don't know what her family would think, though. They're much more involved in our relationship than in-laws here."

"I don't think I'd like that."

"It has its advantages. Access to jobs, holidays in relatives' apartments near Nice, that sort of thing. Very family oriented."

"So that's why you won't marry me; her family."

"I'm committed to Francine, not just to them."

"And after the baby's born?"

"I'll support you, whatever you decide to do. Don't worry."

Chapter 13

Finchie drove up to Mrs Aldrich's ground floor flat in his MG. It was a cold but sunny Monday, so we wrapped ourselves up warmly and kept the hood down. I had a small case with me containing two nighties, a bed-jacket knitted by Mrs Aldrich, toiletries and a fresh smock and underwear. I had also included my A Level books hoping that studying them would reduce my anxiety about what lay ahead. Finchie had given me a filled leather stationery case together with stamps so I could keep in touch with friends if it was difficult to get to a phone box and presumably so I could write to him. We had a Thermos of tea and some sandwiches from Granny Aldrich who seemed to think that Guildford was far away on the other side of the country.

We drove towards the Surrey Hills. We stopped in a sheltered lay-by and warmed ourselves with the hot tea and nibbled at our sandwiches.

"I'm very proud of you, you know," said Finchie, lighting up a Gauloise Disque Bleu, his new cigarette of choice.

"Why's that?"

"Many girls would have gone hysterical and been unable to make any decisions, but you've kept your head."

"Well, I had lots of help."

"Not from your aunt."

"No, but from Granny Aldrich letting me stay with her and not blaming me like Auntie Vi did."

"And your work."

"Yes, Miss Eversley. Who would believe she could be so brilliant. That was your idea. And she came up trumps, persuading Mr Blackwood to let me 'spend a few months nursing my old grandma!' What luck to be able to keep my job."

"I think blackmail came into it too."

"Do you think she'd stoop so low?"

"Well if you've got the ammunition, you tend to use it in a crisis."

"She knew that he'd taken Gladys with him to a book fair for a whole weekend, and Gladys wasn't exactly quiet about it."

"Did you sort out where you're going afterwards?"

"Not yet, but Granny A said if I'm stuck, I could go there for a while."

"I'd like to give your old landlady a piece of my mind."

"No, don't make things worse."

"Of course, I won't, but I couldn't believe it, kicking you out with only 24 hours' notice. So mean minded and suburban, thinking of her own reputation rather than helping you."

I couldn't eat much of my sandwich so I fed it to the sparrows and robins that had come to investigate and we went back to the car.

"Can't we go for a walk?"

"Best to get this over with; anyway, you're not up for walking much."

"I'm so nervous. Will they be kind to me?"

"Do you really think I'd send you to a place where people will be horrid to you? Give me some credit."

"I'm sorry, just got butterflies."

And he helped me into the front seat and we drove off.

***

We arrived at Orchard Court a few minutes later. There were two gates about fifty yards apart. One had an entrance sign below a board saying "Orchard Court. Mother and Baby Home. Matron: Sister Shotley". Presumably there was a sign somewhere saying 'Exit' for the other gate. We drove through the open one. There was a parking area in front of the 1950s building. We got out and walked to the front door. I noticed that the driveway continued alongside the grey walls and disappeared round the back. The building seemed purpose built as a registered Nursing Home and was on the site of an old orchard. Many of the trees were still standing and the one nearest the door had snowdrops at its feet. There were benches beneath what I assumed were two apple trees and I spotted a heavily pregnant young woman reading on one of them.

"She looks about your age," said Finchie trying to reassure me.

"No doubt I'll find out soon enough," I said rather sharply as my anxiety overwhelmed me.

"Good afternoon," said the Matron as we crossed the entrance hall. "We're expecting you, dear."

"Afternoon," replied Finchie. "What's the drill?"

"Well, we'll take Miss Preece up to the ward first and while she's settling in you can come down and confirm the arrangements."

"Thank you," I said more timidly than I meant.

Matron took us up the stairs to a six-bedded ward with views over the orchard.

"It must look wonderful in spring," I offered, trying to appear more confident than I felt.

"Yes. Stunning. And we're usually busy then. It's not too crowded at the moment. Just 4 girls including you, but a couple more expected next week. This is your bed." It was the first one we came to in the room. "Toilet and bathroom are just here." And she indicated a door set into a recess half way down the ward.

"I'll leave you to unpack. If you want some privacy just draw the curtains round."

"Thank you so much," said Finchie. "I'll be down shortly."

He helped me put my few belongings into the bedside table. We both sat on the bed and he gave me an envelope.

"What's this," I said.

"Just a little memento."

I was just opening the envelope when in charged a very pregnant horsey-looking girl.

"Forgot my fags! Oh! My God, Finchie. What are you doing here?"

Finchie leapt to his feet.

"Hells bells, Lottie. Didn't expect to see you here."

"Well," stroking her swollen belly, "bloody Mr N.S.I.T. got me up the duff. Quick drunken grope in taxi. Couldn't wait to get me inside. Mummy and Daddy at the country pile. Wham! Bang! Thank you ma'am. Actually stayed bloody weekend. Very athletic, did all sorts…"

Finchie interrupted quickly: "No details, Lottie, thank you. How's Joly? Still at the bank?"

"Didn't work out. Couldn't keep up with the market traders. Bloody good at sums, those boys. Bit dim in that region, Joly. Estate Agent now."

"Knows you're here?"

"Bloody hell, no Finchie. Chatham House Rules and all that. Supposed to be finishing in Switzerland. Haven't seen you for yonks, not since the wedding. Foxy did you both proud. Bloody Loire chateau and all that."

"Shut it, Lottie."

"Sorry, bloody hell, put my foot in it. What're you doing here?"

"Brought a friend."

"Ah!" said Lottie knowingly.

"Hello," I said, coming forward.

"Ooh, about to drop, are you?"

"In about a week, I think. I'm Christine."

I shook her hand, or rather she pumped mine up and down in a strong grip still looking at Finchie.

"Not a word, Finchie, I promise. Not a word. You too."

"Off you go, Lottie. Got your ciggies?"

"Yah. See you later, Christine."

When she'd lolloped out of the room I looked pleadingly at Finchie.

"I thought you said it was discrete, private."

"I swear it is. Bit of a blow seeing Jolyon's little sister Charlotte here. She won't tell. Not in her interest to say she's been here."

"What's she finishing in Switzerland?"

"Herself!" We both laughed, almost to the point of hysteria, which for me turned to tears.

"Kitty, Kitty, darling. It will be alright."

"You will visit me?"

"Of course. Now be a brave girl and let go of me." I'd been clutching him to me not wanting his reassuring presence to leave me.

"Yes, yes, I'll be brave."

"Any problems ring me at the flat, Tuesday or Thursday evenings." I nodded.

"I'll come down with you."

So we walked down the stairs, and I kissed him shyly as he went into Matron's office.

While he was with her, I walked along the corridor to explore the ground floor. The dining room, which overlooked the side garden, was the first room I came to. It was already set for our evening meal. It felt cosy with tapestry-style curtains, but plastic-looking chair-seats, which looked out of character with the rest of the room. There were carafes of water on each of the 4 tables and pale green bread plates by each place setting. Coming out of the dining room I turned right. At the end of the corridor were double doors with the sign 'Nursing Staff Only' on them. I peeked through one of the round glass windows and saw what looked like the medical facility: a nurses' station and a long passage with three doors leading off each side. It was painted white with only a notice-board for decoration. At the far end was what I guessed was an operating theatre or labour room.

I suppose that's where we give birth, I thought, feeling my stomach starting to turn. I walked back a few steps. Opposite the dining room was a door marked 'Kitchen'. Back on the garden side nearer to the front entrance was a sitting room with a fire in the grate. My back was aching by now so I went in to find somewhere to sit and wait. The alcoves either side of the fire were filled with cheap novels, a few classics, medical books, encyclopaedias and a compendium of games. On a round table in a recess next to the window, were some *Tatler* magazines, *Country Life* and old copies of *Punch*. I sat flicking through one edition, and found myself chuckling at the cartoons and captions.

"I'm off, then," said Finchie who had come out of his session with Matron and had traced my laughter to where I was waiting. We walked together to the front steps. I went with him to his car. And so I said goodbye to my 'sunk asset', my lover, the father of my soon-to-be-adopted baby on the steps of Orchard Court.

Matron came out and waved goodbye at the disappearing car.

"Come and have a little chat, Miss Preece."

"Please call me Christine."

"Fine, Christine it is." We went into her office.

"I'll just give you some information about how I run this Home. We have a few rules and I'm quite strict about them. No smoking in the ward."

"I haven't smoked since I got pregnant; makes me feel queasy," I responded.

"Good. It's such a fire hazard, and goodness knows what it does to your health. Another thing, you must come down for meals, unless of course you've gone into labour, in which case you won't want to eat till it's all over, and then you can have a few meals in bed if you need to. Lights out at 10.00 p.m. and try not to chatter too much in the dark, you need to rest as much as possible. Don't listen to scare stories. It's not a rule, but some of the girls are real drama queens. They've never experienced hardship or pain. Had life too easy a lot of them and they come down to earth with a bump."

"I am quite scared," I confided.

"Understandable. One of the nurses comes into the ward each morning and answers any questions you might have, and leads a stretching and breathing session. That takes about forty minutes. We like you to find a song or a poem to learn, so that you have something to take your mind off the contractions. Can you think of one?"

I had been reading the letter that Finchie had given me when Lottie had interrupted us. It contained the words of a song 'there is a lady sweet and kind' which we had both listened to on the wireless.

"Yes, I think I have a couple. A song and a poem about a cat drowned in a goldfish bowl that I learnt at school."

"Doesn't sound very cheerful. But you've got a choice. Tomorrow I'll have a talk with you about what your decision is about the baby. Of course there'll be papers to sign."

"I have definitely decided."

"Well, it's worth sleeping on it, and I can explain the process, and also how you might feel after the baby's born."

What an understanding woman she was. Not the dragon I was anticipating.

"By the way, the only titles we use here are Matron, Nurse and Doctor."

I was confused.

"You mean…?"

"We have young women from some of the top families in the land, occasionally from overseas. As far as we're concerned you have all been unfortunate, and we're here to help you through your difficulties with discretion."

"So, I call someone, who might be er Lady x, just x, too?"

"Exactly. Keeps the pressure off them. They can relax and be ordinary for the first time in their lives. Not always having to keep up appearances. They have enough constraints and obligations to cope with."

"How egalitarian."

"Society is changing. You've just got to read what's happening in America. It's up to you young things to keep the momentum going."

I was fascinated by her outlook, particularly as she was working in a private clinic, and not a local state-run hospital, but I didn't feel able to probe.

"Off you go now. Get as much rest as you can."

"Can I use the phone?"

"Yes, there's one on your landing for your ward."

"Thank you. Should I be asking anything else?"

"Not as far as I'm concerned. The nurse midwife will talk you through the procedure. We have two so you'll probably meet them both before you go into labour. And two doctors are on call."

"Thank you."

"See you tomorrow, after breakfast."

So I went back to the ward where I noticed the young woman who'd been in the garden sitting by the window, reading, and Lottie resting on her bed.

"How was your talk with Matron? She's OK that one," said Lottie in her abrupt way.

"It was fine. I hadn't expected someone so sympathetic."

"Well, what a shock seeing Finchie. Known him long?"

"A couple of years." I suddenly felt possessive of him, and didn't want to share anything about our relationship with her.

"Quite a dish. Same house as Jolyon. Both in rugger team. Played for the school."

"I didn't know. Explains his nose," I commented.

"Modest, that one. Even about his MC. Known me since I was six. Both dads at school together too."

"What MC?"

"For what he did in the Malayan Emergency."

"He never said."

"Modest, as I said. Think it was something hush-hush. Not like his big brother, Tiffy."

"Tiffy?"

"Yes, his initials, T. F. He'll inherit of course, but he's on some tea plantation now. Such a boaster."

"Yes," I said, never having heard of Tiffy. I didn't want to pursue this conversation so I moved towards the bathroom door.

"Off to the loo?"

"Yes, then a rest. I'm exhausted."

When I returned Lottie had left the ward. I introduced myself to the girl sitting by the window. "I'm Christine, hello."

She offered her hand. I shook it, noticing how soft her skin was and how beautiful she was, with her black hair tied into an elegant chignon, not like my messy beehive, held together with hair pins that fell out if I moved quickly. She inclined her head, but said nothing.

"I'm sorry if I'm interrupting you."

"Not at all, Christine. I'm Fatima."

"Not from England, then," I said.

"Originally from Persia, but came here with my family in 1953 because of the coup." I didn't understand the significance of this at the time.

"How did you end up here?"

She seemed reluctant to confide in me, so I told her some of my story. Then she opened up.

"I was unfortunate. I got involved with a gardener at my boarding school, in the woods."

"Goodness."

"They've sacked him. I'll go back and take my A Levels next term. Going to be a doctor. Everyone thinks I've gone back to my family for a family event."

"And the baby, when it comes?"

"Matron has found a family. Also from my country. I might even know them, but it will all be very discrete."

That night I heard whimpering coming from the far corner of the ward and then, "No, no, Daddy," she shouted over and over again. It kept me awake as much as the twinges and movement inside me together with the difficulty of finding a comfortable position to lie in.

In the morning when her curtains were drawn open, I was horrified to see that the bed was occupied by a child. No more than 13 or 14. Obviously terribly distressed.

"Dad's a bloody earl too," said Lottie when we were walking downstairs to breakfast.

"Do you mean…?"

"Yes, I bloody do. Her mama's going to pretend it's hers if it's a boy. Keep it in the family. No scandal. There are only girls at the moment."

"And if it's a girl?"

"They don't care. Adoption, I assume."

"Poor child. Why only keep it if it's a boy."

"To inherit the title."

"Oh, that's awful."

I felt sick. I'd heard about that sort of thing amongst families where the mother was exhausted from childbearing and the father turned to the oldest daughter, but not in the upper echelons of society, the people I'd been taught to respect by my school and especially by Auntie Vi.

"Poor, poor, kid. How did you find out?"

"My mama knows hers. Both do fund-raising events for the same charity. Bloody shame. Ruined that girl's life. Tried to starve herself, they say."

I could hardly eat my breakfast, I was so shaken up.

I returned to the ward and lay down for ten minutes to clear my head. Lottie didn't appear, so I assumed she'd gone for a stroll.

The child in the corner hadn't come down for her meal, and her curtains were closed.

When I felt more settled, I went downstairs to go through the paperwork with Matron.

"Settling in alright?" she asked.

"Yes, but I'm worried about that little girl in the corner."

"Supposed to be hush hush. Don't get involved."

"She cried all night, and shouted about her…"

"I know. Just be kind to her," she interrupted. "We'll give her all the help we can. Now, back to you." She walked over to a filing cabinet and brought out a brown folder.

"I've got your details here, next of kin, Aunt. Address etc.," she skimmed through the form.

"Can I change that to someone else?"

"Why?"

"Well, we've sort of fallen out. Over me being pregnant."

"But she is your next of kin."

"Can I add someone then, my grandma?" I said, not saying that Granny A wasn't a blood relation.

"As a second contact then. Now, what are your plans when the baby comes?"

"I've talked it through with several people, friends and Andrew. Adoption. It's the only way."

"And your aunt? Did you discuss that with her?"

"Pretty much disowned me. Kicked me out so, no."

"I'm sorry about that. We'll make sure baby goes to a lovely family. We have quite a waiting list. Some want a girl, some a boy. And some are just desperate for a baby, they don't mind either way, as long as it's healthy."

I suddenly had a different perspective on the whole situation.

"So, keeping the pregnancy could be seen as a way of helping others?"

"A good positive view to take, Christine. You've obviously given it a lot of thought. And apart from being illegal, an abortion can have serious consequences, infection leading to infertility, even death."

"Goodness. I'm so pleased I avoided all that, instinctively."

She nodded. "That's sometimes why a woman needs to adopt. So I take it you are happy to sign the consent papers?"

I nodded and signed.

"Did you know I was adopted by my aunt and grandma?"

"No." There was a knock on the door. "Come in." She turned back to me. "Christine, you must tell me about your life when we have a chance. You are very different from our usual clients. Much…" I wondered if she was going to say "More ordinary".

One of the nurses had entered the room with a bunch of papers. Matron smiled at her and turned to me.

"Do you know what to expect when you go into labour?" she asked.

"Sort of."

"Well, Nurse Blackie has arrived with her usual perfect timing to lead you through the process."

"Thank you, Matron," I said, as I was ushered out by Nurse Blackie. I was amused that her name reflected the colour of her skin.

"We'll go to the examination room and I'll take down your medical history and talk you through what will happen when you go into labour."

"Thank you," I said as I followed her through the 'Nursing Staff. No Entry' doors. We went into one of the door on the right.

After she'd made notes about my vaccinations, measles, chicken pox, suspected scarlet fever, avoidance of polio and so on, she took my blood pressure, asked me to supply some urine and told me to undress from the waist down. I struggled to get onto the couch.

"Obviously not long to go," she observed.

She listened to my bulge with a trumpet thing and felt round my pubic hair line really hard.

"Ouch," I squeaked.

"You'll have to get used to a bit of pain."

"Can't you knock me out?"

"No dear, we need you to do all the hard work. We can't do it all for you. You have to keep awake for that."

And she talked me through the different stages of labour.

"You'll have to obey orders too."

"I'm not very good at that," I laughed.

"Well, when I tell you NOT to push, that's very important."

"Aren't you going to do an internal?"

"No, I don't want to start you off today, I've already got one on the way."

"Who's that?"

"Big Charlotte, Lottie."

"But I was only talking to her at breakfast."

"Waters broke as she left the dining room."

"Oh, gosh. Having it here?"

"Yes, unless there are complications, then the ambulance takes you to hospital."

"Have you delivered many?"

"Too many, my dear. A bit more restraint wouldn't come amiss amongst you young things."

"I was told there were no judgments here," I was shocked by her comments and my bravery in challenging her too.

"Sorry, but I have my private opinions. I dread to think what the morals of this country will be like when more people go on the Pill."

"But it sounds like a good way to space children," I said thinking of the families who have lots of babies one after the other, hardly giving the mother time to recover.

"When they're married, fine. But let's hope the unmarried girls don't get hold of it. It could be the end of marriage as we know it."

"Or you'd be out of a job here," I said.

"I certainly hope so. Don't get me wrong. I love my work, but there's a lot of sadness here too."

"Like that little girl in the corner of my ward."

"Wouldn't help her. Anyway, we're here to help you."

So she talked me through what to expect, and I felt reassured that I was going to be in Nurse Blackie's experienced hands.

"Off to check up on Charlotte now, big Charlotte that is."

"Oh, who's little Charlotte then," realising that there must be another one.

"Little one in the corner of your ward."

"So, she's Charlotte too." After that I thought of her as 'Charlottetoo'.

***

"Breathe, breathe. Stop!" I had entered the ward where a younger nurse called Nurse Rowley had started a series of exercises.

"Come in and grab a cushion; watch the others and join in when you're ready."

I heaved my bulk down onto the mat on the floor and leant against a large V-shaped pillow beside the wall.

"And, breathe, breathe, breathe. Stop! Pant, Pant, little breaths, faster than that, little girl. Pant, pant, pant, pant. Well done."

We continued like this for a while. When Nurse Rowley had gone and Fatima, Charlottetoo and I had struggled up, I introduced myself.

"Are you OK?" I said, plunging straight in.

"Yes," little Charlotte replied.

"When's the baby due?"

"Any time now, I think."

I couldn't think of anything else to say without giving away the information I'd recently heard about how she came to be pregnant, so I just said, "I'm exhausted after all that puffing and panting. I'll have a rest until lunch."

"Me too," said Charlottetoo. Fatima put on her coat and left the ward. Having no-one to chat to I lay on my bed flicking through my history notes, trying to focus on where I had left the Hapsburgs with their long chins through interbreeding and their Austrian dynasty.

***

My first full day had passed quietly, reading, walking outside and writing to Clemmie, Granny Aldrich and Miss Eversley to let them know I'd arrived and that everything was fine. I'd been disappointed that I wasn't allowed out of the grounds to post my letters, but as Matron said, "While you're in my care, I can't have you walking that far and maybe going into labour. What would happen then?" I'd slept reasonably well too. I woke up to find Lottie back in her bed sleeping soundly. I wondered how it had been for her, and what they had done with the baby.

She was wakened by Nurse Rowley, who examined her behind the closed curtains. After drinking a cup of tea and being led to the lavatory, she returned to bed.

"Bloody painful. Not going through that again, not for all the tea in China. Absolutely pooped!" She gave a blow by blow account to Charlottetoo and me, interspersed with some choice swearwords, many of which I'd never heard before. Charlottetoo started crying. I went over to her and gave her a hug.

"It can't be that bad," I said hopefully, "Otherwise women would stop having babies and the human race would die out. Anyway Lottie likes dramatizing things. Come for a walk. It's quite sunny now."

So we walked in the garden looking at the crocuses and snowdrops vying for attention under the apple trees.

"You still at school," I asked.

"Yes."

"Going back?"

"Yes, after half term."

"How is school? Do you like it?" She nodded.

"What do you like about it?"

She started crying again.

"Being away, away from…"

"It's OK, It'll be alright." I hugged her and led her to a bench where I rocked her until she'd composed herself.

"I can't bear that Lottie. She's so loud, and her family know mine. Nothing's a secret."

"She won't let on. She's promised."

"Do you believe her?"

"Yes, she's got too much to lose herself. She's supposed to be at Finishing School."

"All she's interested in is 'Coming Out' at the Queen Charlotte's Ball."

"When's that?"

"Some time in the summer."

"She should have her figure back by then."

"Do you think she's ever had one?" said Charlottetoo.

"You naughty girl," I laughed, and she started laughing too.

As the sun went behind a cloud it felt cold, and the wind was starting to blow. We went inside and sat in the lounge. She had left some school books on the table in the window.

"This takes my mind off things. I never thought I'd enjoy schoolwork so much."

"I'm doing my A Levels."

"Aren't you too old? I'm sorry, that sounds rude."

"I didn't stay at school after 15."

"I'd like to stay at school for ever."

"What's your favourite subject?"

"History."

"Mine too. We could study together, if you like."

She opened one of her books.

"Oh, you've got one of Oliver's books." I was delighted to see it was one that I had proof read. "I had a hand in that too."

"Is he the man who…?" she asked.

"Goodness, no! A work colleague; a good friend."

"I'd love to work. What is your job?"

"I work, or worked, for a publishing company. That's one of our school books. He writes a lot of our books."

I felt really proud to see Oliver's writing in a place like this. I wondered whether to contact him, but I didn't want to shatter any views he might have of me.

We chatted for a while, but fell silent when Lottie came down and lit a cigarette.

"Thank God that's over," she said. "Going back to Switzerland next week."

"What did you have," I asked.

"Didn't bother to find out. Going to its family next week. Stiff upper lip and all that." She flounced around in her dressing gown, puffing smoke all over the place, dropping ash. She tried to sit on a chair.

"Bloody hell, ooh a bit sore down there."

Charlottetoo and I looked at each other, and smiled.

"Back to the Dorm, I think." And Lottie stubbed out her cigarette and left us in peace. I followed her to get my A Level work, and returned to study with Charlottetoo.

That evening, being a Tuesday I phoned Finchie at his flat.

"Any news, Kitty, have you settled in alright?"

"They're really nice here. Matron particularly," I said.

"You see, you can trust me to find somewhere nice. Incidentally, don't worry about Lottie. She might be all talk at times, but she's quite a decent type."

"She had her baby."

"That was quick. Boy or girl?"

"I don't know, and she didn't even ask. Can you believe that?"

"She'll want to get on with her life."

"She told me you had brothers."

"And a sister, Alice."

"How come I didn't know before?"

"Can I ever get a word in edgeways when you come and see me?"

"No, I suppose not."

"That's a bit naughty of Lottie, though. What did you say about us?"

"Nothing. She prods a bit, but I don't want to give anything away."

"Quite right. The less she knows the better really."

I lowered my voice, although the phone booth seemed quite private.

"There's a very sad case here too."

"Oh! Who's that?"

"I can't say, but she's only a kid. All sounds a bit worrying."

"Someone force himself on her?"

"Someone," I paused, "In the family."

"Awful, awful."

"Are you coming to see me?"

"Thursday evening alright?"

"If I haven't had it by then."

"The date they gave you was next weekend, I thought."

"They don't always come on time."

"Take care, Kitty. I'm always thinking of you."

"By the way, thank you for the words of the song." The pips started.

"I mean it too. Bye."

"Bye, Finchie, love you."

***

On Thursday evening Finchie arrived carrying a bunch of irises, daffodils, tulips and hyacinths, beautifully tied together.

"They're lovely," I said, "Thank you."

"I know you like irises, and they'll bring a bit of spring sunshine to the ward while you're waiting."

"Gorgeous smell," I responded, putting my head amongst the flowers.

"Yes, the hyacinths."

We were sitting in the lounge. Charlottetoo came in, but seeing us there retreated tactfully.

"What's that child doing here?" said Finchie.

I whispered in his ear: "the one I told you about on the phone."

"She only looks about 10. She's so thin."

"She's tiny, I just hope she can cope."

"Are they helping her?"

"Matron and the nurses are wonderful. She's trying to carry on with her school work and I'm helping her a bit. We study together sometimes."

"I'm sure she'll benefit from having someone like you to talk to."

"Hopefully."

He changed the subject. "Still OK about having the Kitten adopted?"

"Yes, I've signed the forms. The only solution."

"I'll make sure it goes to a lovely home."

"That's what Matron said too. She said there's a long waiting list."

"I bet there is. I'll have a word with her on my way out. I might ask about the little girl too."

"Oh, don't. It's all supposed to be secret. I don't want her to think I've broken all the rules, blabbed my mouth off."

"No, I can just say I noticed her, that's all."

We talked for a while about what was going on in Vietnam, would it ever end, and how different, he thought, from the reasons for getting involved in Malaya. I mentioned the hysterical welcome the Beatles received on their visit to the States and hummed a few bars of *Love, Love Me Do*, and then it was time for him to go, and for me to have my supper and try to sleep.

***

At the weekend another girl arrived, Sophie. She was already having contractions, so, after her chaperone had unpacked for her she was taken downstairs to the Labour Ward.

When she returned to our ward and had recovered, Lottie quizzed her, comparing their birth experiences. She seemed elated by it, so I felt reassured that giving birth could be a pleasant one too. We discovered she'd got pregnant from her French ski instructor who'd had at least three of his students on the go at the same time.

"Very romantic. In the mountains, flowers everywhere. Lovely, lovely time. Of course, I didn't know about the others, only found out when I told them I'd missed the curse. Big disappointment, but, struggle on."

She was actually engaged to someone else.

"Nice man, but fixed up by my family. They've always had social ambitions for me. Title and all that."

"Is the baby going for adoption?" I asked.

"Not sure. It was such a sweet little thing, a girl. I held her. Big mistake. Fell in love. Don't think I can give her up. Break my heart. I'll go down and feed her shortly. But, hey. I'll talk it over with my folks. Fiance might be queer, anyway. He's a bit, you know." She did a demonstration.

"He's a sweet guy, really funny, and I've known him since I was," and she raised her hand from her knee to her hip, "So it's not a problem. I'll take a lover if it is."

We laughed and it took away the anxiety we'd all felt after Lottie's tales of horror. But it also set us all thinking. What if we fell in love with our babies? I decided not to even touch mine when it came out.

***

The Tuesday after Sophie had given birth Fatima went into labour. She started in the early morning, around 3 a.m. so we had a disturbed night. We didn't see her all that day, nor on the Wednesday. Early on Thursday morning I thought I heard the sound of an ambulance, not the Orchard Court one, but a hospital one with its sirens blaring out.

At breakfast the serving staff all seemed subdued.

"Where's Fatty?" asked Lottie, ever the spokeswoman. She'd been quietly tearful for a couple of days and we were thankful she wasn't rushing around, swearing, dropping ash and generally disturbing our preparations for going into labour.

"Got into difficulties," said the waitress spooning out our scrambled eggs.

A sudden hush descended.

"Is she alright?" I said, fearing the worst.

Matron came in.

"I'm afraid I have some bad news. However, Fatima is alright. She lost a lot of blood, had a difficult time, and is at the hospital, being well looked after. We think she'll make it."

"And the baby?" I asked.

"No."

Silence.

Both Charlottes started crying. Even though we didn't want a baby, the thought of having nothing to show for the anxiety and hours of pain at the end of 9 months stunned us.

"We did our best, and so did the doctors," said Nurse Blackie as she entered the room having heard our conversation. "It's very unusual."

"Try not to upset yourselves," Matron added.

We finished our breakfast in silence.

After breakfast Lottie started packing up her things.

"Good luck all." She called out quietly as she left the 'Dorm'.

Charlottetoo and I spent the day studying quietly in the lounge. In the late afternoon we heard a car arrive. After an hour or so the driver got in the car and drove round the building to beyond the medical area. It stopped for about 15 minutes at what must have been a rear entrance, and then drove towards the road. I briefly saw the head of a woman sitting in the back of the car, tilting her head down to something she was holding. *Was it Lottie's baby?* I wondered.

That evening Finchie came to see me.

"The saddest thing has happened." And I told him about Fatima.

He looked visibly shaken.

"Poor girl, is she alright?"

"In hospital still. Lost a lot of blood." I started to cry.

"My darling girl. You will be alright, I know you will, Kitty."

"I didn't realise it could…die," I hesitated over the word. "And I can feel funny twinges in my tummy."

"You'll be fine. It's extremely rare that something goes wrong. And they are very experienced here."

"Oh, yes, yes, I suppose so, but even so, well, you know."

I suddenly jumped up as a sharp pain took my breath away.

"It sounds as if things are starting," he commented and laid his hands on my bump. "Now, now, baby, don't you give Kitty any trouble."

He tried to reassure me, but I wasn't really concentrating. I seemed to be in a bit of a daze.

When it was time for him to go, I went back to the Ward, and rested on the bed. I just couldn't get comfortable, so I walked around for a while.

When I went to the loo, I noticed that a sort of pink coloured mucous plug had appeared. I rang for a nurse.

Nurse Rowley was on duty and came quickly. "Yes, I think you've started. Any pains?"

"Just a few twinges."

"Well, hop back into bed and try to get some rest. I'll come and see you again shortly."

I dozed on and off for a few hours. Then in the middle of the night, things really kicked off. I concentrated hard on breathing as I'd been told, and thought about the song Finchie had written down for me. I rang for Nurse Rowley.

"Let's get you downstairs now," and she held my arm. We stopped half way down the stairs while I held on to the bannister and felt myself almost doubling up with pain. But then it stopped.

"This is most peculiar," I said.

"No, it's all happening quite normally. Contractions come; then they stop for a while, and gradually they build up until out pops the baby."

"You make it sound so straightforward."

"It usually is," she replied.

And so my labour progressed. My poem wasn't much use to me, but I found singing *Mad About the Boy* seemed to take my mind of the pain. My poem and the song Finchie had given me had somehow got muddled up.

"'Twas on a lofty vase's side I knew a maiden sweet and fair." I just couldn't get them untangled. It even seemed in my mind that it was a goldfish giving birth to a kitten.

When it came nearer to the moment of delivery, I was given a mask attached to a cylinder that delivered gas and air. I wished I could stand up, squat down or walk around, but I was stuck on my back with my legs in the air. Then as I started to push I saw my mother. At least, I knew it was my mother from the photo I'd been shown as a child. What was she doing here, I wondered? "Mum, Mummy," I called out. But she'd disappeared.

Nurse Blackie and Nurse Rowley held my feet against their hips as I pushed and pushed on a contraction. Then Nurse Blackie, very fiercely shouted, "Push. Stop, pant, pant, pant," as she checked around the baby's neck in case the cord was caught. "OK push, push, PUSH." I sounded more like a cow in labour than a human being as I obeyed her orders.

And out slithered a baby!

"Well done. Wonderful, you did exactly what we wanted, and, it wasn't too bad, was it?" Nurse Blackie said.

I felt really proud, exhilarated, and not particularly tired. Nurse Rowley mopped my forehead and gave me a hug.

"Do you want to know what it is?"

"Yes, please," I said.

"It's a boy."

"Not a kitten?" We all laughed.

"Whatever got into your head that you were having a kitten?"

"It's just that my boyfriend calls me Kitty."

Nurse Blackie was weighing the baby. "Just under 7 lbs. 6 lbs 10 oz. Perfectly healthy, got everything in the right place."

She pressed a buzzer for the doctor to come and do various tests on the baby and to see if I was fine.

After the placenta had arrived, and been weighed, which I found strange, but apparently it's an important part of the process, Nurse Rowley went to get me a cup of tea.

"I saw my mother."

"When?" asked Nurse Blackie as she wrapped the baby in a white crocheted blanket.

"Just now, when I was giving birth."

"Well, I can guarantee she wasn't here in this room."

"Actually, she's dead."

"Oh! I'm sorry. Sometimes women go onto another plane, spiritual, a different level of consciousness. It's quite possible that you saw her. Did she die recently?"

"No, I never knew her. She died giving birth to me. In an air raid. I wish I'd known her." I started crying.

Nurse Blackie hugged me. "She obviously loves you and is looking out for you."

"I've let her down."

"Not at all. You've had a healthy little baby boy. Do you want to hold him?"

She picked him up from the crib where she'd placed him.

"No. I can't let myself. He's going for adoption." But the temptation was too much. I leaned over the side of the delivery bed and admired the little bundle. It seemed amazing that he'd been inside me. One of his hands was sticking out from the blanket.

"I'll just touch him," I said. So I felt his soft hand, in awe of how perfect the tiny nails and fingers were.

Nurse Blackie swaddled him more tightly and the last I saw of him was the top of his head covered in matted dark hair, as she wheeled the cot out of the Labour Ward.

The doctor came back in followed by Nurse Rowley holding a mug of tea.

She checked me over while Nurse Rowley waved her hand over the tea to cool it down.

"You're fine; and no stitches, brilliant," said the doctor. "I'll just get nurse to give you a bed bath and then, if you feel up to it, you can go back to your ward."

That bed bath was wonderful. My body felt alive so when Nurse Rowley sponged me down it was cooling and sensual. Every nerve was tingling.

"Let's get you up," she said when she'd dried me and put me into my own nightie rather than the backless gown I'd been wearing for the birth. I really felt mothered, even though Nurse Rowley was probably only a few years older than me.

So with her help I walked back to the ward and immediately fell into a self-satisfied sleep. Job well done.

Charlottetoo came over to see me on Saturday morning.

"You alright?" she said as she sat in a chair next to my bed.

"Fine, fine," I said. "It was hard work, but I almost enjoyed it in a strange way."

"Painful?"

"Yes, but it doesn't go on forever."

"Did those songs and poems we're supposed to have ready, did they help?"

"Actually, I think they did, although I got mine muddled up. Takes your mind away from your body somehow. A really strange experience."

"But exhausting?"

"Yes, totally. I could sleep forever."

"What did you have?"

"A boy."

"Oh, I hope I have a boy, then he'll be with me at home."

"I hope so too. Shame we can't find out beforehand."

"Apart from waving a ring."

"They say if it's all at the front, it's a boy."

"Well, I might be lucky," said Charlottetoo looking down at her bump which seemed to be much lower today.

"Are you coming down to breakfast?"

"No, I'll give it a miss. Maybe have it up here and then go back to sleep."

"I'll let them know. Sleep well."

"Thanks for coming over."

However, a few days later my emotions had changed dramatically. I was tearful and my breasts were sore and leaking.

"Here's your medicine, Christine, it'll dry up the milk," Nurse Rowley said as she handed me some tablets.

"I felt so happy, now I feel awful," I cried.

"This is normal; you'll be fine in a few days."

The only thing that cheered me up was the fact that Lottie had gone. I couldn't have dealt with her when I felt like this.

Another girl had arrived in my ward during those few miserable days, but I hadn't taken much notice.

We were sitting downstairs after dinner a few days later when Stephanie, the new girl, felt comfortable enough to share her story.

"Bit embarrassing, actually."

Charlottetoo and I didn't want to pry, but Stephanie continued.

"Embassy May Ball last year."

"Where," I asked.

"Sorry, can't say. Anyway, this man, old enough to be my father," I glanced at Charlottetoo, but she hadn't registered anything unusual. "Took a fancy to me. Followed me around, offered me drinks, went onto the verandah with him. Started touching me up."

"What did you do?" asked Charlottetoo, her eyes wide open.

"At first, I wasn't sure, but the vodka'd gone to my head, and well, I thought, *This is more exciting than playing hostess at tea parties and things and talking platitudes to portly ambassadors*, and he was rather dishy."

"So?" I said.

"He offered to show me round his embassy, and well, we ended up in a cloakroom full of furs and things, and well, that's it."

"What do your parents think?" asked Charlottetoo.

"Well, they're divorced, so I have to be helpful to Papa as the oldest daughter. He had to send me away to avoid a diplomatic incident, he said, so here I am. I'll go back afterwards. Hopefully the weather will be better then."

"Where did you get your suntan?" I asked, having picked up that the embassy was in the frozen north, or east somewhere.

"Oh, he sent me off to a friend in Greece. Luckily, the weather was pretty good and I spent a lot of time outdoors."

"Giving it up?" I asked, "The baby?"

"Definitely. Can't wait to get back to normal. Got my Coming Out in the summer."

"Just like Lottie," said Charlottetoo.

We gave Stephanie a thumb-nail sketch of Lottie.

"Don't think I would have got on with her," she said.

I was starting to work out how they lived. It all seemed to follow a rigid timetable from birth to death, and in between was The Season. Charlottetoo had explained it: The boys were expected to go to Prep School, then Eton, or one of the top public schools, probably the one which their fathers and grandfathers had attended. The girls were lucky if they had a good education. Even the brightest couldn't expect to go to university or work. Even if they did it would be in a fashionable job, an up-market florists, for example, a job where they could take time off to take part in the Season. Nothing too demanding.

I remembered an evening when Lottie had asked how I spent my time, "When you're not bonking Finchie," she said. I hated how she belittled my relationship and tried to turn our love-making into a basic crude physical act.

"Working in a publisher's and studying the rest of the time," I responded.

"Can't find the time. Don't know what I'd do, or if I'd be able to stick at it. Don't know how you people do it. What with exercising the horses, riding to hounds, the shoot in August and all that. Loads of parties, new clubs opening, shopping, travel, skiing. No time."

And Sophie had piped up, "Such a shame it's no longer at Court, you know, coming out. Just parties and Royal Ascot and things. Would have like to have been presented. Mummy was."

"So was mine," Lottie added.

"And mine," chirped up Charlottetoo.

"Bloody exhausting, though. Good fun too. All preparation for marrying, up, in my case, provide an heir to some titled family who need my family's money."

I had glanced at Charlottetoo whose eyes went up to heaven for a moment, then caught mine and we had exchanged smiles.

"Like a business transaction, I suppose, Lottie."

"Yes, marriage by 25 or so, an heir and a spare, especially an heir. Do what I like after that. Chat to friends in the morning, horses, the Hunt, the shoot, entertaining."

"I couldn't bear that."

"Brought up to it. All planned from birth. For generations. Even the boys. Know their path from the off."

I wondered if that was the sort of life Sophie led. Or, suddenly I wondered about Finchie. Had he had that kind of upbringing? I knew he and Lottie mixed in similar circles. The fact that her family had been to his wedding in France and that he seemed to be out of town regularly indicated that kind of life. Possibly.

I'll ask him next time I see him, I thought. However, I never did.

Sophie spent a lot of time in what I discovered was the Baby Unit at the far end of Orchard Court. She came to say goodbye to us the following weekend. She brought the baby into the lounge, which made us a bit uncomfortable as she should have gone home from the back door, but she was happy and excited, a proud mother, so we showed our delight at the tiny creature, with a feathery down of hair of an indeterminate colour, smelling of Johnson's Baby Powder, and with the tiniest hands I'd ever seen. I decided not to touch her though. Sophie smothered us with kisses and thanked us for being so lovely. Her fiancé came to collect her, and they looked like a happy family as he cradled the baby. They got into a smart cream Rolls Royce with a liveried driver to chauffer them. We were all happy for them and it took away some of the distress we'd felt over Fatima.

***

One day after I'd had the baby, I had ventured down to the lounge to give myself some exercise. I flicked through a copy of *The Lady* and was just reading one of the adverts: 'Titled family requires Nanny for impending birth of twins' when I heard Matron's raised voice.

"Is it reasonable that she doesn't know? Anyway, you're jumping the queue…"

"But it's my …" Then a door banged shut.

Nurse Blackie suddenly appeared saying, "You need to rest, what are you doing down here?"

"Just needed to see if my legs still worked," I said.

"Well, let's get you upstairs again, now you know that they do."

She guided me upstairs and I rested in the darkened room conscious much later that a car was leaving from the gravelled drive.

***

A few days after that episode, which had puzzled me slightly, but not as much as the total silence from Finchie, I received a letter.

I recognised his handwriting. I couldn't wait to get somewhere private to open it.

"My darling girl," he started. I skimmed through it. It seemed to be rather formal, so with a feeling of impending doom I read on.

"You have been so brave and sensible about all this and I thank you for it. Your little kitten-boy will have a loving and happy home. I will see to that. And he will have all the advantages in his upbringing that you wish you'd had. Never regret giving him up for adoption. You have created a family out of a couple who could not have children of their own. I write this with tears in my eyes and you must be brave too. I am ashamed that I am too much of a coward to come and tell you face to face, but I am leaving this weekend to live and work abroad. This is the best for all of us. But I want you to know and believe that I have loved you since we first met, and although we won't express our love again, you will always be in my heart. I will cherish the memories I have of our relationship, with a beautiful, intelligent young woman who made my life in London worth living.

You, I'm sure will go on to love again, perhaps marry and have more children. I wish you a happy, contented life.

I will always remember you and be grateful for your gift of love to me.

Your ever-loving Andrew (Finchie)."

I sat stunned in my chair. I read it, and re-read it before I eventually took in the fact that I might never see him again. The date on the envelope showed it had been posted a few days after I'd given birth. How could he be so cruel. I was too angry to cry. I got up and paced around the lounge. Then I stormed out and into the garden, reading and re-reading the letter.

I decided to confront Matron.

"We have signed a confidentiality agreement with all our prospective adopting families. I can't tell you where your baby has gone."

"How could he do this to me. Did he take the baby? Why hasn't he come to see me since it was born?"

"I really can't answer that. I know baby has gone to a good home and will be well-loved and cared for. Now go back upstairs."

I stomped out. When I got to the Ward, I decided I'd had enough of it. I wanted to go home. But where was home? So I phoned Granny Aldrich.

"I want to come back to you. Can I please, just for a while, until I get myself sorted?"

"Yes, dear, yes, Chrissie, come on. You've got a lot to tell me, I'm sure."

When I'd calmed down a little, I asked Matron to book me a taxi to the nearest station. I'd find my way to Tooting somehow.

"It's a bit soon for you to go, you know," she said. "Stay another week just to make sure everything is alright."

"No, I've made my mind up. I want to go today."

"It's been paid for until the end of the month, you know."

"Too bad. Keep the money, it might help someone else."

"If you're determined to go, I feel I must give you some of it. Are you going home?"

"I'll go to my grandma's."

"As long as there's someone to look after you."

"Yes, she will."

I went upstairs to pack and had a tearful goodbye hug with Charlottetoo.

"Please stay till I have the baby," she cried.

"I can't," I said, "But I'll phone you. Keep in touch."

I went downstairs to find both the nurses in the hall. "We are sorry you're going," they chorused out of synch. "Good luck."

When I had fully composed myself, I knocked on Matron's door.

"I've come to say goodbye, Matron." We shook hands. "And to thank you for everything you've done."

"I'm pleased everything went well, but we don't want to see you back here again," she laughed.

"I was dreading the whole thing, but it has been, well an education."

"You have given a lot too. I think the other girls have benefitted from having you around. Society is changing, and it's up to you young things in the real world as I've said before."

"Yes, I learned a lot about their restrictive lives. I don't envy them," I replied, "But I'd like to keep in touch with little Charlotte. If it doesn't compromise her in any way."

"Well," she paused. "But what about you. Any plans?"

"Back to work, I hope, and get my studies completed. Then, who knows."

"Put this behind you and move on. I'm sure you'll have a great life. God Bless." Matron and the Nurses came to the front steps and waved as I got into the taxi. Suddenly Matron rushed forward and pressed an envelope into my hand through the window.

"The address of a doctor to see for your six week check-up. All paid for. Good luck, you were a delight to have here."

"Thank you," I said. "You've all been so kind." I started to cry. The taxi drove off. I opened the envelope. As well as a letter addressed to a doctor in Harley Street there were four £5 notes.

By the time I got to Guildford I had calmed down again. I paid the driver and carried my small case into the station. I realised I hadn't even worked out how I was going to get to Granny Aldrich's.

The man at the ticket office suggested two ideas. Change at Clapham Junction and take a bus to the Northern Line, or go to Waterloo and get the Northern Line there. I chose the latter option as I had memories of Mr Blackwood dropping me at Clapham Junction and my complicated journey to Northfields. But no, I wasn't going to Northfields, but to Tooting Broadway, to Church Lane, where Granny Aldrich had her ground floor flat.

She was delighted to see me, complimented me on the flowers I'd picked up for her on my way from the station, berated me for my extravagance and sat me down with a cup of tea.

"Well, tell me all about it." And so I did, even including the letter from Finchie.

"That's typical of those posh types. Love 'em and leave 'em. Just like sailors they are, a girl in every port."

"Not now, Granny," I said, "I know he's not really like that. It must be his upbringing."

"Sending them away to school when they're barely out of nappies, and then on to those schools, you know the sort. I've read 'Tom Brown's Schooldays', I have."

"I don't think it's like that now."

"Shame he's not here, I'd give him a piece of my mind."

"I know you would, but I'm really tired, let me go to bed."

In the morning she gave me a cup of tea in bed. She heaved herself up beside me and we carried on our conversation. It was such a relief to pour everything out to her, about the birth and the experiences I'd had.

"Do you know, those girls came from a different world. I felt sorry for them. Not as free as me, not able to have a choice about their lives. They even used different words. They'd say 'Go up', if they were talking about someone going to university, and then 'come down', 'come out' She's coming out in the summer,'" I said, mimicking Lottie's accent. "Finchie and my brother were in the same 'hice' at school." We laughed. "And Lottie went to get 'finished'."

"Finished off more like," laughed Granny Aldrich. "Best to stick to your own."

"But what if you're not sure what 'your own' is?"

"Well, folks like us. Hard working, happy to talk to anyone. You know, normal people."

Chapter 14

"Good to see you again," said Mr Blackwood. "Miss Eversley will be too. She's had a lot to put up with recently. Grandma recovered?" he said.

I wasn't sure what he was talking about, so I just said, "Yes, thank you." And went downstairs to my desk.

"What's been going on," I asked Gladys.

"We've had some funny types here while you've been away. Poor Miss Eversley has been tearing her hair out."

"Why?" I asked.

"A stream of temps. Not very good ones either. You should have seen their spelling, and they didn't wash the cups properly. And they wanted to call Mr B and Miss E by their Christian names."

"Well, perhaps that's the way things are going. They call you Gladys, and me Christine."

"Yes, but, well, they're the bosses."

Then Miss Eversley walked in.

"Oh, how lovely to see you back, Christine."

"Thank you. It's a relief to be here again."

"Come upstairs and tell me all about your Grandma," she gave a wink and smiled.

"I'll bring some tea."

"Make mine coffee, if we've got some."

"Fine," I said.

After I'd given her an account of my experiences and she'd sympathised with my feelings about giving up the baby I asked what new books were being prepared.

"We're doing something on the Empire."

"Ours or the Roman one?"

"Ours. And we've asked Oliver if he can write the chapter about the Malayan Emergency."

"What does he know about that?"

"He was there doing his National Service."

"Oh, I didn't know." Suddenly my worlds were starting to collide. Finchie had been in Malaya. How dare he come into my work-place? I pushed thoughts of him from my mind and concentrated on what Miss Eversley was saying.

"That's what turned him into a pacifist."

"Hence the Peace News he gets," I added.

"And his Aldermaston Marches, and CND. Mind you, I'm going on the next one, at Easter."

There was a growing anti-war movement in the country strengthened by the threat of nuclear weapons.

"I'd like to come too. I don't like the idea of war. Look what it did to my family."

"Of course, I remember you telling me soon after you joined."

"By the way, thank you for covering up for me with Mr Blackwood."

"Well, he's not as pure as the driven snow, neither is Gladys, so I took a chance."

"Blackmail?"

"No, of course not. Just a knowing look, and he agreed you could have three months to look after your Grandma. But you're back early, so you're in everyone's good books, especially mine."

Then she asked me to contact Oliver to find out how he was getting on with his research.

"Back again, then?" he said, when I got through to him on the phone at his mother's house. "Grandma OK?"

Oh dear, he doesn't know.

"I need to see you, and tell you all about it."

"Well, I'll have to come in next week to give Connie some copy."

"Connie?"

"Yes, Miss Eversley."

"Gladys was complaining that the temps who replaced me used people's Christian names, even Mr Blackwood's."

"It's what people are doing in other places, so, why not us."

"I suppose so, but I think I'd find it a bit informal for work."

"You'd get used to it, and Connie is quite matey with you anyway."

"But we keep a distance."

"Anyway, what were you ringing about?"

"Just to get an update for 'Connie'"

"Tell her I've written the chapter but just have to check a few facts, and discuss how to anglicise the Chinese words."

"Do you speak Chinese then?"

"A bit, and some Malay. From my time there. But only simple words and probably inaccurate, so I need some help."

"I can't wait to read it."

"I'll see if you can proof-read it, and perhaps do some picture research."

"I'd like that, it would take my mind off…"

"Off what? Have you got a problem?"

"Not really, but I'd like to talk to you."

"We could have lunch together next week when I come in."

"Yes, perhaps away from the office."

"This sounds serious. Anything I can do to help?"

"No, not really, but it would be good to talk to you."

When Oliver came in to Blackwood and Green's I gave him a hug, which surprised both him and me.

"Now, now," he said.

"Sorry, I'm just pleased to see you."

He went up to 'Connie's' office and I followed.

"Are you ready for some tea, coffee?" I asked.

"Yes please, Christine," she replied. "Coffee for me. Oliver, what about you?"

"Tea, Chrissie."

So I made the drinks and wondered at my behaviour towards Oliver when I'd unexpectedly found myself giving him a hug.

"Oliver's suggested you could help with some picture research for his chapter."

"I'd love to. Not quite sure where to start though."

"We've got a file on Picture Libraries, obviously there's the BBC one, and all the main newspapers have their own pictures of the Emergency, as do Reuters and a few others. Contact the ones on our list for a start and find out what they've got, can you visit, and how much they'd charge for use in an educational publication."

"Sounds straightforward."

"It's the actual selection of which image to use which can be the tricky part. But now, Oliver was asking about your Grandma. Can we talk about the situation?"

"I'd rather speak to Oliver myself. Perhaps at lunch."

"This sounds ominous," said Oliver.

"No it's not, but it's rather embarrassing."

"Fine, save it for lunch."

"Take as long as you like," said Miss Eversley.

And so I busied myself phoning picture libraries and making a list of possibilities for the section on Malaya wondering if the emphasis was too narrow if it focussed only on the Emergency.

At 1.00 p.m. Oliver and I walked round to the sandwich bar.

"Let's go to that little Italian place round the corner," he said.

"Ooh, that would be a treat."

As we walked there I started to tell him about my relationship with Andrew (as I now called him).

"I knew you had someone special, for a couple of years too."

"Well, it ended up with me getting pregnant."

"Oh, you poor thing. Did you have an abortion? Is that why you've been away?"

"No, I had the baby. It's been adopted."

"That must be so hard."

I burst into tears. "I don't think I've got over it yet. And then Andrew went away. He was married; I didn't know till too late."

"What a bastard."

"No, not really. But I kept it secret, and Miss Eversley made sure my job was still here for me, which was wonderful. Everyone else thinks I've been looking after my Grandma. Granny Aldrich isn't really my grandma, but it was a useful ploy. And, incidentally, she's not ill at all, just a bit slow on her legs."

By the time we'd got to the restaurant I'd cheered up. Oliver was concerned that I'd had to go through something like that without him knowing.

"You were working somewhere else."

"Yes, but I'm on the phone. And my mother's a nurse so you could have come to her for help."

"I didn't think of that, and anyway I was ashamed."

"Nothing to be ashamed of. It can happen to anyone. And you're fully recovered?"

"Yes, apart from getting weepy when I think about it. I've still got to have a check-up; my six week one."

"Do you know who's adopted the baby? What was it, anyway?"

"A boy. It's gone to a family who can't have children, that's all I know," although I did have my suspicions.

"Well, after all that you need to eat something nourishing," said Oliver.

I laughed. "You're starting to mother me."

"As long as I'm not smothering you."

So we had a wonderful meal of osso buco and salad, followed by zabaglione which we shared. I didn't have wine, thinking of the work I had to do that afternoon, but Oliver had a glass of chianti from a raffia covered bottle. *Very stylish*, I thought.

After lunch, which had taken us more than our allotted hour, I walked with him to the School of African and Oriental Studies where he was meeting a lecturer to discuss the relative merits of Pin Yin and the Wade Giles system of anglicising Chinese and to decide which of the many Chinese dialects to feature, if any. I walked back across the square to the office feeling relieved that I'd told Oliver about the baby.

"You took your time," said Gladys, "Miss Eversley was looking for you."

"She knew where I was," I told her and went up to her office to apologise for coming back late.

"No problem. I said take as long as you needed. I understand how difficult it must be to talk about what happened. More to the point, did Oliver understand?"

"Yes, I thought he'd be disappointed in me, but he was very sympathetic."

"I thought he would be. He's a great person; we're lucky to have him writing for us."

That Friday Oliver had collected some papers from the Messenger, and was loitering outside my office. It was obvious that he was waiting for Gladys to leave the room. I went out into the hall.

"What is it?" I asked.

"Wondered if you'd like to have lunch with us this Sunday."

"That would be lovely. Does your mother mind?"

"It was her idea, actually, but I'm all for it too."

"It will do me good to get out of Granny A's hair for a while. How do I get there? I've only been in Mr Blackwood's car for that Christmas Eve party."

So we planned my route, and Oliver offered to pick me up at New Malden station.

Mrs Mooney welcomed me from the kitchen in her soft Irish accent. "Won't be long. Hope you eat anything."

"Yes, I do, thank you."

"Go in and sit down, will you. Oliver, give the girl a sherry," she called out.

So I sat on the red settee holding the flowers I'd brought for his mother.

"Sweet or dry?"

"What're you having?" I asked, not being used to sherry.

"Harvey's Bristol Cream. I actually bought it when I was last in Bristol. It's sweet."

"I'll have the same, then."

I put the flowers on a side table, and had just taken my first sip of the sweet syrupy liquid when Mrs Mooney walked in, taking off her apron.

I stood up and held out the flowers, a mixture of tulips and narcissi. She stretched up and kissed me.

"That's kind of you. You didn't need to, you know. Thank you, they're lovely. I'll put them in water in a minute. But first of all Oliver told me all about your misfortune, and I want you to know that if you need any help I'm here, a trained nurse."

"Mainly working in the limb-fitting department, mind," said Oliver.

"I don't think I've lost a limb, but at times it does feel a bit like it."

"Go and pick some spinach, Oliver dear, while I have a little chat with Christine."

When we were alone she asked about the birth, "If it's not too painful to talk about it."

So I gave her a brief summary, and told her that I was going for my six week check-up the following Tuesday.

"You've been very brave, you know. Back in Ireland a lot of girls got caught and didn't want to give up their babies, but the nuns made them. They were dreadfully unhappy. You seem to have thought it all through, and made a proper decision."

"I hadn't realised how hard it would be afterwards though."

"It's the hormones. It takes a long time for the body to recover. Almost as long as it took for the baby to grow."

Oliver returned with the perpetual spinach clumped in his hand.

"I'll just give that a rinse. The food's ready apart from that." And Mrs Mooney went back into the kitchen.

We had a splendid lunch. Beef, Yorkshire puddings, roast potatoes and spinach. Then an apple pie and custard.

"Of course, I learned how to make Yorkshires. Didn't have them in Cork. Well Kinsale, actually. My father was a fisherman."

"Mum was a child when the Lusitania got sunk."

"Oh, my goodness. That must have been awful."

"My parents took in some children whose parents had drowned. It was a terrible time. I was only young, but I remember more the emotion rather than any facts."

Mrs Mooney told me how she'd been brought up in a tiny fisherman's home, one of the Ferryview Cottages, overlooking where the fishermen mended and stored their nets.

"You can't imagine what an upheaval it was for me to go as far as Cork. I picked up a letter to find I'd been accepted for nursing training, and suddenly had mixed feelings. Collywobbles. To leave Kinsale, when I'd only travelled a few miles inland before, to lose my friends and family! It was a wrench, but there was no work for me in Kinsale at that time. My dad took me in a pony and trap for the long bumpy ride to Cork. The roads weren't all made up then; many of them were just tracks, smoothed down by horse and cart, the occasional farm vehicle and perhaps one or two cars. What an uncomfortable ride. I enjoyed the training, but it was like being in the army. Orders, orders all day and night. 'Obey the sister, or matron will be after you'. There was an advert in the nurses' home asking for nurses to come to England as there was a severe shortage. So I replied and came over to work in Roehampton Hospital. Just in time it turned out. Cork was devastated, burnt out."

"I didn't realise," I said, knowing little of what happened in Ireland.

"Yes, by your lot," she laughed. "But I don't hold it against you, you know."

I blushed. I knew there were still problems, the IRA and all that, but hadn't met anyone it had affected.

"Anyway, that's where she met my dad, in the limb-fitting centre," continued Oliver, covering up my embarrassment.

"Yes," continued Mrs Mooney as she looked up at a photo of a handsome man in army uniform. "He died in 1956, mainly from recurring infections, in spite of all the medical attention I could offer."

"Oh, I'm sorry, I remember seeing that photo of him at the party, but I didn't realise he'd died. Was he injured in the First World War?"

"He was in constant pain. Best thing for him, dying, after everything he'd gone through," Mrs Mooney continued. "But it wasn't from fighting. He caught meningitis in Africa where his regiment had been sent. He'd only been there a month or so, in 1915. He got gangrene. That's how he lost his legs."

"Before penicillin," added Oliver.

"But tell me what you're working on now you're back at work." As Mrs Mooney changed the subject, I caught a glimpse of her sadness, as she picked up the photo and held it quietly for a moment or two before replacing it on the piano and turning to focus on me again.

So I described my first foray into picture research, and Oliver praised my 'eye' for spotting appropriate pictures.

After lunch Oliver and I washed up.

"I like your mum," I said. "She's really interesting and caring. A lovely woman. I didn't know about what happened in Cork, though."

"British forces, yes."

"And yet she's made her life here. You don't count yourself as Irish, do you?"

"No, in spite of my name. I'm not a secret IRA person, don't you worry," he laughed.

"I'm so sorry about your dad."

"He was good fun when he felt well, and he wrote a bit. Mostly short stories for magazines. He was worried he'd end up selling matches on the streets, but he discovered a talent for repairing rush-seated chairs."

"So that's why you have so many."

Oliver laughed, "Too many."

We chatted about the chairs for a bit and then he asked: "Are you coming on the march?"

"Which?"

"At Easter."

My heart sank: I had promised Grandad Preece I'd visit him then.

"I'll have to check. I'm supposed to go to Eastbourne to see my grandad. I'll let you know. Who else is going?"

"Well, Connie came last year. You know her family's Quaker. Her dad was a Conscientious Objector in the war. Had a hard time. Her brothers are going too, I think. It won't be as chaotic as last year. It's only one day this time."

"I'd love to come. The more I hear about war the more I can't believe it solves anything. And now the bomb!"

"Well, it's a way off, so no need to decide now."

When I felt it was time to leave, Mrs Mooney said, "It was a treat having you here, it was. Come again."

"I'd love to. Thank you for everything."

"Give me a ring after your 6 week check-up."

"I'll do that. Thanks for taking an interest."

Oliver walked me to the station.

"She made me feel so much at home."

"She loves having another woman around. She sees too many of my men friends and not enough girls. And the rest of her family are still in Ireland."

"In Kinsale?"

"Some are. Others mainly in Cork now. It's becoming quite a smart city."

We talked about when he'd been over there last for a cousin's wedding.

"It's quite primitive in places; in the countryside you still see people drawing water from pumps, and there's still a distrust of the English."

"Oh, yes, the IRA."

"They're still against the Treaty, and, I gather, there are rumblings, mainly near the border."

"Do you think it'll flare up again?"

"I wouldn't be surprised."

When Oliver left me at the station I felt more calm and relaxed than I had since I'd received Andrew's letter. It was good to have a real friend who didn't demand anything of me.

***

The following Tuesday I went for my check-up. As I was sitting in the waiting room I flicked through a copy of *The Times*. Amongst the Births, Deaths and Marriages I spotted an announcement: "On 3rd March 1964, a son, William Arthur George" etc. to "Viscount and Lady…a brother for Charlotte, Emily and Georgina." Charlottetoo's baby!

Thank goodness it was a boy. I promised myself I'd contact her.

After my examination, I walked slowly back to the office, thinking of what I'd say to Charlotte. I found a phone box in New Cavendish Street. I dialled her number. A man answered the phone.

I put on the elocution voice that Clemmie had forced on me.

"May I speak to Lady Charlotte, please."

"I'm sorry to inform you that Lady Charlotte is not receiving calls at the moment."

"Is she ill?"

"Are you a friend of hers?"

"Yes, we met recently. Can you tell me if she's alright?"

"She's indisposed at the moment. Can I take your name?"

So I gave my name and Granny Aldrich's phone number.

"Please ask her to phone me when she's feeling better."

"Yes, miss."

And that was that. She never phoned me.

In the evening after my check up, I phoned Mrs Mooney to tell her that I'd been pronounced fit and well; everything in order.

"I did enjoy having you here. Come again soon."

"If it's not too much trouble, I'd love to," I replied.

And so we arranged for me to have Sunday lunch the Sunday before Easter 22nd March.

Lunch was late that day as Mrs Mooney had been to church. She gave me a plaited palm blessed by the local priest.

"I'm not religious," I said.

"Nor are we, but I like to keep some of the traditions. Habit more than anything, and the chance to catch up with a few friends from Ireland."

"Is Oliver a Catholic too?"

"No, doesn't think any of it can be proved, but he was christened as a baby."

"Where is he today?"

"He won't be long. He's just making some arrangements for next Sunday. A group of his friends are going on the March."

"Oh, yes, the CND one. I can't go this year. I've promised my grandad I'd stay with him over Easter."

So we chatted about Eastbourne, my family and our tastes in food while I helped her set the table and dish up the vegetables, which she put to keep warm in the oven.

At about 3.00 p.m., Oliver arrived.

"Sorry about that. Couldn't get away. Getting some banners ready, and making sure we have enough badges. Here, you have one, Chrissie."

"I'm not coming."

"Wear it anyway." So I pinned the CND badge onto my coat which was hanging over the bannisters in the hall and we all went into the dining room overlooking the garden.

We ate our belated lunch and I could see that Oliver was distracted by his preparations for the following Sunday, so I helped Mrs Mooney wash the dishes, and we talked about her family in Ireland. I walked myself to the station.

***

The following year I saw more of Oliver, having lunch with him occasionally when he wasn't working for B & G and helping his picture research when he was. We'd also been to see some new French films which Connie had praised and which we discussed at length in the office. Fortunately for me they had subtitles as I still only had a minimal French vocabulary. He was becoming a valued friend and seemed patient with my many questions about his political views.

"You'd be a great lecturer," I said, praising his clarity of thought and ability to express complex issues in easily digested bites.

"I nearly was," he responded. "A friend's father offered me a post, but I couldn't see how I could combine it with my writing. It might even have curtailed my political involvement, being part of a well-known university. They might have disapproved."

His mother had me to lunch every few months and even invited Granny Aldrich to come with me. Fortunately they got on well, and Granny A was able to tell Mrs Mooney about my early days, from her point of view.

One Thursday, just before Easter, I was flicking through a newspaper in the doctor's surgery whilst waiting for Granny A's heart medicine prescription. A familiar name caught my eye. Charlottetoo had died, aged only 16! Tears of anger and sadness welled up. I felt as though I'd stopped breathing. The receptionist came over to see if I was alright.

"No, no, I've just read that a friend of mine has died."

She made me a cup of tea and held my hand.

"Very close, were you?"

"Yes, yes." But I couldn't say any more without breaking a confidence.

When I got up to leave she called after me.

"You've forgotten the prescription."

Not only had I forgotten why I was in the surgery, but I was so distracted I was nearly knocked down by a car as I crossed the road. Who could I talk to about her?

I reminisced about the conversations I'd had with her at Orchard Court, her studies, her frail looks. Had she gone back to school, I wondered. I wanted to tell the world about her, and it took huge restraint for me to avoid confronting her father in a public place now I knew for certain who he was and the government position he held.

Fortunately I became distracted by preparations for the CND march which Oliver and Connie had invited me to join.

But when I arrived, that Sunday, I spent a good hour trying to find Oliver in the huge crowds moving from Hyde Park to Trafalgar Square. We'd agreed to meet at a particular spot near Lancaster Gate Station. When I couldn't find him there, I'd searched the faces in the procession and then started my zig-zag hunt up and down the lines of people, bumping into placards, home-made signs and pushing between families with push chairs and generally annoying the people I'd disturbed. It transpired that Oliver's group had walked all the way from High Wycombe and had taken the opportunity to collapse on the grass and tend their blisters so I had missed them, assuming that they'd moved on towards where the speakers were assembling. When I eventually found them, the crowd was so dense that I could barely elbow my way through.

"Glad you could make it"; "Better late than never"; "You almost missed the fun" were some of the greetings I received.

"Thought we'd never find each other," Oliver said. "Fabulous turnout." And so we walked, some of his group were carrying banners saying 'Ban the Bomb', others were wearing clothing with large CND logos painted on. Still others were carrying, or even wearing, gas masks left over from the war.

"I can't believe how many people there are," I said.

As we turned a corner, a girl came bounding up to Oliver.

"Haven't lost your politics then, Ol," she said. Oliver laughed as she gave him a hug and kissed him. She left as suddenly as she'd arrived with her arms round two men's shoulders, looking like a glamorous Juliette Greco with her dark eye make-up and long dark hair. I suddenly felt possessive.

"See you, Jane," he called after her as the three of them sashayed through the crowds.

"Who was that?" I asked.

"Old girlfriend, from Bristol."

"She's come a long way for this," I commented.

"Her uncle's an academic; something in the anti-apartheid movement. She's a serial protester."

Our voices were drowned out by the crowds, but I felt upstaged, jealous, which surprised me.

Miss Eversley, or Connie, as I now called her and two men wriggled their way through the crush to join us.

"What a turn out! I'd like to think that we'll be listened to now. Soon there'll be no more war, or at least a different kind of war, not with the horrendous devastation of the A bomb."

"It won't be that simple," said Oliver. "Once something's been invented it's too tempting to use it."

"But look at all these people, thousands and thousands. They must listen to us," I said.

"It depends who 'they' are," said Oliver.

'They' now included Charlottetoo's father, which gave a further impetus to my protest.

We walked for what seemed miles, stopping and marking time on the spot when the march got snarled up, or just taking stock of the people around us, smiling in solidarity with complete strangers. Some people were singing Bob Dylan's *Blowing in the Wind* and gradually we all joined in. Eventually we got to the edge of Trafalgar Square, near the Canadian High Commission, having jostled our way as near as we could to the speakers. Suddenly the crowd became silent, the silence spreading like a wave. The speeches had started. In spite of the polite attention of thousands of people, it was difficult to hear what was being said. The sound undulated, so sometimes I could catch a phrase, then it went. Then a few words were carried on the breeze. Then a change of voice from a male one to a female one. Often we had to rely on resumes passed on to us like a Chinese whisper.

"Don't worry, it will be reported, on the news and in the press," said Connie, reading my facial expression. "The important thing is being here. Showing solidarity and all that."

"Coming for the picnic afterwards?" asked, Victor, one of the men with her, who I later found out was her twin brother. I looked questioningly at Oliver. "Yes," he said, nodding to me. "Where?"

"By the Lake, South side. There's usually some pelicans there. We'll pitch camp under the trees."

Over the next hour or so we extricated ourselves from the crowds and walked through the Mall to St. James's Park. When we got near Waterloo Place I stopped suddenly, remembering a snowy afternoon when my friend Clemmie's car wouldn't start.

"You go on. I won't be a minute, I'll catch you up at the Lake."

The rest of them turned to walk across the grass parallel to Horse Guards Road.

I walked up the steps, turned left into Pall Mall and right into Duke Street St. James's. But there was no sign of life. No lights on in the block of flats either. Being Easter the shops were shut and apart from a few stragglers from the march the street was deserted. I don't know what I'd expected. I cursed myself for hanging on to the past, and ran through the streets and the park to join the picnic.

"You're quiet today," said Oliver as he escorted me towards Charing Cross station that evening. "Crowds got to you?"

"No, just a bit tired."

"See you on Tuesday then." And he bent down and kissed me on the cheek.

On my way back to Granny Aldrich's my mind was whirling. *What was I feeling about Oliver? Jealousy? And about Andrew? Relief? Surprise?* I couldn't pin anything down.

Granny A was sitting in her chair when I returned.

"Are you alright?" I asked.

"Just had one of my dizzy spells."

"I'll call the doctor."

"You'll do no such thing. I'll be fine. Anyway it's Easter, he won't be on call."

"If you're sure."

"Look, Chrissie, don't fuss. I've had these turns before. I just need to sit for a while."

So I went into the kitchen to make her a cup of tea and a hot water bottle. Just as I was burping the bottle to let out some of the air, she called.

"Perhaps some rum and hot milk would do me some good."

As I was warming the milk, I heard a sharp intake of breath and a groan.

"What is it? Are you alright?" I called as I rushed in. But I could see she wasn't. She'd slumped over and her breathing was very rapid. I called an ambulance and sat with her on the journey to St. George's.

"Heart attack, but she's recovering," said the doctor in A & E after he'd put a monitor on her chest and done various checks. "We'll keep her in tonight at least. Just got to wait for a bed, then she'll go up to the ward."

I sat with her for a while.

"You go now, dear," she said quietly. "I'm in good hands."

Reluctantly I left her and walked through the dark streets back to Church Lane.

However, at 3.30 a.m. the phone rang. I hadn't got undressed; I was just lying on top of my bed dozing, but I sprang to the phone, knocking over a glass of water on my bedside table.

"I'm very sorry, but Mrs Aldrich passed away a short while ago. She had another heart attack."

And that is why Easter 1965 sticks in my mind.

I gave myself a few moments to recover from the shock. I made myself a cup of tea, drank half of it, and put on my outdoor shoes and coat.

I walked back to St. George's. The receptionist directed me to the ward where Granny A was. It was only when the nurse drew back the curtains and I saw Granny Aldrich's lifeless body that I broke down in tears, as much for myself as for her. She was like family to me, having helped at my birth and given me more mothering than Auntie Vi. She had even taken me in when Auntie Vi and my Northfield's landlady had kicked me out when I'd got pregnant. *Would I be able to stay in her flat*, I wondered selfishly.

The nurse gave me an envelope containing her wedding ring and the St. Christopher's that she wore round her neck.

"She had you down as her next of kin," she said.

I hadn't realised that, and it started me crying all over again.

I started to wonder who I should notify. She had a sister somewhere in Australia, and a nephew and niece too, but I didn't know where they lived.

When I got back to her flat, I sat with another cup of tea and started to make a list from the address book I found in her handbag by her bed. There were only about 20 people in it whose names hadn't been crossed out. Old friends who'd died, I supposed. I found her birth certificate: she was 84. I hadn't realised she was that old as she had a lively mind and, apart from her legs, and what she called 'a touch of angina', seemed to be in good health.

I thought I should notify the Jennings. They'd been neighbours for many years and still lived a few streets away. I walked round there and knocked on the door.

"What is it, Chrissie," said Mr Jennings still in his pyjamas, "It's only just gone 7 o'clock, and it's Easter Monday, a holiday."

"Sorry, sorry, but Mrs Aldrich has died."

Mrs Jennings appeared behind her husband.

"Come in, come on in," and she put her arms around me and held me while I sobbed my heart out.

Over the next few days, they helped me contact her relatives. The funeral took place two weeks later to give her sister and nephew and niece time to get flights. Mr Blackwood gave me a few days off to sort everything out.

I was still living in the flat, but after I'd notified the Registrar of her death, a letter came from the Council telling me I had no right to live there. However, when I objected the Council said they would give me a month to find somewhere else.

Granny Aldrich had left me £1,000; more money than I'd ever had in my life. The solicitor told me it would take a few months before I could have the cheque, but I was already planning what to do with so much money. I wondered about putting it down as a deposit on a flat of my own, but then unexpected issues arose.

I went to my bank to find out about mortgages. I was told I would have to have a man as my guarantor! Imagine my anger. I stormed out of the bank. The following week I was still fuming from such an insult. I tried a Building Society, its Head Office in Baker Street, but the answer was still the same.

Mrs Mooney sympathised and even offered to let me stay in her spare room.

I was tempted to take up her offer, but decided instead to rent two rooms with shared kitchen and bathroom on the top floor of a house in one of the roads off Charlotte Street. The area was disturbed by the building of a huge tower which people said was going to be higher than St. Paul's Cathedral. The reason I chose to live there was it was cheap, I could walk to work, walk to the theatre and be reasonably near to Regent's Park. Above all I wanted to be independent.

I still went to Mrs Mooney's for lunch every few weeks, and it was there that I moaned about how difficult it was to get a mortgage without a male guarantor.

Oliver took me into the garden while Mrs Mooney was preparing the tea things.

"How do you feel about getting married?" he said.

"Well, when I find the right person, I might consider it."

"No, I mean, to me."

"My God, Oliver. Do you realise what you're saying? I don't know you like that, I mean, we're friends, work together. I'm fond of you, but marriage."

"Do I have to get down on my bended knees?"

"No, Oliver, what brought this on?"

"I have been thinking about you, not as a friend, but more than that. Well, definitely since the march at Easter. Maybe even since I met you on the doorstep your first morning at B & G. And I think you've shown some interest and affection, too."

"Well, you were wonderful, you and your mother, about the baby, and especially when Granny A died. I thought you were just comforting me in my loss, making me feel wanted."

"It was around that time that I came to the conclusion that it **was** more than that. I was almost experiencing your pain. It sounds like a soppy film, but I realised, well, I think I'm in love with you."

"Oh, Oliver, I've been so confused. My emotions have been all over the place, what with the baby last year, Finchie just leaving like that, and now Granny A dying."

"I feel I've been through it all with you, just a bit."

"But marriage? I'm just about settling into my flat, being independent."

"I wouldn't shackle you to me. We could lead our own lives, we've still got our work."

"I need to think about it."

"Can I take that as a little bit positive."

"Yes, shall we 'walk out together' as Granny A. would have said, and see if we're OK?"

"Girlfriend and boyfriend?"

"Yes, but it sounds a bit corny. How shall we manage it at work?"

"Well, I've got some work to do for another publisher."

"Traitor!"

"I'm freelance, I've got to take what's offered, so I won't be at B & G's much in the next two months."

"What shall we tell your mum?"

"I've already told her what I feel about you."

"What, before telling me?"

"I had to talk to someone, to help me clarify what I felt. She's very fond of you, and thinks we'd make a good match."

"Well, I certainly feel comfortable here, and actually, when your old girlfriend leapt out at you during the march, I must say I felt a bit jealous."

"You didn't?"

"Yes, I did."

He kissed me on the forehead.

"That was all over a long time ago; just friends now."

We walked back up to the house arm in arm. I felt relaxed, unbelievably happy and relieved that at last I could identify and express the emotions that had been bubbling around inside me.

We had tea and exchanged secret glances until Mrs Mooney eventually said.

"Now, Oliver. What's going on?"

"We're going out together," I said.

"As a couple," said Oliver, "just to see how things go."

"Well, good luck both of you. I think you suit each other." And she turned to me and said, "I gather you've got yourself a nice little flat in town, tell me about it."

So I explained about the rooms, and that it was an opportunity to get my head together after everything I'd been through.

That summer Oliver and I spent many nights there, discovering our new relationship, sitting up all night talking in detail about our feelings, beliefs, philosophy of life, and even about Oliver's past loves. He wouldn't talk much about his National Service days, although I picked up some understanding of what it must have been like for him in one of our conversations about pacifism.

"Do you mean that no one anywhere should fight? I can't see that being realistic. You've only to look at what goes on in the playground: 'My toy!' 'No, mine!' Snatch, snatch, hit, hit. And before you know what's happened, other children have launched in, and without a teacher's intervention full scale playground war breaks out."

"It would be perfect for no-one ever to fight, but, as you say, unrealistic, human nature being what it is."

"And why do people make war anyway? It's not always property. I know about the fights to succeed to the throne, and expand one's land. Oh, and the religious wars, Catholic versus Protestant."

"Wars based on different beliefs can't be solved by diplomacy, certainly. It's not just Christian against Islam, but Sunni against Shiite, sect against sect, ideal against ideal. It seems we have to impose our beliefs on other people."

"Thinking, misguidedly that we're saving them from hell and damnation," I added.

"So often it's to do with valuable resources, diamonds, gold, and so on."

"How do you justify being a pacifist if other people are doing the killing for you? I could never work out how people could be Conchies and perhaps let Hitler walk in and take us over, change our whole way of life."

"It's my experience that makes me hate war. I've known what it's like to kill; to see the life leave someone's eyes, the collapse of their body, the smell, the blood. My shame."

"Oh, Oliver, I didn't mean to upset you. It must have been awful." We sat quietly for a while, and didn't discuss the matter for many years.

But being together and getting to know both the breadth and boundaries of our growing relationship felt exciting, even a bit clandestine, as we were not letting the people at our work in on our secret.

As Christmas 1965 approached, we felt ready to tell people that we were getting married. Mrs Mooney invited our colleagues from Blackwood and Green, together with some of my friends and several of Oliver's to her house ostensibly for a Christmas Eve party.

"Slainte," cheered Mrs Moody.

We had a few drinks and then Oliver stood on a chair. He tapped a knife on his glass to call us all to order.

"I have some exciting news to announce. Chrissie and I are getting married."

I waved my hand in the air showing off the solitaire diamond ring that Oliver had presented me with a few days before, but which I'd taken off until he'd made the announcement.

Well, the moment's silence was palpable, and then everyone started clapping, and saying things like "You dark horse", "What a lovely surprise", "How did you keep that a secret for so long".

James and a heavily pregnant Clemmie hugged me. "You didn't let on, how come you could keep that a secret?"

I smiled. Maggie and her boyfriend jumped about excitedly, as did Mr and Mrs Jennings, but Toby looked a bit put out.

"I think Toby had designs on you. He's always fancied you."

"Well, he's too late. Anyway, he's more like a brother."

John gave me a hug and said, "He's perfect for you."

"But you've only just met him," I replied.

"I can tell," and he tapped the side of his nose.

Some of Oliver's friends took him to one side and congratulated him.

Connie and Mr Blackwood came over to me, and Connie said, "I knew it would take some time, but I could see it coming, even when you first met. There was a chemistry between you."

"Looking back, I realise I felt comfortable with him, and now that's grown into, well, hopefully a foundation for marriage."

Mr Blackwood said, "It's the first time our company has become a marriage broker. Well done. I'm sure you'll be very happy."

Gladys gave me a hug too. "Do you think you'll have children," she asked.

"One thing at a time," said Connie, giving me a conspiratorial look.

"I'd love to get married and have children, two, one of each," said Gladys.

"Come on, Gladys," said Connie, "Give them time to get over the excitement of being engaged first. When do you think you'll get married?"

"In the spring, I hope. We haven't decided yet."

***

In fact we waited until the following June. We were married at Kingston Register Office, and the bride wore ivory. My bridesmaids were Sandra, Clemmie and Maggie. The Jennings family came and proudly watched as their daughter walked cautiously behind me without the aid of crutches or callipers. Oliver's best man was his cousin, Kieran, who had flown over from Ireland for the event. We had our reception upstairs at a local pub with several other friends and some of Mrs Mooney's too, including her neighbour, Mrs Pak. We invited Mr Blackwood and his wife, and Connie came with Victor and her man friend, Philip, who apparently she'd been living with for many years. Auntie Vi had declined my invitation as she and her husband would be in Spain buying a small apartment near Elche.

Our honeymoon was a present from Mrs Mooney's relatives in Kinsale and we left Heathrow Airport a few days later. It was my first trip in an aeroplane. I found it particularly exciting as we felt the thrust of the take-off which pressed me into the back of my seat. We were met at Cork airport by Kieran and his wife. They drove us to the most beautiful fishing village I've ever seen, where we stayed in a small B & B overlooking the harbour. Kieran and Mary apologised profusely for not being able to put us up at their home, but they only had two bedrooms and one of them was taken up with their three small children. Oliver and I were relieved as we wanted to be on our own, but as the honeymoon accommodation was a wedding gift to us from my mother-in-law's relatives, we were obliged to spend some time with them. Oliver wanted to visit the two forts he remembered from his visits as a child, as well as other historic places in the surrounding countryside. He took copious notes particularly when we visited the star-shaped James Fort and the later Charles Fort.

"You never know when I might be asked to write about the construction of castles and forts," he laughed when I scolded him for working on our honeymoon.

As Oliver's Uncle Joseph had retired and had more free time than the other relatives, he became our chauffeur whenever we wanted to visit places as far apart as Killarney, Clonakilty, Blarney, or Cobh. We packed in an incredible amount of site-seeing in 8 days, but spent our last night in the Imperial Hotel in Cork before catching our flight home.

I realised that my new life with Oliver would be comfortable, that I would be looked after and loved, but that I had to make room for his research and writing as well as cope with his sleepless nights when memories of his National Service took hold. He would wake up drenched in sweat and terrified for a few moments until he'd become aware of his surroundings and my arms holding him.

Part 3

Chapter 15

Scrape, scrape, pull. At last the strips of wallpaper were coming off.

"I couldn't bear the heavy pattern. It really darkened the hall," I told Clemmie.

"Give me the scraper, and I'll help while the little one is asleep."

"He certainly takes up all your time."

"Keeps me occupied certainly. Nappies, feeding and all that. Hardly any time to myself."

"I bet James does his bit, though."

"You are joking! He's so exhausted by work he's hardly capable of functioning when he's at home. And he's not at home much; his hours are a real challenge. So many nights."

"But he's a proud father."

"I suppose so. He's a bit distant though."

"Probably the shock, and it's such a responsibility supporting you both."

"He'll be a consultant one day, then he'll have more control over his work load I expect and there'll be more money so we can go out more. I really miss our theatre trips."

"But you're pleased you married him?"

"I don't really think about it. I suppose we're in the same situation as lots of couples with a baby. The baby gets all the attention and we focus on him rather than each other."

"So not as romantic as it seemed a few years ago."

"A bit like you, I suppose. It must seem rather mundane, married to Oliver, after all the drama of the last couple of years."

I stopped my scraping and pulling and looked at her.

"What do you mean?"

"Oh, you know; exchanging the hurly-burly of the chaise-longue with the deep-peace of the double bed, or something along those lines."

"Well, I've certainly got the deep peace bit. And I value it. I could have done without all the drama."

"My parents were surprised that someone would want to marry you with your past, especially having had a child."

"What an old-fashioned attitude. Oliver has never criticised me for what happened, just admired me for how I dealt with it. I'm glad he didn't have your parent's attitude. Anyway, you didn't have much say in your marriage, did you?"

"Oh, yes, I did."

"I thought, they'd engineered the whole thing; you, the daughter of a pharmacist, marrying a doctor. Come on Clemmie."

"It wasn't quite like that. OK they did make sure I met the 'right kind of boy', but we got on and one thing led to another."

"Almost an arranged marriage, then."

"Not quite, but I can see how you must view it, compared with your experience of love and lust."

"Now, now, Clemmie. What I had with Finchie wasn't just lust – well, so I thought at the time. And it's given me a more equal relationship with Oliver. He'd had quite a few affairs before meeting me."

"Well, it's alright for blokes."

"No, it isn't just OK for blokes. Why can't we play the field, as they say, particularly now the pill is easier to get."

"I still think it should only be available for married women."

"Oh, Clemmie. Don't be such a prude."

"Well, it makes marriage less, oh, I don't know, viable, necessary."

"It's still the place for bringing up children, though, isn't it. And girls can avoid the terrible dilemma I had."

"I suppose so. Anyway, let's see round the rest of your house and go for a walk before Damian wakes up."

We put down our tools and cleaned ourselves up in the bathroom that had been converted from a third bedroom several years before.

I showed her our bedroom and the spare room, both of which needed decorating.

"Is this where you'll put a baby?"

"Goodness. We haven't got round to thinking about that yet. I don't know how I'd feel about it quite honestly. It would rake up painful memories."

"I thought you'd got over that."

"Would you ever get over giving your baby away? Imagine what it's like. Your little one being taken away before you've even held him." I started to cry, but stopped myself before I gave Clemmie more ammunition to pity me or even to criticise me.

"Let's go downstairs, I'll show you the kitchen and living room," I quickly added to change the subject.

"I've seen the kitchen."

"So you have. Well this is the living room and the garden room; it's got double doors so we can open it into one room if Oliver isn't working."

"It must be a challenge having him about the house so much."

"It sounds like the opposite to your situation. But he goes away to do research, and meet his friends, of course."

"Jane, you mean."

"Watch it Clemmie. She's OK. I've got over worrying about her. We meet up, all of us, with her new bloke at parties."

"Now I am jealous: parties."

"I bet your parents would babysit. You could come with us."

"I'm not sure about Oliver's friends: load of beatniks, into demos and riots."

"Not riots, no. Yes, they are political, but peaceful. I like them."

I could see this could turn into a row, so I continued the tour of the house.

"The kitchen's primitive but I like the window here, and the door into the garden."

"And this door?" she inquired as we moved back into the hall.

"Cellar."

"You could convert that."

"You can hardly stand up in there, anyway, it's where we keep the coal."

"Not much furniture," she commented as we put on our coats.

"It will take time. All our savings went into the deposit. Mustn't forget my keys. I'll show you the area."

So we took the baby in its buggy and walked down towards Mortlake High Street and the river.

***

Sitting by the pond in Barnes Clemmie breast-fed the baby.

"No wonder I'm tired. Sleepless nights and all this really drains me."

"Don't talk to me about sleepless nights. Oliver wakes up a lot."

"Oh, don't complain about too much sex, it gets less and less, I know about that."

"No Clemmie, it's not about that. He has nightmares."

"Bit old for those, isn't he?"

"We all have them sometimes, just he has rather a lot of them."

"Get him some sleeping pills."

"I have suggested that, but he doesn't want to talk about it."

"Off to the psychiatrist then. That'll make him open up."

"He's not mad, just worrying about something."

"What's his mother say about it?"

"I haven't mentioned it to her. I'm still getting to know her, and I don't want her to think he's unhappy."

"Well, you should take a robust approach, or put him in the spare room."

"Clemmie, not so much of the 'should'. I'm confiding in you for support, not to be told what to do."

"Only being practical."

"Yes, alright. Thanks."

***

Oliver returned from a meeting with some friends in a local pub.

"You seem a bit down. Come and have a cuddle." He led me to a beanbag on the floor in the front room.

"It's Clemmie, she really gets on my goat."

"It always ends up like this, doesn't it. You look forward to seeing her and then complain that she's been bossing you about."

"Well she does. Just because she's older, but she irritates me with her advice."

"What this time? Why have you moved into such a small house? How can you bear to eat off orange boxes and sit on cushions and beanbags."

"Not quite, Ollie, she didn't go that far. It was when I told her I woke up in the night a lot."

"Oh!" Oliver went quiet. "Best not to tell her about intimate things."

"It was worrying me, but I didn't disclose anything important."

"You know it's difficult for me. Things happened during National Service. I can't seem to process them. I can't talk about it."

"Sorry, Ollie. I hoped I'd be able to help."

"You do, just by being here. I do love you."

"I love you too, that's why I want to help."

"One day."

And so we let it lie.

***

A couple of days later, I was back at work with Blackwood and Green when the phone rang. Rather than a voice speaking I heard a jazz riff playing.

"It's arrived," I exclaimed.

"Yes, Mum was as good as her word."

"Where did you put it?"

"By the dividing wall."

"No, what about the neighbours."

"Only joking. The wall dividing the front room from the hall."

I laughed. "That's perfect. Give me a concert when I get home."

Connie called out, "If that's Oliver remind him there's some work here for him if he wants it."

"I'll pop in next week, tell her."

"I could bring it for you."

"No, I've got to talk about various things with her and Mr Blackwood, like more money," he whispered.

"I'll tell her you'll pop in. Love you."

"You too."

"Oliver's piano's arrived," I proudly told anyone that would listen. "And, Connie, he'll come and see you next week."

I enjoyed getting down to work again. Oliver and I had discussed how important it was to keep our individuality as much as possible. We were both used to being independent.

"You're so much older than me..." I'd said one day during our many walks along the river bank.

"Now hold on. Not all that much."

"But you've had time to find out who you are, establish a career, define what you stand for."

"I'm still searching, I'm a work in progress; so are you."

"But I'm worried I might lose my identity, be overwhelmed by you."

"I don't see myself as on overwhelming sort of person, Chrissie. Is that how you see me?"

"Well, you are adamant about your political beliefs, which is good, but I'm worried I won't be able to 'grow up' into me. Do you understand?"

"You are already, you, a unique being. That's who I fell in love with, not a disciple!"

We both laughed at that.

"So now you're Jesus," I went into hysterical giggles.

"Only if you want me to be," he retorted.

"I don't think your mother would like that much. That role has already been taken, she thinks."

"Quite. I'll still be doing my own thing, as will you. Particularly with work."

I felt reassured, and that's why work and my studies continued to be important, even though it meant I had very few evenings free.

However, on one of those evenings when we were strolling by the river, Oliver said, "A penny for your thoughts. You're not your usual chatty self, rabbiting on about whatever comes into your mind."

"Do you know what day it is?" I responded.

"Not until you tell me, no."

"21st February."

"Oh, darling, I forgot. How thoughtless of me." He stopped me mid step and drew me close to him. I could smell the smokiness of his clothes and hair. I melted into the security of his arms.

"I really thought I'd got over it, I really, really did."

"It must have been hard being with Clemmie and her baby; I assumed you were just annoyed at her for her language, her bossiness, 'You ought to do this, not that, you must, you should' etcetera, but seeing her with the baby…difficult, I imagine."

"I didn't realise, but yes, it could have been that. I wondered what the Kitten would have been like at that age."

"Running about and getting into everything, I expect."

"And I'm still not certain who adopted him."

"I thought you were convinced it was the father."

"Well it sounded like that, from what I thought I'd over heard, but not knowing is frustrating."

"I could have a look at Somerset House, birth certificate and that."

"No, Ollie; it's my problem. Please don't. I'll manage, it's just that it comes into my head now and again. Or rather, I feel a physical yearning."

"But…" he paused.

"What, Ollie, what?"

"Just shut me up if I'm putting my foot in it, but how would you feel having a baby with me, a baby of our own?"

"I think it's too soon. I'm not sorted out enough, and anyway I've read that people bring children up in the way they were brought up."

"And you don't want to be cruel, I understand that."

"Auntie Vi wasn't cruel, just frustrated that her own ambitions were thwarted, but she did hit me a lot."

"But there would be two of us, and I was never hit as a child, well, only at school. Those priests…"

"You've never even held a baby, let alone changed one."

"Well, have you?"

"Only little Sandra when she was born. She was like a doll, so active and then…"

"But you saw how she managed at our wedding. Without her callipers, no stick or anything."

"Look at those two swans, no, over there. There, Oliver," I pointed. "Look as though they're going hell for leather, what a fight."

And that closed the subject of babies for a year or so, while it wandered about in my subconscious.

***

One Sunday after one of Mrs Mooney's filling roasts and apple pies, I was sitting in a deckchair next to her listening to the sound of children playing in the next door neighbour's garden. Oliver was washing up.

"He's quite domesticated, isn't he," I mentioned.

"I should hope so, he's been trained by me."

"Did you ever try for any more children?" I paused. Was I being too abrupt? "I'm sorry, that's a bit rude, too personal."

"No, it's alright. I would have liked another but it was difficult with his Da as he was. Why?"

"I'm just thinking really."

"What, about having a baby?"

"Just mulling it over."

"It must bring up lots of memories for you."

"Well, there's that. Yes. I'm not sure I've got over that yet."

"Perhaps you won't. But a baby could help with the healing."

"I wouldn't want one just for that."

"I've never worked in maternity, well, not since my training, but people have them for many reasons, not just for the baby's sake. Sometimes it saves a marriage."

"Or the reverse."

"That's true too. Oliver would be a good father, I'm sure, but it's up to you. Certainly, it takes two, but it's the woman who has to go through with the birth and the feeding, sleepless nights and so on…here he comes."

"Not on about my sleepless nights, you two," Oliver commented as he brought us cups of tea.

He sat down on the grass.

"Not really, just bemoaning women's lot."

"Ah, a feminist meeting. I should have guessed. Shall I, the poor weak male, go away?"

We laughed and the conversation switched to Oliver's latest piece of writing for children about the new Hovercraft and how it worked.

***

"This is my last packet of pills," I stated when we got into our bedroom that night.

"The clinic's open tomorrow, you could pick some up then," Oliver said casually as he changed into his pyjamas.

"No, I mean I'm not going to take any more."

"Ah. Does that mean what I think it means?" he said smiling broadly. "Has my mother been going on to you about her becoming a grandmother."

"Not at all, but I did just talk around a few issues."

"Well, it's your decision, and, of course, I'd be delighted to become a daddy."

Chapter 16

I met Jane, Oliver's girlfriend from Bristol, at parties and on demos. One evening in a flat in Finborough Road she expressed her surprise that we'd got married.

"I don't know how you can stand it. He gets so remote, caught up in his work or his causes. Like a Rottweiler and its prey. Can't let go, can't get distracted."

"I like being able to do my own thing. Quite happy having time to read, go to talks, galleries, focus on my work, well, when I was working," I replied.

"Yes, but he seems absent; can't talk about his emotions."

"Perhaps, but I've found he can generally communicate well."

"On paper, yes, but…"

"No, I have a totally different perception of him."

"Maybe you bring something out of him that I couldn't."

"Maybe. We seem to suit each other."

"Does he still play jazz?"

"Occasionally. I hope he'll carry on with it. I think he's brilliant."

Suddenly there was a buzz going round the room.

"Let's go, come on you lot, stop chatting."

"Where are we going?" I asked.

"Over the road, to the Troubadour," Oliver said. "Are you OK for that? Not too tired?"

"I'm fine," I said.

Jane helped me up from my chair. "Ol and I heard Bob Dylan there a couple of years ago."

"How wonderful. Oliver thinks of him as a poet as much as a musician."

"I agree. He's been a hero since Blowing in the Wind, a voice of protest."

Jane and I walked arm in arm down the street, me waddling from side to side, and she steering me through the crowd gathering outside the café.

Once inside we found a corner where I could sit to relieve the ache in my back and groin.

We found ourselves in a group of people talking to some men who'd just returned from the States.

"Can't believe they're escalating the war," one of them said.

"I thought it was easing up," I commented.

"Quite the opposite. Talk to Gary here," said Oliver. So I met an authentic anti-war voice: our new American friend.

"Yeah," said Gary. "The Tet offensive caught us off guard. And even our troops are brutalised, doing horrendous things."

Oliver nodded in agreement.

"That's why I quit," continued Gary. "They called me up: got my notice to serve, the draft. But I found the thought of killing those poor guys... I couldn't do it. Not as if they were going to invade the U.S. Cowardice they said. Thought they were going to put me in jail so I nipped over the border to my cousin in Canada, who got me to Ireland, and then came here." He took a long drag from his spliff.

"A Conchie, like Connie's dad," Oliver said as he turned to me.

"No one understands. It's a futile war over artificial boundaries. We shouldn't have gotten involved." Gary'd pronounced it 'footle'.

"All war is futile," said Oliver. "What can we do about it?"

"There's a Stop the War rally coming up in your big square soon," said Gary.

"Trafalgar Square?" I said.

"Yup, I'll sure be there."

"I won't. Look at me." I pointed to my huge belly.

"I will," said Oliver. "Can't have our little one growing up with Vietnam in that state."

"Do you know when?" I asked.

"I'll be in touch. It'll be quite soon," said Gary and he and Oliver went to the bar to 'refresh' our glasses, as Gary put it.

By this time my energy was waning. Oliver offered to take me back to our Victorian terraced cottage, formerly owned by the local brewery and sold to us for just under £6,000 which seemed an absolute fortune in the mid-60s. We just hoped that Oliver's income was going to cover the mortgage repayments, utility bills and petrol and maintenance for our old banger of a car. Oliver had persuaded Mr Blackwood to say he was on the payroll to make it easier to get the mortgage, and, of course, I had recently stopped work so we were totally reliant on the variable income from his freelance writing. He didn't seem worried about any financial issues facing us.

My main concern that evening was to get comfortable and have some rest as I was exhausted. He tucked me up in bed with a hot water bottle as there was no heating in the bedroom, and put an extra blanket over my feet. I don't think he realised that I had quite enough heat internally from the baby I was carrying.

"You go back, you were having such an interesting chat. And there'll be some good music shortly." So he went back to the Troubadour. It took me a long time to get comfortable enough to sleep, so I looked round the room designing how I'd like it to be. At that time we only had a double bed, two bedside lights and some crates in our bedroom: no dressing table or wardrobe yet. We had Oliver's old cot waiting in the baby's room. Downstairs was a put-you-up sofa from Mrs Mooney's as well as some planks on bricks which created a set of bookshelves. Oliver had brought his desk and typewriter from his old study and created an office corner in the back room and, even though he wasn't exactly a handyman, had managed to put up some shelves on brackets in an alcove to store the essential part of his reference library.

I loved the feel of the house. It had many of its original Victorian features including the fireplace where slightly embossed cyclamen graced the tiles either side. We had put an electric fire in the grate as when we'd first arrived in the midst of winter the smoke from the fire had filled not only the living room, but the bedroom above. The other heating we had was a paraffin stove, which meant we had to walk to the nearest garage and fill our can with Esso Blue paraffin when it ran out. Somehow I managed to doze off and didn't even hear Oliver return in the early hours of the morning.

***

"The demo's going ahead," he said one morning when we were having our breakfast.

"When?"

"Next weekend."

"Well, I definitely won't be going. I'm already a couple of days overdue."

"Do you want Mum to come and stay?"

"That would be really nice. Are you working at home today?"

"Yes. Just got to finish off this section. I'll take it in tomorrow, rather than post it. Quicker that way."

"Want me to proof read it?"

"That would be great. Give me, say, two hours."

"I'll go round the corner and pick up a few things."

"Can you manage?"

"Don't fuss. I'll be fine. Give you a coffee when I get back."

He kissed me lightly on the lips and went to his corner in the back room to get down to work. I washed up the breakfast things, had a brief sit down at the kitchen table and reminded him to get some coal up from the cellar for the boiler.

When I came back with the shopping he was nowhere to be seen.

"Oliver! Oliver! Where are you?"

There was a muffled sound coming from under the stairs.

He'd gone down to the cellar, but the ill-fitting door had stuck, and he couldn't get back into the hall.

I tugged and tugged at the handle. It came off in my hands.

"Hang on, I'll get a screw driver."

So I found one and unscrewed the door.

"Get out of the way," he shouted. "I'm going to give it a push."

And down it came into the newly painted hall revealing a dirty figure holding a bucket of coal. He reminded me of one of the Black and White Minstrels I'd seen in a show at the seaside. I could hardly stop laughing.

"We must get something done about that," I spluttered. "What happens if I get stuck down there? Or the baby crawls in."

"I feel bent in two. I was just hoping you didn't meet anyone and decide to go back with them for a coffee or something."

"I don't know anyone here yet, only a few shopkeepers who always ask how I am. How long have you been down there?"

"Since you went out. I thought I'd get the coal immediately, otherwise I'd forget. I get so engrossed."

"Oh you poor thing."

So while he was cleaning himself up, I popped next door to find out if the neighbour knew anyone who could do a few jobs for us, the priority being that door.

"Oh, at last," said a woman called Josie. "I wondered when we'd meet." So we chatted and I told her Oliver worked from home quite often.

"Oh, I hope our baby doesn't disturb him."

"Not at all. Apart from the nappies in the garden we wouldn't have known there was a baby next door. How old?"

"Nearly a year now. I take him to a playgroup each morning; I have to stay with him. When are you due?"

"Should have been the 10th."

"Won't be long then." I was so relieved to have a neighbour with a child. My first friend in the neighbourhood.

***

The weekend of the demo arrived. Oliver had deposited his copy with the publishers on the Thursday and had spent the following days designing and making posters and placards with the help of various friends who turned up unannounced at our house. He collected his mother on the Saturday morning, and together we put blankets on the put-u-up in the living room. On Sunday 17th March, he met up with a group of friends who helped him carry the various badges and placards to their rendezvous point in the West End. That night he hadn't returned. I wasn't concerned as he would often stay overnight with friends if they'd been on somewhere. I was more concerned that I had started to go into labour. My mind couldn't cope with anything else. Mrs Mooney timed my contractions, and when they were about every 10 minutes apart she phoned for an ambulance. I was whisked off to Queen Mary's Hospital in Roehampton. She stayed for an hour or so to make sure I was getting the best treatment possible, and then returned to Mortlake. When it got light Mrs Mooney started to worry as there was a news item on the radio about some riots in Grosvenor Square. She phoned the local police. After being transferred to different stations she got through to a more central one. Oliver had been arrested and put in a cell with a group of protestors.

"They can't do that," she had informed the helpful police officer. "His wife is giving birth AT THIS MOMENT." The officer told her that he'd find out where he'd been taken.

"Bow Street Magistrates Court," he informed her. "Due to go before the beak at around midday."

Mrs Mooney arrived at the Court. When she told me about it I had visions of her turning into the Grandma figure in the Giles *Daily Express* cartoons.

Apparently she burst in and shouted to the Magistrate, "His wife's gone into labour. You can't send him down!" When they'd calmed her they let Oliver go with a fine and a promise not to get involved in such behaviour again.

"Only if the police respect my right to protest," he declared.

"Off you go," said the Magistrate. "Your wife needs you more than we do. Get out."

He and his mother took a taxi to the hospital. At 11.25 a.m. I had delivered a baby girl weighing 8lbs. 7 oz. on Monday 18th March 1968.

When he walked into the ward, I gasped. He looked as if he hadn't slept a wink and hadn't even shaved, but above all he was wearing damp crumpled clothes.

"How wonderful," he said. "My own little girl; what a sweetheart. Look at her, the tiny thing. And lots of hair too. I'm so proud of you, Chrissie. And to think I was trying to get all the wars in the world to stop so my baby daughter could grow up in peace." He gazed at the little bundle in the cot beside my bed.

"I hope you succeeded. You look a fright."

"D'you know what, they arrested me for shouting and singing, 'Hey, hey, LBJ, how many kids will you kill today!' not for violence. You know I wouldn't behave violently on a demo. And everyone was jostling and pushing in the Square. Utter chaos. And to think it was a peaceful protest until we got to the U.S. Embassy. When the police arrested us, just a small group, they put us all into a cell, and guess what. They decided the cell wasn't clean enough, so they hosed it down, us included, calling us 'Commie bastards'. No wonder I look a mess."

"Can I see the baby," said Mrs Mooney as she walked down the ward. She'd discretely let Oliver see the baby first.

"My grandchild; a granddaughter. So sweet. Look at those tiny hands, Oliver, perfect little fingernails." And she started to cry. "Your Da would have been so happy."

We all hugged each other and Oliver said, "I haven't even brought you any flowers."

"There'll be time for that. I have to stay in hospital for 10 days apparently."

"Do they know it's actually your second? They might let you go sooner," whispered Mrs Mooney.

"They want to make sure I can feed and bath the baby first. I haven't had that experience yet."

"Well you know where I am if you need any help."

And she left us to marvel at the little person we'd created. Oliver cried as he held the baby for the first time. I couldn't wait for him to pass her back to me. She still seemed part of my body.

After Oliver had gone and I'd attempted to feed and change the baby, I went to sleep. The cots had been taken into a side room so we new mothers could get some rest. However, in the night, when all the lights had been dimmed I found myself walking along an unfamiliar corridor in the maze of one-storey wards at the rear of the hospital.

"Where are you off to?" a nurse I hadn't seen before challenged.

"I don't know. I'm looking for my little boy," I replied automatically, realising that I must have been sleep-walking as I had no notion of how I had come to this unfamiliar part of the hospital.

"Which ward are you in?"

"I don't know." I started to cry.

"When did you have your baby, was it today, yesterday?"

"Yesterday, I think. I'm so confused."

"It's the shock." She took me by the hand and walked me back to my ward.

"This lady's looking for her baby boy. Is he in with the other cots?"

"But she had a girl," said the nurse on duty.

"She seems to think she's had a baby boy."

"Don't worry dear, I'll bring her to you, so you can see that you had a baby girl," said the kindly night nurse. She thanked the nurse who'd rescued me and brought the cot to my bedside. She checked the label on the cot, 'Teresa Rose Mooney' after Oliver's mother and mine. She pointed to the pink band on the baby's wrist 'Baby Mooney' and my name on my wrist. "Here she is, your little baby girl. I don't know why you thought she was a boy." She placed her in my arms so I could cuddle her.

I kept my thoughts to myself. I realised I'd confused the birth of my Kitten-boy in 1964 with what I'd experienced on 18th March when I'd given birth for the second time.

When I told Oliver, he was really sympathetic.

"You obviously haven't stopped grieving for him. Time will heal."

"But I've hardly thought about him since I got married."

"I expect it was something to do with going through the same physical process again. I'm sorry I wasn't here to be with you."

"They don't let the fathers in. That's why there are all those men pacing up and down in the corridors smoking frantically."

"I'm here now, and I'll look after you." He visited every day.

Chapter 17

"Please don't take her, Oliver, no, please, no."

"I only want to take her to the shops to give you a break."

"Don't take her away, no, please."

"Just round the corner."

I burst into tears and grabbed little Teresa out of his arms and rushed upstairs. I threw myself on our bed holding the baby tight.

"It's alright, Chrissie, it is. Let me hold her, you're squashing her."

"No, no, you'll take her away."

"Chrissie," he said sternly, "That's the last thing I'd ever do, you know that. I'm here to stay with you and baby."

"But how do I know?"

"I promise, on everything I hold dear. Just let me cuddle her. Yes, that's right let her go."

He gently lay down beside me and took baby Teresa and we held her between us.

"Oh, Ollie, I'm sorry. It's so difficult."

"It'll take time. You're doing really well. You let my mother hold her yesterday."

"But you were going to take her outside, I wouldn't be able to see her."

"Let's go downstairs. Make some tea, sit in the kitchen. Then I'll carry her into the garden."

"No, no."

"Yes. You'll still be able to see us."

My stomach did a double somersault. I felt blood rushing in my ears.

"OK, I'll try."

I carried Teresa into the kitchen. Oliver made us cups of tea. He rolled me a cigarette and lit it at the gas stove. He put it in my mouth as he gently prised the baby from my arms. My breath came in short bursts but I tried to suck at the cigarette to calm me down. Then I seemed to stop breathing altogether.

"Come back," I called. "I can't breathe."

"Drink your tea," Oliver called from just outside the kitchen door. "And breathe in and out really slowly. You're doing fine."

He'd taken six steps into the garden. My eyes were fixed on him. The tea was hot, but I sipped it and gradually my breathing returned to normal. I looked at him proudly holding up our baby. He twirled around with her in his arms, and walked slowly back to the kitchen.

"Well done," he said. "But I'm holding her now, till you've finished your tea and your fag."

I felt I'd made an important step, but it was so painful.

The next time I went to the clinic to have Teresa weighed, I mentioned to the nurse that I found it difficult to leave Teresa with anyone else, especially if I couldn't see her.

"Does it make you feel depressed?" she said.

"I'm not depressed at all, I'm very happy. But my mind races and I imagine someone's going to take her away or they'll be run over, or they'll fall over, even in the house and she'll be hurt, or even killed. And everything goes too fast for me, and my head aches and my stomach churns over and over. I just want to run away with her…" My heart was beating faster and faster as I was talking. Eventually I just burst into tears.

"I'll write a note for you to take to your GP." She held my hand and stroked Teresa's head. "What are you up to, little one, making your mummy so worried?"

"No, no, it's not her fault, it's me," and out it came: all about how my Kitten-boy had been taken away from me, and how I'd pushed all those feelings down and how Oliver was trying to help me, but I was upsetting him because I couldn't let Teresa go.

"It's understandable; you buried so much about your first baby. But Oliver is Teresa's daddy. He has as much right to her as you. You must let him hold her, change her, bathe her. Do it bit by bit. Otherwise you'll wear yourself out, and then you'll be no good to anyone."

"I feel so stupid, but it's like a physical pain when I stop holding her."

"Talk to the GP; I'm sure he'll give you something to help."

"But I'm still feeding her, I don't want her to be drugged, it could damage her."

So I went to see our GP who had a surgery in a house beside Barnes Pond. He gave me some Valium, which made me feel a bit floaty and relaxed, but I was still conscious of the physical yearning for my baby when she was out of my sight.

However, gradually I allowed Oliver to take over more of Teresa's nappy changing and bottle-feeding. After two months, I slowly came off the medication.

"You've given Teresa double-love, you know. All the pent-up love you had for your other baby."

"Oh, Ollie, I don't know how you've put up with me for the last six months. I'm so, so sorry."

"You don't have to be. I knew it might be difficult for you, but not that bad."

"You had every right to leave me."

"No! I would never do that. And anyway, Teresa is my daughter as well as yours. I won't leave you."

"And I feel mean to your mother; she offered to have Teresa overnight, so we could meet up with our friends. I still can't do that."

"How about if she stays here with the baby? Could you manage that?"

"I could try, if we don't go far. I might be able to let her baby-sit here, I think," I said slowly, thinking I could nip back to check on Teresa.

"Well, let's plan a little treat for ourselves. We haven't really celebrated with our friends yet."

"You've downed a few beers though; wetted the baby's head and all that."

"But not with you."

So we organised a small gathering, starting out at The Sun Inn, a short walk away, followed by a visit to the Bull's Head for some jazz.

We invited our neighbour Josie and her husband, Mike, as well as Jane and her latest beau. Oliver asked some of his co-demonstrators as well as Connie from B & G and her partner. My old friend Maggie was delighted to join us as she'd felt I'd cut her off, particularly as I hadn't been to her recent wedding as it would have meant leaving the baby. John Jennings and his boyfriend Carl phoned to say they would come later as they were working on a show at Richmond Theatre. Toby was sadly detained at Her Majesty's Pleasure, and although John cheekily devised a cunning escape plan, it was a fantasy that would never be fulfilled.

It was through talking to him that I realised my problems were tiny compared with what he'd had to face. His work as a carpenter in the theatre introduced him to colleagues who were quite open about life choices which were still frowned on in other places of work, whether it be living with a girlfriend or boyfriend or being open about their sexuality.

"Mum was OK about it, sort of. She said how different I was even as a child compared with Toby."

"I've heard stories about him; very much a womaniser, isn't he."

"She was more worried that I might get beaten up or arrested, 'and we've already got enough prison experience in this family, thank you very much,' she'd said. She was scared I'd get hurt in some way outside one of our clubs."

"And your dad? I can't imagine he was delighted; he was always very straight-laced."

"Goodness. You should have seen him when I brought Carl home! I thought he was going to have a heart attack."

"Because your date was a boy?"

"No, because…well, his actual words were: 'I can't believe you've brought that half-caste boy home. What his parents must have thought, marrying outside their own kind.'"

"'But, Dad, both his parents are white,' I told him."

"'Well, she's no better than she ought to be, then, having an affair with a darkie.' Dad said."

"'No, it is not like that.' I told him."

"'Why we brought so many of them over here, I don't know. We could manage the transport and hospitals quite well.'"

"No; I said it's not like that at all. Carl's family have been in this country for centuries. The eighteenth century in fact."

"'There weren't no darkies here then,' retorted Dad."

"'One of his great, great, greats worked in the docks. Had a child with a local girl. He has a wonderful line when people tell him 'Go home nigger'."

"You talking about me and your dad?" Carl joined in.

"Tell her, Carl, tell Chrissie what you say."

"'I bet my family have been here longer than yours. Where were yours in 1790?'"

"I can't imagine that goes down well," I said, thinking to myself that I hadn't realised black people were in England that long ago either.

"Sometimes it does, sometimes it doesn't." said Carl. "Do you remember what your dad said then, John-boy?"

"How can I forget! 'And now he's a homo like you!' Mum intervened then as she could see how upsetting it was for all of us."

"'Don't go on about it so,' Mrs Jennings said. 'Can't you see the boy's happy. In fact both of them are. And it's legal now, so you've got to change your attitude.' That told him."

"But it didn't change his attitude, did it, Carl? 'I'll think what I like,' he said." John paused, looking down at the floor. "Actually, I haven't seen him since."

Our conversation put my problems into perspective. What it must have been like for John, being in fear of the law for so many years.

I was really proud of myself though. Apart from one small panic earlier in the evening when we were greeting people at the Sun and I phoned home to check that everything was alright, which of course it was, I enjoyed the evening, and felt as though I'd re-entered into society.

Chapter 18

"Ring, ring! ring, ring!"

So typical! I was in the middle of changing Teresa's nappy and couldn't get to the phone.

After cleaning off the nappy, I was in the middle of putting it in the blue-lidded bucket and topping up the solution, when the phone went again.

"Hello!"

"Mavis here." It took me a moment to work out who Mavis was. "I'm afraid your grandad has had an accident. He's tripped on some steps and hurt his ankle. I've taken him to hospital."

"Oh, no! You're such a good neighbour. Are they keeping him in?"

"No, it turned out it was a sprain, but he has to rest it up for a few days."

"Is he at home now?"

"Yes, but quite immobile."

"I'll come down. Oh, just a moment. Oliver won't be back for a couple of hours. He'll drive us down." I cursed the fact that I couldn't drive.

"That'll be good. I'll give him some lunch. Look forward to seeing you later then, and the baby."

I forgot to ask if he needed anything, but I could always pick something up from the local shops.

I went back upstairs, checked on Teresa who was sound asleep in her cot, and packed a few things in case I had to stay overnight. Teresa's things took up more room than mine: nappies, creams, nappy bucket, muslins, sleeping suits, day clothes, bottles, steriliser, baby milk powder. What a palaver!

Oliver came back at four o'clock and agreed to drive us down. I hadn't packed for him assuming that he might return home leaving us there.

"I'd better take at least a change of underwear and my shaving things," he said. "Just in case."

So off we went in our second-hand Ford Prefect.

I really liked being in the car while Oliver drove. I found lots of memories floated up, and somehow sitting side-by-side helped me to pour out some of my supressed feelings.

But this autumn day I wasn't thinking about my Kitten-boy, or even my anxiety about Grandad Preece. Through the turning leaves I spotted a sign for East Grinstead.

"Guinea pigs!" I exclaimed.

"Teresa's too little for one of those yet," laughed Oliver.

"No, not that sort. Did I ever tell you about one of my first secretarial jobs with a man who had virtually no face?"

"My goodness. No. That must have been a shock."

"Well, I must admit I gasped when I first met him. D'you know, the agency didn't even warn me. I was only 16, or so. I'd seen injured servicemen selling matches or shouting 'Star, News'n Standard', but I'd never come across such a badly injured person before".

"Yes, the visible signs of war are still around us."

"I felt really embarrassed by my reaction, Ollie, but he was so kind. He seemed to take it in his stride. I can't have been the first to react that way. He turned away from me towards the office window overlooking Piccadilly Circus and asked me if I'd heard of the Guinea Pig Club."

"Had you?"

"No. I felt really anxious about what he was going to tell me. Anyway, he said he'd been a pilot. RAF. In a Spitfire. Battle of Britain apparently. The Germans were attacking the South Coast. He and his lot were trying to stop the Luftwaffe bombing the shipping convoys. Apparently he was shot down early in his flight so there was lots of aviation fuel on board. The plane burst into flames. Lucky to survive. Dragged away by some farmers who hosed him down. He said he'd have been even worse if they hadn't done that. They got him to a small hospital and they couldn't do much. Went to a burns unit in East Grinstead."

"So that's what triggered the memory. I must say, you seem to remember so much of what he said."

"I think it's imprinted in my mind because I was so shocked. Anyway, a man called Archibald McIndoe, I think it was, patched him up. It was all trial and error in those days. Hence 'Guinea Pigs'. I remember asking him if anyone else was injured in the plane, and feeling stupid when he said, 'Single seater. Only me.' I apologised for reacting so badly. He was very gracious saying he knew he looked a fright, but at least he was alive."

"What was the damage?"

"In spite of years of plastic surgery he had no hair, not even eye-lashes. Only two holes for a nose, and a hole for his mouth, but no proper lips. I can see him now. His skin was a patchwork of varied colours ranging from brown through pink to white. His ears were misshapen and one of his hands was a mere claw. But he still managed to hold a ciggie."

"What was the company?"

"I can't remember, but he started it before the war. He praised his staff. They seemed to look after him, and stuck by him when he came back."

"I'd love to write about those unsung heroes and the medical people who were brave enough to experiment and, hopefully, give them back their lives."

"You will, you will. And you can now add that South African doctor. What's his name?"

"Christiaan Barnard. The heart man."

"Fancy replacing someone's heart. Amazing."

"My mother looked after some of the war casualties who'd lost limbs. Couldn't replace them though. I don't remember her talking about the ones who were badly burnt, but some of them must have been. This is why we're fighting so hard to make sure there are no more wars."

"You'd think I would have been protesting against war earlier, bearing in mind my parents' deaths."

"Depends how conscious you were that you could influence things. When I first met you, you put that burden on the politicians, I seem to remember, and didn't recognise the power that we, the ordinary people, have in making change happen."

"Auntie Vi didn't encourage any criticism of our leaders, our betters, as she called them. She stifled any disapproving noises I made of what the politicians did, and always voted for whoever her dad had voted for. Same as Mr Jennings, making his wife vote the same as him. Probably told Toby and John to do the same."

"I can't imagine them doing what he told them to do in the privacy of the polling booth."

"He was grateful for the war. Thought it was the best time of his life, and it gave him the skills to become a mechanic. He said once that after the war he had no direction and missed the strong sense of purpose and committed comrades."

"I doubt if he used the word 'comrades'," replied Oliver with a smile.

Teresa started to cry, so we stopped and I went and sat in the back with her on my lap.

On the approach to Eastbourne, we avoided the town centre and took the windy road near Beachy Head.

"I love this place," I said. "We had some wonderful holidays with Grandad."

"Well, perhaps Teresa will too," Oliver suggested as we drove past the hotels, the Wish Tower and Bandstand on towards Marine Parade.

As I carried her from the car, it struck me that this was the very first time she was breathing in sea air. I stood with her gazing out to the familiar horizon.

Mavis greeted us.

"What a pretty little thing," she said as she admired the baby and stroked her hair.

"Thank you. She's so good too, no trouble at all on the journey. Just made one short stop. Have you been with Grandad all this time?"

"No, just brought him some shopping. He's resting, but I'll leave you to it."

"I can't tell you how grateful I am. He's lucky to have you living next door."

"I hardly see him usually. Just see him go for his stroll along the prom sometimes, or bump into him at the shops."

"He won't be doing that for a while," I commented as I watched Oliver help Grandad to the outside lavatory.

"Well, I'll be off. Let me know if I need to get anything for him."

"Thank you so very much. Hopefully we can sort him out now."

I tidied up the compact kitchen and found some tins in the Easiwork. I set about heating up some food for us and warming Teresa's baby food while Oliver sat with Grandad.

"I wouldn't mind going into a home," said Grandad as I interrupted them with bowls of steaming tomato soup. "I don't suppose you remember that big house we visited, when you and the boys were creeping about as commandos."

"Vaguely," I said, concentrating more on feeding Teresa than on Grandad.

"Well, I've heard that they've turned it into a retirement home. I might have a look at it."

"Surely you want to be independent, don't you?" I ventured.

"That fall really shook me up. What if no one's around? Mavis found me on the pavement. I could have been there for hours. Or at night. What if I'd fallen on my way back from the pub, or the chippie?"

"It's a big decision, Grandad."

"One of my mates is thinking about it too. He served in the Great War."

"So you have lots to talk about," I suggested.

"No. Too horrible. You know what I mean, don't you Oliver?"

"I still wake up at night; find I can't talk about it either."

"The worst thing I did was try to strangle my lovely wife."

"What!" I exclaimed, shocked that this gentle man could do something like that.

"I was woken by her screams, luckily. I thought she was the enemy. Just shows how these things prey on us for years and years."

"And come out in our dreams," added Oliver, glancing at me.

"How's the writing?" asked Grandad, sensing that the atmosphere needed changing.

"I've got plenty to do at the moment. Our next door neighbour works at the brewery, Watneys, you know."

"And Josie, his wife was helpful after I'd had Teresa," I added.

"Through him I met someone at his work who was creating an archive in preparation for writing a history of the brewery. I told him that's the sort of writing I do."

"It came just at the right time as Oliver could work nearby."

"I showed them some of the things I've written, and they got me involved."

I went into the bedroom to change Teresa and heard Oliver describing how he organised the archive into a sequence to develop into a book. The sky was darkening but there was still an orangey glow coming through the window reminding me of evenings when the Jennings boys and I snuggled up in one bed with Auntie Vi on the other and listened to stories beginning, "It was a dark and stormy night," against the creepy sound of the lightship out in the channel. But none of those childish excited fears were anything compared with what Grandad and Oliver had endured in different wars, one in Europe, the other in Malaya. I wondered whether Oliver would ever manage a whole week without waking in a cold sweat with staring eyes hiding what visions were lurking there.

When I returned to the living room, Oliver had embarked on a description of the local pubs.

"Although it's only just opened, the Charlie Butler, it's quite popular."

"I don't get it," I added. "It's a Young's pub in Watney's territory."

"Well lots of locals knew him when he was Young's head ostler. That's why the pub has his name."

"What a tribute. To have a pub named after you!" said Grandad. "You must be experts with so many in your neck of the woods."

"Yes. We're pub connoisseurs," Oliver admitted, grinning.

"You should see us on boat-race day. Sometimes we walk down to the river and meet up with friends at The Ship, quite near the finishing post. Our nearest one, though, our local, is The White Hart. We watch it there if the garden isn't under water."

"I'm still waiting for Oxford to win," bemoaned Oliver.

"Didn't you go to that left-wing college?" asked Grandad.

"Ruskin. I suppose it was left-wing compared with the rest of the university. We'd got there through the Workers Education system."

"That's how I got introduced to books, the WEA. Could hardly read before I went into the army. Then they couldn't stop me gobbling everything up!"

"Sort of City Lit, I suppose. Lots of different subjects to help people who'd missed out at school, or left too early," I suggested.

"Or who hadn't developed the skills of studying until they were older, or in my case frogmarched into National Service before I'd decided what I wanted to do," Oliver added.

"But your favourite pub is The Bull's Head in Barnes, really, isn't it Ollie?"

"Of course, because I can sometimes play there; only as an amateur. But now I can play at home since the piano came."

I noticed how dark it was getting, and broached the subject of us staying.

"Not at all," Grandad said firmly. "You young things have got your own life. I can manage perfectly well now. Just help me to the lavvy, Oliver, then I'll get to bed."

So we returned to Mortlake, promising to return frequently. The visit had persuaded me that I needed to learn to drive so I could come independently to Eastbourne and anywhere else I fancied.

Chapter 19

We were sitting on the grass in Hyde Park. Little Teresa and Nathan were running round us giggling, oblivious to the 'Rolling Stones' playing in the distance. We'd just finished our picnic with Josie and Mike when a group of Oliver's old friends wriggled through the crowds and hauled Oliver up.

"Be back shortly," he called out as he disappeared into the crowd.

We were so busy enjoying the music that we hadn't noticed how long Oliver had been gone.

Had he gone home without us? How were we going to get back? Oliver had parked the car in one of the side streets off Bayswater Road, and I still couldn't drive. We gathered up our things and put the children into their pushchairs and started walking towards the nearest gate. We spotted Oliver with a group of what could only be described as tramps, bearded young men, with lanky hair swathed in smoke from their spliffs.

"Ollie," I yelled. "We'd given you up for dead. Where did you get to?"

He moved over to us and kissed little Teresa on the head.

"Just a crowd of people without anywhere to stay."

I lowered my voice to a whisper: "You haven't invited them home, have you?"

"No, but they've invited me to join their commune."

"Oh, yeah?"

"Don't be ridiculous. Someone mentioned my name and I got involved chatting, that's all. They ridiculed my bourgeois life-style a bit, but they're OK really, just finding it difficult to get accommodation."

"It's becoming a challenge, I know. We're so lucky."

There had been articles about homelessness in cities in 'International Times' as well as the mainstream press.

On the way home Oliver mentioned that he'd lost contact with most of his friends from his protesting days.

"Just as well," said Mike, who was sitting in the front beside him. "You must be nearly forty: time to hang up your marching boots."

"I'll keep going on demos if the cause is just," Oliver retorted. "Those youngsters are the next generation and things are difficult for them, particularly in relation to the police."

"But you had your run-ins too, Ollie," I piped up from the back.

"Yes, against the H-bomb in 1961; and, of course, Grosvenor Square last year, but there seems to be more violence now. I was lucky getting duffed up a couple of times for specific reasons, but they seem to be picked on constantly for doing virtually nothing. Even for sitting on the pavement."

"Perhaps it's the way they look," said Josie. "They look disgusting."

"Part of the beat generation fashion," I suggested.

We continued our observations when we got home. Josie and Mike stayed for coffee and cheese and biscuits and we put Teresa and Nathan to sleep upstairs.

***

A few months later, Oliver bumped into one of the dishevelled crowd he'd met in Hyde Park.

"I was just walking down Piccadilly, when I saw him. An American guy with a small group of friends."

"Did he look as bad?" I asked.

"No, funnily enough. They'd taken over a huge building that used to be a ballet school or drama college or some such. Luckily the man who was going to develop it decided to keep the water and electricity on, so they were able to keep reasonably clean."

"So they were squatting there."

"Yes, and they showed me round. A very elegant building with a grand entrance hall and stairs to the right of it. The upstairs rooms were pretty big too, with marble fireplaces, and lots of mattresses on the floor. They'd painted the walls with slogans, and some psychedelic patterns, but apart from that, it was reasonably well kept."

"I'm really surprised. I expected they'd wreck a place like that."

"Hopefully they won't. There are about twenty people in there, mainly students and American backpackers, and yes, a few of them are stoned out of their minds. Others are writing poetry or chatting up girls. But it's a valid protest about the housing problems and the number of empty properties in London. Most of them are interested in CND too; in fact I helped them make a banner using a hub cap for the circle, and 'We Love Peace' on it, and some normal peace signs."

"Isn't that breaking copyright?"

"You should know, with your picture editing. The man who designed it ensured anyone in the peace movement could use it."

"So no copyright. Very generous."

"Reflected his views. He was a conscientious objector."

"Ah. But you're not going to join them, in the commune."

"No. It made me recognise that, although my principles haven't changed, the way I live my life has. I can't just hang out spending time reminiscing about the past with my mates; I'd rather focus on building a future with you and Teresa and developing new interesting friends."

I hugged him. "Just what I wanted to hear."

Chapter 20

Walking along the river one day, we were taking it in turns to push Teresa in her pushchair when Oliver suddenly turned to me.

"I couldn't bear it."

"What, what?"

"If I had to go through what you did. Have a baby taken away. You must have built a strong wall. I don't know how you did it. How you cope."

I didn't know how to answer. Did I cope? I certainly had a searing pain that welled up frequently, particularly on my Kittenboy's birth date, and it seemed worse since having Teresa.

"I don't think I do cope. I'm still in pain. But I push it away. I distract myself as I can't do anything about it."

"Do you feel the need to find him, reclaim him?"

"I feel that would be disloyal to you, and to our baby. It would upset everything we've got. And how would you feel?"

"I'd do anything to take away your sadness."

"Oh, Ollie," my unbidden tears trickled down my face. "Why was I so taken in?"

We stood by the river and he held me close. He wiped away my tears, stroked my hair and whispered:

"You were young and in love. No, not so young, just very trusting, and it was your first love. No one can blame you."

We walked along silently for a while immersed in our own thoughts.

"I could help find him," Oliver suddenly announced. "Tell me again, what exactly did you overhear?"

My heart raced for a moment. I felt slightly sick.

"It's difficult to remember exactly, but something like Matron talking about not jumping the queue."

"But he was the father. He'd have the right. What was on the Birth Certificate?"

"The Birth Certificate," I repeated. My eyes widened and I felt a shudder run through my body. "I never saw it. I don't know."

"I could find out. Andrew Finch, wasn't it?" I could sense he was starting to gear up for the challenge, as though his research antennae were starting to twitch as if it was a new leaflet or book that he had to write.

"No, it's my problem. I'm not sure about it. It would upset everything. Leave it, Oliver, please leave it."

We started walking again, focussing on helping little Teresa totter along the tow-path, even going as far as crossing Barnes Bridge, hoping for a train to run along beside us, but it didn't. We walked for a while along the wooded north side of the Thames only returning as the circling swifts indicated that it was time to go home.

Chapter 21

"Oh no! Conservatives; Edward Heath of all people."

"I really thought it would be Harold again," I commented.

"No cause for celebration then."

It was in the early hours of the morning and we'd both been watching Cliff Michelmore on our new Radio Rentals T.V.

"But I have got something for us to celebrate."

Oliver turned to me with a secret smile on his face.

"I think I can guess what it is," he paused dramatically. "Could it be a brother or sister for Teresa?"

"How did you know? I thought it would be a surprise."

"Well, I know your body almost as well as you do, and I did notice that your 'monthly', as my mother would put it, hasn't appeared recently."

"So I don't have any secrets from you," I smiled, and we both hugged each other, delighted that Teresa wouldn't be brought up as an only child as we both had been.

"It's a bit early to phone Mam, but I'm too excited to go back to bed. Could you manage a very early breakfast instead of going back to bed?"

"It's so light I don't think I could sleep. Yes, why not. It's nice to have time to ourselves while we eat. Anyway Teresa will be up soon and, well, I'm so pleased that you're pleased too."

"Did you doubt it?"

"No, not really, just I wanted to be sure before I told you, and what with the distraction of the election, it got a bit obscured."

"So now both of our children will be able to vote at 18 too."

"I don't think I was ready at that age. I still feel I don't know enough to make an informed choice, even though we both went to those meetings. So much is at stake."

"We can only go by what we're led to believe, that's one of the issues, so we have to balance that with our own experience of life."

"I remember Auntie Vi telling me to leave off complaining; that our betters know what's best for us."

"Certainly with regard to capital punishment they did. I honestly think that some elements in the population would have wanted it to continue."

"That's one of the issues, we're not educated to think through the impact of major decisions in parliament. I don't remember anything at school related to politics."

"We did something called British Constitutions, but it was really National Service and my experience in Malaya that woke me up."

"I'm so glad you've had some respite from those night terrors."

"Yes, somehow they have quietened down; not disappeared entirely, but that course of stuff from the GP helped."

"And he seemed to understand and help you to talk about it."

"Quite a good psychiatrist in his way. Mainly asking gentle questions and allowing me to be silent if I needed to. I think that helped me to put things in perspective and find alternative ways of responding to the dreams. Hopefully they'll go altogether. They're still lurking waiting to grab at me, particularly when I get over-tired or something during the day triggers a memory."

"Perhaps what you were writing for B & G early on when I first knew you brought it back."

"My book on the Malay Emergency, you mean. Yes, I thought it would help, but it didn't. I remember those days because that's when you told me about your first baby."

"I thought you'd no longer be my friend, I was so worried."

"You didn't need to be. I think I was already in love with you then."

"Not jealous?"

"No. That's a feeling I've conquered. It's destructive to the person that feels it, I've always thought. And anyway, it assumes you own the other person."

"I think that's the problem with Clemmie. She feels she owns James, and when he's late back, or stays overnight at the hospital she imagines he's with one of the nurses."

"I wouldn't be surprised if he was, the way she goes on at him."

"Oh, Ollie, what a thing to say!"

However, it turned out he was right. When I phoned Clemmie the following month when I was sure the baby had properly taken root, she told me that she and James were splitting up.

"Oh, Clemmie, I'm so sorry."

"I daren't tell my parents. They are so snooty about divorce. No-one in our family has done it, and it meant all that sordid going to a hotel and getting a private detective to verify that adultery had taken place."

"How horrid."

"But now we just have to wait for two years, if I agree, then he can have the divorce."

"Will you agree?"

"I don't know, at the moment. I've got Damian to consider, but I don't want to be with James if he doesn't want me."

"Has he got someone else?"

"I bet he has. He hasn't said so, but I know there's someone, one of the nurses, a theatre nurse he's worked with. He's talked about nothing else: how efficient she is, how pretty and good with people, and how she respects him and looks up to him."

"Don't you?"

"Not now. He's always doing things I don't like, like taking our little Damian to rugby matches, and excluding me. All boys together and that sort of thing."

"I'm sure it will work out."

"And where will I live?"

"You'll sort something out." Suddenly I felt tired of her. All I'd intended to do was let her know about the baby, and she hadn't commented on it or congratulated me. Just 'Oh, OK,', then launched into her problems. At least she hadn't told me what I ought or should be doing. 'Mustabation' Oliver now called it. Which made me laugh thinking about the word.

Chapter 22

By the time little Margaret was born in 1971, fathers were allowed to be with the mothers during the birth.

"Here, I'll mop you again," Oliver said as I sweated through a contraction.

It was a relief to have him there calming me down, but I had forgotten what a gruelling process it was, even though the actual labour was shorter than with Teresa.

As I made the final grunting push, Oliver even helped to pull the baby out.

"It's a girl," he shouted triumphantly.

I was so exhausted all I could do was sink down into the bed and hold the heavy bundle when it was presented to me.

"I'm sorry about all the swearing, Ollie. Forgive me."

"Nothing to forgive. Thank goodness men don't have to go through that. I don't think I could bear the pain."

"Well, there wasn't time for much gas and air. Isn't she sweet. Look at her hair. I'm so glad they both had hair."

"More than I've got now," responded Oliver.

I gave him the precious bundle to put into the waiting cot while the nurse sponged me down and helped me into a clean nightdress. Oliver went to phone his mother who was looking after Teresa at our house.

I only stayed in hospital a week this time. Oliver enjoyed being a 'hands-on' father to Teresa while I was away; he brought her each afternoon to see her baby sister. I could see they would get on well by the way Teresa stroked the little hand that had disentangled itself from the loose swaddling of the cellular blanket.

"It's certainly given him an insight into what we go through," Mrs Mooney commented when she visited us on our return to the house.

"I hope it hasn't put him off," I said.

"You're not thinking of having another one, are you?"

"No, I wasn't thinking of that." I was actually worried that it would shatter his illusions of me, having heard me swear, and seeing me in such an ungainly animal-like situation.

"Here's your post." Oliver came into the bedroom carrying a small pile of what looked like cards.

"Oh! One from Auntie Vi. I can't believe it. She didn't send one for Teresa's birth."

"Actually, it's a post card, from Elche: 'Glad everything went well. Welcome to baby. Our apartment overlooks this garden. Even better than Kew. From Vi and Herbie'."

"I didn't know that she knew."

"I sent her a telegram. She must have responded immediately."

"Are they there all the time now?"

"No, just while their new house is being done up. He's Assistant Bank Manager now, so they've moved to Sutton. She phoned when she got the news."

I wasn't sure if I was pleased or not. Auntie Vi had kept her distance, apart from a change of address card.

"Do you want her to be godmother?" asked Mrs Mooney.

"Not under any circumstances, thank you. Although I'm grateful to her at one level, I don't want her too involved with us. Anyway, she's now got airs and graces: reflected glory from Herbie's job."

"She told me she's been going to flamenco classes," said Oliver.

"She always wanted to be a dancer. I think that's how she met Herbie, at ballroom dancing sessions."

"Well, we've got our own little dancer here. Come on Teresa, pull that thumb out of your mouth and come and talk to your little sister."

"My baby," muttered Teresa and put her cheek next to Margaret's.

We all smiled at their relationship developing.

Mrs Mooney made us a wholesome stew and offered to stay overnight, but I really wanted time to adjust to being a family with two children, so Oliver drove her back to New Malden.

***

Oliver was a great dad, getting up in the night to carry Margaret around the bedroom when she disturbed my sleep, changing Teresa's nappy and making her breakfast while I was breast-feeding, and generally taking a full part in their care.

"Life is precious," I heard him tell Mike one day, who thought it was unmanly to be so involved. "They reward me with their little smiles and Teresa's funny mispronunciations as she struggles to find the words to express what she's trying to say."

"I bet you'd have liked a boy, though."

"Not part of my thinking. I'm happy with the girls."

I felt proud that he felt that. I wondered what he would feel if my Kitten-boy came into our lives. Perhaps I would ask him to check the records at Somerset House.

Chapter 23

The looks Oliver gave me when he was sitting by his alcove supposedly working made me feel warm and well loved. He just glanced at me with a tiny curling of his lips which broke into a smile when he'd noticed that I'd registered him looking at me. Then he'd go back to his writing, still harbouring a secret smile.

One day, I had just spotted his gaze, and I felt we were so secure that I could suggest we tried to find out about 'our' Kitten-boy.

"He'd be your son too," I said.

"Please, my love, don't get your hopes up too high."

"And the little ones would adore having an older brother."

"But he'd be settled with whoever it was took him in. It would disrupt his whole life."

"But what about us? I feel able to look after him and deal with the adjustment. Yes, it would be a challenge, but I feel ready for it."

"Well, if you're certain, I'll try to find out."

After that conversation I did have misgivings about having a big brother for Teresa and Margaret, who seemed so content with each other. Part of me wanted them to know him, but part of me was tearing at myself for even thinking of it. I kept coming out in hot sweats about it. I was now the person waking up in the middle of the night, not Oliver.

In the meantime, the girls were starting to develop their awareness of the world around them.

We navigated our way gingerly through their observations of people on the buses or walking past on the pavement.

"Why is that lady so fat?"

"Sh, darling, she's got a baby in her tummy."

"Was I in your tummy, Mummy?"

"Yes, sweetheart."

"How did I get in?" and, "Has that man got a willy, like Daddy?"

At home we welcomed their uninhibited curiosity. We thought we were open and liberal about most things, but trying to be honest as well as respecting the sensitivity of bus-loads of passengers, tested us sorely.

"Why is that man shouting? Is he cross with us?"

What could we say about the behaviour of someone with mental health issues striding up and down our tube carriage other than "Keep quiet, darling. Look the other way. We'll talk about it later"?

Whereas in my childhood, I'd accepted that there were many limbless men, they were mainly men, working sharpening knives or selling things on street corners, my children had to accommodate a different type of casualty as people with disabilities became more visible.

Gradually, instead of nurses caring for them in 'special' institutions, trained teachers started to take over the education of children with disabilities in 'special schools', helping them develop their potential. We often saw specially adapted transport taking children from their homes to these schools, and gradually Teresa and Margaret started to wave at them as the passengers turned to look at the street. Of course, they had met Sandra and seen pictures of her when she wore her callipers, so Teresa assumed that every child with a disability would throw away their sticks, or magically move about without relying on a wheelchair. We had a lot of disenchanting to negotiate.

***

It would take many years to describe the up-bringing of our two delightful girls. But there were certain highlights I remember. For example, when Margaret was about 3 and Teresa about 5, we decided to give them a pet to foster feelings of responsibility in them.

My friend Maggie had always loved cats. She phoned one morning in the school holidays just after I had dropped the girls off for a play day at a friend's house.

"Guess what, Chrissie. Tabby has given birth to five kittens. We've been up all night watching her licking them all over as they came out. It was wonderful."

"Congratulations. What are you going to do with all of them?"

"Well, I'll keep one of them, but, I wondered if you'd like one for the girls. I know you said you might be interested. What do you think?"

"When do you think they'll be ready to leave their mother?"

"Ooh, in about eight to ten weeks."

"Let me come and have a look. I could come over now. The girls are at a friend's house."

So I went to see them.

"Aren't you driving yet?" commented Maggie when I arrived.

"Not yet. I want to find a really good teacher. My tummy turns over thinking about it."

"Brilliant woman in Edwardes Square taught me. Passed first time. She's doesn't let you drive until you feel really confident about all the mirror, signal, manoeuvre stuff, and then you go round the square a few times until you feel self-assured enough to go onto Ken High Street. That was a bit scary, of course, but she's got pedals too. And once you're in the traffic she talks quietly to you and driving starts to come naturally."

"Yes, I really must. It would help going to visit Grandad, and shopping and everything really. I nearly did my back in carting pushchairs on and off buses, and as for all the steps at stations, well."

"Anyway, come and see the kittens. Now they've dried off they look soft and fluffy."

We went upstairs to the airing cupboard where Tabby had given birth.

"Oh, they are adorable. I'd love the girls to see them."

"Or do you want it to be a surprise, perhaps for Christmas?"

"Maybe at half term, because little Margaret is going to nursery in September, and it would be a treat after the shock of having to conform to the system."

"That should work well. How does Oliver feel about it?"

"I haven't seen much of him this week. He's up in York doing some research for a book. I'm sure he'll be happy."

"Which one do you fancy?"

My eyes moved from one to another. I held a couple of them tenderly. They were so light and delicate.

"Male or female?"

"I think female. Then we can have the pleasure of her having kittens, and providing some sex education too."

We both laughed.

Margaret held up a pretty little one with tiger-like markings. "This one is really cute. Would she do?"

"Definitely. Don't let anyone else have her."

After an hour or so, I went home determined to phone up the driving instructor and get to grips with becoming independent.

***

Half term arrived. The autumn day had been warm and bright as I made my first solo journey to Maggie's house half an hour away. My chest filled with pride as I parked faultlessly in her drive and marched up to ring the doorbell.

Maggie was already standing there. She'd been watching from the downstairs window.

"Brilliant! I bet you feel pleased with yourself."

"I couldn't believe how quickly I learnt. And then that test! Well, the examiner assumed I'd been driving for ages. In fact it was well under three months."

"Down to business. I've got a box ready for you. Here are some pouches of special kitten food. Did you buy a litter tray?"

"That's the bit I'm not so keen on, the training."

"She's pretty good actually. Not many accidents. She was trained by her mother."

I drove home as if I had some eggs on the back seat. Oliver was waiting, looking quizzically at me.

"It was fine. I didn't bump into anything. In fact it was strange being on my own in the car, but I felt really confident."

"And proud, I bet. Quick come in and let's hide the kitten in the kitchen. The girls are next door; I'll go and fetch them."

"We've got a surprise for you!" I called out as they entered the hall. "Come in here, in the kitchen. Surprise, surprise!"

And I held out the wriggling box as the kitten tried to get out.

"I know what it is, it's a surprise," said Margaret.

"So it is," I said as Oliver took the box and struggled to keep the lid on.

"Ta dah!" said Oliver holding out the little tabby kitten.

Margaret burst into tears. "But it isn't. That's not a surprise."

Oliver and I looked confused.

"Did you tell her?" I asked Oliver.

He shook his head, and inquiring lines appeared on his forehead.

Teresa explained:

"Nathan got a surprise: a guinea pig, so Mags thinks that's what a surprise is."

"Oh, darling, a surprise is something you aren't expecting. It's a happy thing, not an animal. It could be any animal," I explained.

"Or a piece of luck, or a birthday present, or Granny Mooney coming to stay," Oliver hugged Margaret and wiped away her tears.

"Well, if she doesn't like it, I'll have it," said Teresa as she grabbed at the kitten.

"No, no, I want it," Maggie said as she released herself from her father's arms.

"It's for all of us. We have to look after it carefully," I explained. "It's still only a baby."

The next decision was what to call it.

"It's a kitten so it must be called Kitty," Teresa explained.

Oliver and I looked at each other.

"Um, it sounds a bit ordinary, don't you think, Chrissie."

"How about Stripey, or something that describes what it looks like," I contributed.

"It looks fluffy. We could call it Fluffy."

"To my mind that sounds more like a name for a rabbit. What about Tiger," added Oliver. "It's got those sorts of markings."

"But it's a girl," I argued.

"Tiggy, Tiggy," shouted both the girls in unison. So Tiggy it was.

That evening Oliver dawdled over coming into bed.

"Kitty," he said.

"Don't call me that, please."

"No, I meant, we both had a reaction when Teresa wanted to call the kitten Kitty."

"It just shows how the past catches up unexpectedly."

"On that subject: while I was doing my research for the new book I went to Somerset House, on the pretext of looking up a person who might be registered there."

"And, and?" I felt my knees shiver under the covers, and my stomach seemed to turn itself inside out.

"Don't get your hopes up. I couldn't find any entry for a child born to you and Andrew."

I burst into tears.

"You must think I dreamed the whole thing. Honestly I didn't. I don't understand it. No birth certificate."

Oliver took me into his arms.

"Of course I believe you. Never ever think that I don't. I just thought I'd better let you know."

"Does it mean that my Kitten-boy doesn't exist?"

"He could have been adopted and his new parents had a new birth certificate registered."

"Or, if Andrew kept him, it could have been registered somewhere else."

"Unlikely, because Somerset House keeps all the certificates of births, marriages and deaths. But all the public records are moving so I could try the new location in case some of the files have already moved."

I was silent. I sighed deeply.

"Leave it, Oliver. I think it's best if I don't know. I must reconcile myself to the fact that he's gone for ever."

"You've got us. Perhaps that's meant to be: just we four. And we all love you very much, you don't need anyone else. It could be just curiosity, not a real yearning."

I sobbed myself to sleep that night. No one could know what it was like to have a baby, and for him to be whisked away before I had a chance to build a relationship with him, even though he'd been part of my body. I knew it was a real physical yearning, however much I might love my girls, I still hoped my Kitten-boy would come back to me.

Chapter 24

Bringing up two children, let alone three, on an irregular income, was a source of anxiety for me more than Oliver. This was made worse by some intense industrial action in the 1970s. The 1970 dock workers strike had affected many imports. Lavatory paper was rationed. Even the paper used for printing books was hit.

"We're one cheque away from disaster," said Oliver one day as he opened the morning post. "Publishing is grinding to a halt and even B & G can't employ me at the moment."

"I'll see what I can find, tucked away," I replied, wondering where I'd hidden my savings for Oliver's birthday present.

"Got a secret stash, have you?"

"Just a few pounds, for Christmas and things."

"Could be useful for this electricity bill."

So I used his present money to settle that account, and Oliver got a scarf made from retrieved wool from an old jumper, and some of the girls' paintings which we'd fitted into a cardboard frame.

"Do you know, Chrissie, I actually prefer these presents to any shop-bought ones."

"You're so positive. Whereas I can't help thinking we're going back to the days when I lived with Auntie Vi, scrimping and saving, wearing cast-down clothes, buying things on tick and her going down to the pawnbrokers regularly and not always being able to buy back the bits of jewellery she'd taken to 'uncles'."

"I think you're around the house too much, worrying rather than getting out, getting more stimulation."

"You're right. Being with the little ones and doing housework doesn't exactly stretch my mind, and I feel guilty that I'm not bringing in any money."

"You could get a part-time job, maybe in a local shop or use your picture research skills."

"I'd like that, but who's going to collect the children from school?"

"I'm quite capable you know, and my work is generally flexible, that is, when I've got some."

So next day I asked a few of the parents at the school gate if anyone they knew wanted some paid help, as I couldn't see anything suitable in the local newspapers or on the board at the library.

A few weeks later, I had a phone call from a local writer who wanted some pictures found for her book about ballet. What a joy! She lived nearby and would pay for my time up to a maximum of eighteen hours a week for two months. It gave me a chance to meet people at most of the major ballet establishments: the Royal Academy of Dance, the Royal Ballet School, Ballet Rambert at Sadlers Wells and the Arts Educational Trust, and to visit the Opera House in Covent Garden and the rehearsal rooms of the London Festival Ballet. I had the authority to agree fees too from a set budget, and the money I earned made our life more comfortable. One of the bonuses was that occasionally I would be given tickets to shows, mainly at the Royal Festival Hall. It helped mend my relationship with Auntie Vi ('please call me Violet now') whose legs danced while she was watching the ballets that she would have loved to perform when she was younger.

This work led to more freelance research work including some for a solicitor trying to trace information about a house in Kew that his client felt belonged to him by rights, even though the last member of his family had lived there in the early nineteenth century. There seemed to be no details of an exchange of deeds or a bill of sale. I did what I could but a judge ruled that they had no rights to the property. I found the work somewhat dry and hoped I would return to the world I knew, that of publishing.

We could now pay our electricity bills before the red notice arrived, but in early 1974 we were often plunged into darkness. The Prime Minister, Edward Heath, had ordered the Three Day Week to help conserve power supplies affected by the striking miners, so we used candles more often than our light switches.

Occasionally when I collected the girls from school and nursery, the shelves above the radiators held candles in jam jars to illuminate the corridors on darkening afternoons. They, of course, thought it was great fun, but I was constantly worrying about the danger of fires and how we would cook our food. Oliver was upset that so many pubs closed early, or even didn't open at all on the days when there was no electricity.

Gradually I started to build up the confidence to use some of the contacts I'd made at B & G's. I was introduced to a publishing company based in Fulham Palace Road, within a reasonable distance from where we lived.

"I'm sorry we don't have anything permanent at the moment," apologised the person who interviewed me.

I was ready to go away, disappointed but pleased that I'd had the courage to get myself to the point that I could sell my experience to a stranger. The man flicked through some papers, and made a quick phone call to someone in an outer office.

"Have you got anyone to do the picture research on that new line? No? I'll get back to you."

He turned to me as I was putting my coat on ready to leave.

"Don't go yet. It seems there might be something, just occasional work, on a daily basis. Shall I introduce you to my colleague who's working on some new information publications? She might have something that could use your skills."

So I met my future boss. A charming, rather scatty woman named Victoria, whose fair hair escaped from her chignon more often than she pinned it back.

"Most of our publications are novels, so we're a bit clueless about this new one." She looked through my references. "I think you are just what we need, someone to do picture research. Ooh, yes, diagrams too." She licked her finger and turned a few pages of what looked like the contract. "You could deal with the people who do the diagrams too. What do you think?"

"It sounds just what I'm looking for. How many days work would it be, do you think?"

"At the moment, I'd say about three days this month; rather more for the next three months, then not much more unless you'd like to go to the printers to check the colours and so on. I'm sorry I can't be more specific. It's our first time with this sort of book."

"Can I just mention, that I might find it difficult to work in the school holidays."

"Same as me. I try to schedule things so that I get most of my work done before the summer. It's a bit of a balancing act."

"How many have you got."

"Two, a girl and a boy."

"Mine are both girls." I blushed, suddenly feeling disloyal not mentioning I had another one, a boy.

"Not pregnant are you," she laughed. "I thought you went a bit red then."

"No, no. Just happy about the work, and relieved that it's quite flexible."

In my delight at my success and that it would fit in with the children's school timetable I forgot to ask about the daily rate of pay. I berated myself on the bus going back to Mortlake hoping I wasn't going to be underpaid as I knew how challenging some jobs could be.

"Always ask how much," Oliver said after he'd congratulated me at home. "They get away with as little as they can."

I quickly phoned up Victoria. She told me the rate: way above what I'd expected.

"It's because it's not regular," she said. "I hope that's alright with you. I don't have any say in it; it's all set down in the budget I've been allocated. Tell me if you're not happy."

"No, that's fine," I said.

When I told Oliver he nodded. "You must have made a good impression. I thought I might have to teach you how to negotiate."

"Not necessary. Just hope I don't let her down."

"You won't. Have faith in yourself."

We both felt more relaxed than we had in ages.

Chapter 25

"Our Father, what art…"

"Who art, Nathan, who art."

"Who art in heaven. Goodbye."

"We had a brother, but he died."

I was hanging up the washing in the garden when I suddenly stopped. It was Margaret's voice.

"Really?" said Josie. "I didn't know that. Perhaps it's too sad to talk about."

"No one's told us, but that's what we think happened," said Teresa in an authoritative voice.

"Is he buried, like my guinea pig?"

"I expect so," answered Margaret.

"Oliver, Oliver," I whispered as I moved towards the kitchen door which Oliver had been painting.

"What's going on?"

I told him what I'd heard.

"Do you think we should tell them? I don't know how they got that idea. I wonder if your mother said anything."

"I'm sure she wouldn't. Perhaps they've heard us talking, or your Auntie Vi said something. Or even your grandad."

"I can't imagine any of them would. It must have been us. Let's find a moment to tell them. I don't want them to think we've hidden something so important. The idea that he has died. How did they think that?"

So when the girls came back we asked what they'd been doing next door.

"Poor Piggy. He died. So we buried him. In a box, and put flowers on top," said Margaret.

"Then we said prayers so he'll go to heaven," Teresa added.

"It must have been a little grave for a guinea pig," I observed.

"He was quite fat, but he went into a shoe box," said Teresa.

"With lots of tissue paper round him, and a cross, don't forget that Tessa."

"Nathan made it from two twigs tied together."

"What a lovely ceremony," I said. "I thought I heard something when I was hanging out the washing. Something about a brother too."

Teresa and Margaret looked at each other.

"It's all right. Tell us what you think," intervened Oliver.

"We think we had a brother but he died," Teresa said making a sad face.

"Did he, Daddy, did he?" Margaret hugged Oliver as she spoke.

"No. We think he's alive," I said.

"But why doesn't he live with us?" Margaret asked.

"It's a long story, but he was taken by another family," I said.

"No. He was stolen!" Both girls looked horrified.

"No, no, that's not right. I shouldn't have said taken. He was adopted."

"Your mummy had him when she was young, and she couldn't look after him, so another family look after him," Oliver came to the rescue.

"Aren't you sad, Mummy?" asked Teresa.

"Sometimes, but I've got you two, so I'm really very happy."

"Can we meet him? He could come and play with us," said Margaret.

"Perhaps one day. But we don't know where he is now."

"Is he happy?" asked Teresa.

"Yes, I'm sure he is. He's very happy." I blinked back my tears.

"Do you think we should let Josie know?" Oliver asked.

"Well, it's private, but I suppose it's not a secret. I'll tell her next time we have a coffee. I don't want to make a big thing of it."

"Private, but not secret," copied Teresa. "So we shouldn't say anything about it."

"I suppose you could say it's family business, not for everyone to know."

And the girls ran off, saying, "Private, not secret. Private, not secret," as if they were working out the difference.

***

The next day I invited Josie to come for a walk round the pond in Barnes.

"Sorry to hear about Nathan's guinea pig," I said trying to introduce the subject of my Kitten-boy casually.

"I'm quite pleased; it smelled and Nathan wasn't very good about cleaning him out. It became another job I had to do. And I've got my O.U. studies, which no-one thinks about. He was upset, of course, but he's not responsible enough yet to have another pet."

"The girls are lucky we only have a cat. They don't have to do much apart from feed it, and stroke it."

"That's the good thing about cats: independent. By the way, I wanted to ask you something, but I don't want to upset you."

"I think I know what it is. I was in the garden and I heard what the girls were talking about. No their brother didn't die, he was adopted. I had him when I was young, before I knew Oliver. Actually I knew Oliver. We worked together, but I was going out with someone else; I didn't know he was married. So I had the baby and he was adopted."

"He didn't die?"

"No. He's alive and well and living somewhere, I don't know where."

"Do you wonder where?"

"Yes, I wonder, but I've no way of knowing where he is."

"Does Oliver know?"

"Yes, he was one of the first people I told. He was very supportive. We were already good friends, and one thing led to another, and we got married a few years after."

"You're so brave."

"My aunt thought I was stupid. I'm not brave, I just get on with things. The girls are my focus now. But it's private, so I'd appreciate it if you didn't mention it to anyone. It's all in the past."

"You needn't have said that. Of course, I won't. But it must have been hard."

"We've mentioned it to the girls now, and they are trying to weigh up the difference between private and secret."

"They must wonder where he is though."

"Yes, I think they'd like to have an elder brother, but I can't see it happening. Anyway, how's the studying?"

"The essays are difficult, but I went to a summer school. That was brilliant, we even challenged the lecturers at breakfast, we were all so keen. Mike moaned about having to look after Nathan on his own. He thinks we're growing apart because I'm becoming better educated than him."

"Is that really the case?"

"Well, as you've shared something private, I know I can tell you something. I've always felt a bit unconnected with Mike. Not his fault. I occasionally meet up with a couple of girlfriends I met at art classes."

"Ah, I think I know what's coming. Do you think you're more attracted to women than men?"

"That's just it. I'm wondering if I am. There was nothing in the '67 legislation about women, so I don't know what people feel about it. I know Mike hates the whole idea of homosexuality, so I can't say anything to him. He thinks being lesbian is a mental illness or something enacted for the titillation of men. I've been going to a club, Gateways in Chelsea, sometimes instead of my art class. I'm still not sure, but I think I'm going to explore the idea."

"That's the only way. My friend John, I think you met him at a party, his father is very anti the whole thing, but his mother is relieved that he's happy. He had a tougher time, but luckily found a permanent boyfriend quite early."

"I'm not ready to say, yes I am gay, but I do feel attraction to one of the girls at the club."

"Well, good luck. Now we know everything about each other, it's time for a drink. How about the Sun Inn?"

"What, to celebrate?"

"Why not."

So we drank our shandies, and then went to collect the children from school.

Chapter 26

"Satu."

"Satu" came a little voice.

"Dua."

"Dua," repeated the same little voice.

"Tiga."

"Tigger; bounce, bounce bounce," said another voice belonging to Mags, who'd decided she didn't like the name Margaret.

"No not Tigger. T. i. g. a. Tiga. Three."

"Tiga," replied both girls.

"Empat," said Oliver.

"Umpa, umpa stick it up your jumper!" they chorused.

"What are you lot up to?" I said as I could hold back my curiosity no longer.

"We're learning numbers in Malay," said Teresa.

"I don't know when that'll come in useful," I said.

"Well, some of my friends at school know numbers up to ten in lots of languages, so Dad said, 'Let's do it in Malay'."

"There won't be many of them who know that," I commented.

"Mei Lin's father's from Singapore," Teresa replied.

"Well, she might, but her parents would speak Chinese," said Oliver.

"And Rosnah, might. She's from a place called Kay El."

"Ah, Kuala Lumpur, the capital of Malaysia. She's bound to know," said Oliver. "You could try saying 'Selamat pagi', good morning to her."

"Where did you learn it, Daddy?" asked Teresa.

"In Malaya; it's called Malaysia now, but I was there when they had some terrible fighting going on. I like to think I helped them keep the country for themselves."

"Can we go there, Mummy, tell Daddy to let us go there, please, please," asked Teresa.

"Maybe one day," said Oliver, "But it's a very long way away."

I left them to hear Oliver's description of what it was like, the jungle, the climate and the people. He didn't tell them about what it was like fighting the Communists in the Emergency though.

That evening we talked through the implications of continuing to be part of the Common Market and whether it was affecting our commitments to the Commonwealth. Labour's manifesto had promised a referendum on the subject.

"I can't understand why we need to have one, when we've only been a member for a couple of years," I queried.

"We didn't really have a say in the decision then. It was Heath's lot that made the decision."

"If Labour get in, I think we'll get more information before we have to choose. He keeps saying it's *our* decision. What a responsibility. We need to find out more."

So Oliver used his researcher's nous to find out what the new terms of the negotiations would be, and we both decided to vote 'Yes', when Harold Wilson's new government honoured their manifesto promise, even though Oliver's heroes Michael Foot and Tony Benn were against the idea.

"I can't believe they have the same attitude as Enoch Powell," I said, remembering the uproar at his 'Rivers of Blood' speech a few years previously.

"But Benn has acknowledged that it's the British people's decision, but doesn't think the European Union is democratic. He fears for Britain's sovereignty, our ability to be self-governing."

We would have to wait and see whether the resounding "Yes" result made a marked difference to our lives, and, as Oliver once observed, "It might help other nations to see us as part of a wider community, Europe, rather than a country whose empire is shrinking."

Chapter 27

So much was happening in the '60s and '70s that was to change peoples' attitudes. I remember going on a demonstration against the proposed amendments to the 1967 Abortion Act in June 1975 and consequently falling out with Oliver's mother.

"I know I'm not one of the best Catholics," she said, "But abortion is wrong; it's killing a child."

"But, if it's done early enough, surely the embryo isn't yet a child?"

"I am surprised at you, Christine. You who understand what it's like to have a child out of wedlock. Just think of all those families who can't have children naturally. You are depriving them of adopting one."

"I personally would never have an abortion. But I think a woman has the right to choose, not have some men in Parliament deciding for her. And what if she's raped?"

"That would be a challenge, but, again, the child could be adopted."

"What must it be like to carry a baby inside you that's the product of rape."

"I can see your point, but I still think abortion is wrong. I am not in agreement with the Act anyway."

"I think the '67 Act is comprehensive enough. I'm worried about the changes which would limit women's rights even further."

At which point Oliver came in.

"So are you going on the Demo, Chrissie?"

"Certainly, but I don't think your mum's happy about it."

"No, I'm not, but at least you both stand up for what you believe in. I have the right to do the same."

"Well, we'll make it a family outing, take the girls."

"I'm happy to look after them if you like."

"No, I think it's important we all go. They need to understand that we can influence things, not just by voting, but by coming out in large numbers to show our strength." And so Oliver closed the discussion.

I felt proud that our daughters were more politically aware than I had been as a child. They joined us on more marches, particularly those against nuclear weapons, and even visited me when I joined the protests at Greenham Common. I'd heard about a group of women from Wales who'd set up camp there to protest against the UK Government's decision to allow the Americans to base their Cruise Missiles at a former RAF airfield. That was in September 1981. However, it wasn't until Christmas of the following year that I joined them as we all held hands around the base. Most of us were mothers, horrified at our government allowing nuclear weapons that could attract other countries to bomb our children, let alone allow another country to use our land from which to launch the missiles. We were also indignant at the treatment the protestors had received. Although it was a women-only movement, when we helped create a human chain from Greenham to Aldermaston, Oliver, some of his friends and the girls came too to support us. I wasn't one of the brave women who stormed into the base and got arrested, but felt proud that I had at least displayed my objection by being there, albeit for a short time.

***

In the meantime, Oliver's work had hit another barren period. There was more competition from less established writers. He wondered if his style was too didactic or whether fewer information books were being produced. However this gap provided an unusual opportunity for our family.

Oliver was helping out at the CND Bookshop in Seven Sisters Road, North London. Although it was a long way from Mortlake to Finsbury Park Station and the pay was only just adequate for our needs he was inspired by the conversations with people who had the same ideals. He loved reading the pamphlets and books when the shop wasn't busy, but above all it kept him in touch with any demonstrations against the nuclear threat, which felt increasingly real as the political situation between the USA and USSR worsened.

The shop was asked to display posters for a weekend music festival connected with CND: Glastonbury 1982. The shop also distributed the tickets and Oliver bought 3 full price tickets, and one free one for an under 14 year old. He brought them home.

"We *are* going to have a holiday this year," he declaimed as the girls greeted him on his return from the shop.

"Where, where, Daddy?" they screamed, leaping about in excitement.

"We're going camping."

When I heard this, my heart stopped.

"Oh, no. I don't do camping."

"I bet you've never tried it. Anyway, this is camping with a difference. We're going to Glastonbury."

"Is that the event that raised lots of money for CND last year?" I asked.

"Yes, and it's our turn to contribute and to have a great time."

Teresa piped up, "Some of the 6th form went last year. It's pop music, and dancing and partying 24 hours a day. Wow!"

"I've always wanted to go camping," said Margaret.

"Let's hope it doesn't rain," I said.

"Don't be a spoil sport, Mum." Teresa looked at the tickets. "It's in the middle of June. It'll be summer, lovely and hot."

"Right," I said. "No pocket money for a month," and they all groaned. "Then we'll have enough money to buy a tent!"

"Yes, yes," the girls shouted and danced around the house.

So we went on what Oliver called "half rations" and saved in any way we could.

"I'm over 14 now," Teresa said. "I can get a job."

"No, no," both Oliver and I protested. "Concentrate on your studies. You're coming up to some important exams. Focus on them."

But, when Oliver and I thought she was doing revision with a friend, it turned out she was washing up in a local café. I cried when she presented us with the £30 pounds which she'd earned over six weeks. She had earned £2.50 an hour and had done 2 hours on Fridays and Saturday evenings.

"I don't know whether to be cross with you, or proud of you, darling," I said.

"Proud, I think," said Oliver. "What an enterprising young person you are."

"I didn't like it much, but Mr Colley was pleased to have some help, and he doesn't mind if I stop now. He said, any time I need a bit of cash he's always happy to have someone to do the dirty work!"

"We can't take all of that," Oliver said. "You keep £10. You've earned it."

And so, with the savings from my intermittent work too, we had enough money to buy our tent. It was a four-berth in dark green.

"Let's try it out," said Oliver, one Sunday morning the weekend before our trip. So we went onto Barnes Common, and, amid much swearing and re-reading instructions, eventually got to grips with erecting what would be our temporary home.

A couple of Oliver's friends were going to be working as Car Park Attendants so we travelled with them in their pale blue Dormobile on the Friday.

"I wish we'd bought a Dormobile instead of a tent," I moaned as we tried to cope with the horrendous downpour that flooded us out that night.

"I'm not going to the loo all weekend," said Margaret after she'd tried out one of the trench toilets which had overflowed in the deluge. "Absolutely revolting!"

"We can't sleep in those," Oliver stated as he tried to wring out water from the sleeping bags we'd bought when we gathered the necessities listed in the 'Protect and Survive' leaflet that had arrived on our doormat a few years previously. What a bad start! Fortunately the Salvation Army came to our rescue and lent us some blankets. Oliver went on a recce to find some better loos, and found some flush toilets in the admin area, so we slurped our way through the mud in the dark hoping that other people wouldn't follow us.

I don't remember the music much that night as all we were interested in was keeping dry. However, the following day was a slight improvement, and the girls went off to get their hair plaited, and their faces painted, while Oliver and I wandered around occasionally bumping into people we'd met on demos, and making new friends on the various stalls. There were lots of jokes from some men about the Talk of the Town cabaret theatre closing down, and what would happen to the high-kicking dancers and whether they could become an attraction to raise CND funds. When evening came we were treated to our first experience of a laser light show. And Van Morrison, who I'd heard of, but never actually heard. "Van the Man," people shouted when he came on stage.

We loved watching films outdoors: Dr. Strangelove was shown, particularly poignant for a CND event, and *My Brilliant Career* which the girls found inspirational.

However, the lasting impression was one of mud, mud, glorious mud, and the odour of overflowing lavatories mixed with cooking smells from the various primus stoves and food cooked directly on open fires. None of us went to Glastonbury again, particularly as Oliver was searched by the police as we left. "I'm getting too old for all this hassle," he remarked.

Chapter 28

And what about Grandad Preece? Well, with the girls growing up and my work developing, I'm afraid I neglected him somewhat. Having been determined to visit once a week, the gap lengthened to once a fortnight, then once a month. At one point I didn't see him for six weeks.

"It's alright, Chrissie, I know how busy you are."

"But I feel so bad about it, particularly as you seem to need your neighbours' help more and more."

"Don't fret. I have a plan."

And he told me about the friend he'd been visiting in a home for retired soldiers.

"One of the helpers at the lunch club took me. It seems comfortable; they've got a lift. There are lots of people of my age so I wouldn't be lonely. You must remember it. Springwell. Where you played commandoes when you were little, and…"

"Yes, you told us about it, when Teresa was a baby, and you'd had that fall."

"Well, I've been looking at this," and he handed me a brochure, or rather a folded piece of A4 paper with a photo of the mansion on the cover.

"If you're determined we could go and have a look, or at least phone up to find if they've got a vacancy."

"Yes, dead men's shoes, and all that."

I brought his phone over to him. I had insisted he got connected so he could summon help if he had an emergency, but he'd hardly used it for that reason, mainly to call his bookie.

"Why don't you speak, Chrissie. You know the sorts of questions to ask."

"I think they'd prefer it coming from you. They might think I'm trying to put you away… Oh, hello. I'm making an inquiry about the accommodation you provide." A voice at the other end of the line asked if it was for me.

"No, no. For my grandfather. He's here. Perhaps he should speak to you."

"Hello, hello. You might remember me, I'm Preece. I visit one of your residents occasionally."

He held the phone so we could both hear what the woman said.

"I'm thinking about joining you, becoming a resident, signing up, so to speak."

"Ask if they've got any vacancies, Grandad?"

"Have you got any rooms available?"

I couldn't hear what she said next, but Grandad looked disappointed. Then his face lit up.

He covered the mouthpiece: "Could you run me over there today, Chrissie?"

"Sure. When would be best?"

"When would you be able to see me?" A pause, as I imagined her looking in an appointment book. "Yes, that would be fine. Tickety-boo! We'll be there at 3.00 p.m."

I put the phone back on its hook.

"Can we make it in time, I'm not sure how long it takes to drive there."

"If we leave in half an hour we'll be early. You can meet Johnny."

I hadn't realised how slow he was. He shuffled along almost tripping himself up, but managed to get into his coat with my help as his arms didn't seem to have the strength to lift themselves up. How had I missed his deterioration? He was in his early 90s I guessed, but having been a fighting soldier who'd survived the First World War, he had maintained a certain style and dignity. It was sad to see how difficult it was for him to get his legs into the passenger seat of our car. He didn't seem in pain, just not very flexible.

As we drove up the drive, arriving only just in time due to his inaccurate memory of the way he'd been taken before, and my insistence at stopping to look at the map as I realised Grandad couldn't see well enough to help, we saw an elderly man leaning on a stick waiting on the steps. As we approached, a woman joined him.

"Just there's fine," she said as I parked on the gravelled half-moon shape near the entrance.

"I heard you were coming. Coming to join the comrades?" It was Grandad's friend, Johnny.

"I hope so. This is my granddaughter, Christine." So we exchanged pleasantries while the woman steered us into an office to the right of the main doors.

"Tell me about yourself," she said.

So Grandad talked a bit about how he was finding it difficult to manage at home on his own, but how healthy he was, and how he'd heard great things from his war-time colleague, and thought:

"If it's working for him, it'll work for me."

"It's always wonderful to welcome an old soldier here. We're impressed with how you stick together, have lots to talk about and generally keep yourselves active."

"You weren't sure about a vacancy," I added, before Grandad got too excited, and then disappointed.

"If you could manage in one of the smaller rooms, we have a vacancy probably from next month or so. The larger rooms and the suites are all occupied, and will be for some time."

"Could we have a look, do you think?"

"I could manage a small room, I think," said Grandad. "I won't be bringing much with me. I think Johnny just brought his favourite chair and a chest of drawers."

"The room could take more than that. Let's have a look, and then we'll go through the charges. We have a discount for men who fought in the First World War, you know. It used to be a training ground for the forces, and they left some money, an endowment, when they turned it into a residential home."

"A bit like the Royal Hospital, Chelsea," Grandad said.

"Something similar but no uniform. We also have a couple of women here; they've got some connection with the forces. Mostly army."

I laughed as I noticed Grandad's eyes light up.

"I'm never too old for a girlfriend."

We both laughed, but then I thought, *No, we shouldn't make a joke of it*. Perhaps that's what's kept him young since Grandma died, chatting up women on the sea front. He may even have had a girlfriend. No, you're never too old.

So we took the lift to the second floor. His friend Johnny came with us. We walked down a short corridor which had rails just above the dado, which helped Grandad to maintain his upright demeanour.

"Here we are," said Miss Byers, who seemed to run the place. "Big enough I think if you don't have too much large furniture."

The room looked as though it had been recently occupied: the bed had been stripped, but a heavy armchair still had cushions on it, patterned with country scenes. The dressing table masked part of the window, and a heavy oak table had three chairs round it: two were tucked in, the other looked as though someone had just vacated it. There was a matching desk with a fourth chair tucked under it. I wondered where the previous occupant was. I shivered.

The room was light, partly because it was south facing and decorated to take advantage of that. There was a view over a formal garden and onto what looked like a field that sloped down towards woodland.

"On a clear day some of our residents say you can see the sea, but quite honestly I think it's wistful thinking. The cloud patterns in the low-lying part over there could be misinterpreted as sea, but I don't like to disabuse them."

"I'll take it," said Grandad.

"Hang on, you haven't seen the bathroom, or heard the price," I whispered.

So we looked into the en suite bathroom, which was really a shower room with a toilet and wash-basin. It was quite small, but equipped with rails.

"It's enough for a wheelchair, if ever you need one. Just about," Miss Byers assured us.

"I won't be using one of those," insisted Grandad.

"My room's on the other side of the corridor, overlooking the drive," said Grandad's friend.

"Isn't that a bit noisy?" I asked having heard the sound my car made on the gravel.

He lifted up a wisp of hair.

"Got these, can turn them down if needs be." He proudly indicated his hearing aids, as well as a box-like object hanging from a cord on his chest.

Having admired the room we went into a huge sitting room on the ground floor. The floor to ceiling windows overlooked a long patio with stone balustrades. Miss Byers ordered tea and we talked through the costs. I didn't know much about Grandad's financial situation but he came into the category where he could receive a large discount on the fees. He would have to pay extra for meals and laundry, and outings, if he fancied a concert or the theatre. He seemed happy with the arrangements particularly as he'd no longer have to pay for the upkeep of his flat, which he had leased ever since he and Grandma Preece had moved to Eastbourne.

"When do you think he can move in?" I asked.

"Well, that depends. You probably realised that the room's only just been vacated. We are keeping it for at least a month, just in case the previous occupant needs it. However," she lowered her voice, "he's been moved into a hospice, and we are waiting for the family to let us know what's happening. It won't be long; he's been ill for a while and it reached a crisis. I wish we had facilities here, you know, a medical wing, but we don't. It would be easier for some of them, being able to stay in their home. It does become their home, you know."

"I'm sure Grandad will be very happy here. Let's hope it's not too long before he can move in. He's got the bit between his teeth."

We laughed.

Part 4

Chapter 29

"We've had a job offer," said Teresa one day many years later when we went for Sunday lunch in their Leyton flat. "Marcus spotted the advert and it would be a wonderful opportunity. Imagine teaching in a country with palm trees and exotic animals."

My heart sank. I would miss Teresa dreadfully. It had been bad enough when she'd left to go to college. I'd cried for a week. I hadn't even cried that much when Grandad died 2 days before Teresa's 21st birthday. He'd been well looked after at Springwell and died in his sleep after going to his room for a lie down after lunch. And 99 was a remarkable age for someone who'd lived through two World Wars.

"Where is it, Teresa, Africa, West Indies?"

"Singapore," said Marcus.

"I hardly know where that is. Is it near China?" I asked.

"No, it's at the tip of Malaysia. Had a terrible time during the war," Oliver said. "Interesting part of the world. Not that I was there at the best time, but now it's an independent country, Singapore. Lee Kwan Yew has transformed it into a thriving economy. I wouldn't mind visiting it again. I only went there briefly in the 1950s when it was impoverished and over-run with jungle."

"Of course, you must visit, and Mags too."

"It seems such a long way away. But what an opportunity. What sort of school?" I asked.

"It's Independent, but pretty much like the Comprehensive we're working at here in Leyton."

"Similar sort of curriculum. Not much different, same exam system, just private," said Marcus. "Multicultural because of all the ex-pat children."

"Quite near the centre too, so we won't be cut off," added Teresa.

"It's only the size of the Isle of Wight; you won't be cut off. You can reach everywhere easily now they have a Mass Rapid Transit system in place. Air-conditioned too. I was amazed when I read about it as lots of the land is marshy, but apparently the engineers did a magnificent job; it works really efficiently and goes from North to South and East to West." Oliver's ability to hoard information was proving relevant and useful to real life as well as for his writing.

"It's a miracle to find a post for both of us. I'll carry on teaching history, and Marcus will be Deputy Head of Maths."

Teresa and I went into the kitchen to wash up.

"I thought you were thinking of starting a family."

"We are, Mum, but these things don't happen overnight."

"They did to me, pretty much," I responded, "even when I least expected it."

"Yes, Mum. That must have been terrible, but you survived."

"You helped. When you came along you were a source of healing, even though I didn't recognise it at the time."

"I know you were very possessive."

"Obsessed, more like."

Teresa passed me some cups to dry.

"But you let me go. And Mags. You didn't phone her every day when she left home!"

We laughed.

"You just wait till you have little ones."

"Anyway, we thought we'd leave it a year and then maybe try for a baby while we're out there. Childcare is brilliant there, so if I time it right I can carry on teaching."

"How organised you both are. I'll miss you desperately, but it sounds like an opportunity you can't turn down."

"Both in the same school too; it's amazing. Just like here. But a much smaller school."

"Where will you live?"

"They have a sort of resettlement officer who helps find accommodation. She's already suggested that a place called Holland Village would be convenient for work, and the flats are really nice, air-conditioned and with servants quarters. Not that

I'll need a servant, in fact I think I'd find it awkward having one. Against my principles."

"You might need one in that heat."

"I'll see when we get there."

"So have you given in your notice?"

"Not yet. After Easter is when we have to do it, but we've already accepted the jobs and we mentioned it to the Head, informally. He thinks it's a wonderful opportunity, but will miss us."

We continued our talk when we went for a walk round Coronation Gardens.

I thought this part of London looked quite run down, but the gardens brightened things up.

"Oh, I forgot to ask, will you be teaching in English?"

"Yes, Mum. But a lot of the children are bi-lingual, French, German, et cetera, and they learn Mandarin and Malay. Some speak Tamil, so a really exciting linguistic environment. You must come and visit us."

Chapter 30

So we did. Not just Oliver and me. Eighteen months after Teresa and her husband Marcus had started work in Singapore Margaret and Kevin got married. They'd lived together since their last year at college. Now they both worked as physiotherapists, Kevin specialising in sports injuries in a health club, and Margaret working in a hospital. They'd suddenly decided to regularise their situation with a small register office wedding. For their honeymoon Teresa had invited all of us to Singapore. The honeymooners stayed in a hotel near Orchard Road, the main shopping street, and we followed a week later and stayed with Teresa and Marcus.

"I feel as though my sense of smell has been lying dormant all these years," I said to Oliver as we went out of the cool airport into the humidity to wait for a taxi.

"Rotting vegetation, mixed with frangipani and durian," he said. "Phew, I'd forgotten how hot the breeze could be, let's hope the taxi has air-con."

We joined a short queue of people of all nationalities. When it was our turn a pale blue taxi moved alongside. The driver put our cases in the boot and we got in. Although the plastic smelled a bit at least it was cool. Oliver gave him Teresa's address in a mock-Chinese accent, which I thought disrespectful; however the driver understood, so perhaps it was near enough to the local accent.

"I've never seen so many flowers by the roadside. Look, they're wonderful." In between the palm trees there were shrubs laden with pink or cream coloured flowers.

"I'm all in," said Oliver. "That long journey's catching up with me."

"I thought you'd slept most of the way."

"Not really, I was disturbed by memories of when I was last in this part of the world. I can't say I'm looking forward to going into Malaysia."

"Well, we've got three days to enjoy Singapore first; try not to spoil your holiday."

We arrived at the apartment. Oliver paid the driver and said something that sounded like 'shey shey'. A Sikh concierge took our cases from the taxi boot. The entrance hall was cool, almost too chilly, and had marble-type flooring. We went up to the 3rd floor in the lift and Teresa was waiting for us as we stepped out into the apartment.

We both burst into tears as we hugged each other. Oliver collapsed into a chair and Marcus went over to him and poured him a Tiger beer.

"Welcome to Singapore!"

Teresa showed me round the apartment quickly and took our cases into our bedroom. En suite! What luxury. From the window I could see the swimming pool in the garden framed by banana trees and palms. And the air-con was wonderful.

Quite suddenly, as though someone had closed shutters over the moon, it turned dark.

"The same time every evening," explained Teresa. "So near the equator, you see."

Oliver and I showered and changed from our crumpled clothes into our English summer clothes.

Mags, as she liked to be called now, and Kevin joined us for dinner which we ate on the balcony overlooking the garden.

"I must say, you two have landed on your feet," commented Oliver.

"It's wonderful," said Teresa. "Hard work, but coming back here is such a treat. I jump straight into the pool and then get on with my marking."

"I tend to get involved with various meetings in the evenings, but apart from that we can go exploring the island, and even go into Malaysia for holidays. We're looking forward to doing that trip with you, especially as you know the country well, Oliver." Marcus had organised a few days in the Cameron Highlands for us, followed by Kuala Lumpur and then returning to Singapore via Malacca and Johor Bahru State.

"I hope it's not going to be too exhausting," said Oliver, who seemed to be taking a long time to recover from the flight and jet-lag.

"No, I've hired a mini-bus with air-con, and I'll drive. It will be fine."

"We've booked a place overlooking a tea plantation. It's cooler there, and you can go on jungle walks," Teresa added.

"We went into the jungle part of the Botanical Gardens yesterday," said Kevin.

"Lovely," said Mags, "But I sat on the grass and got bitten by some nasty ants. On my behind too!" We all laughed.

The next day Oliver and I explored the island using the MRT system. It meant we didn't experience the constant sweating and exhaustion occasioned by the extreme heat and humidity. But Oliver was more tired than usual, and we had to cut short a visit to Jurong Bird Park and take a taxi back to Holland Village.

"What about a boat ride to Sentosa," suggested Teresa when she returned from school the following day.

"That sounds relaxing," we agreed. But we found our visit to the Museum distressing.

"What they must have gone through," I commented.

"And all because the War Cabinet couldn't envisage the Japanese invading from the North, so all the defences were in the South."

"And yet, look around. There are lots of Japanese tourists too. I wonder what they feel seeing these enactments of the Japanese surrender."

"And the Singaporeans. They seem to accept them now, in spite of the cruelty of those days. But what must the older people feel? They suffered most. But now driving the economy is all important, so presumably they must welcome tourists from anywhere."

When we returned to the flat, we recounted our feelings to Teresa and Marcus.

"We have heard terrible stories about people being beaten to death for picking up a few grains of rice from the road. I don't think they've forgotten, but, yes, bringing money into the country is important and the Government here has done a lot to create a welcoming environment for visitors, as well as showing the benefits to the locals." Marcus was impressed with the work-ethic of the Singaporeans, and their dedication to education.

"I hear they still have National Service. We saw soldiers marching on our way back," I commented.

"Yes, they join the Army, Navy, Air Force or police; that's why it feels as though there's a policeman behind every tree sometimes."

"A bit like Big Brother is watching you?"

"Sometimes. But it's created a safe society. You can go anywhere and feel reasonably safe."

"We hear debates about what to do with crime in the UK," said Oliver. "Bring back National Service, they say, but judging by my experience it wouldn't help. 'Who plays the piano?' shouted the sergeant major. 'I can, sir.' 'Well, move this one then.'" We all laughed, but for Oliver it had been abhorrent; the bullying, the lack of privacy and affronts to personal dignity. Above all he'd hated the training; the exhausting and demoralising attempts to turn decent young men into killing machines to be deployed in Africa and South East Asia.

"You'll be alright in Malaysia, Dad," sympathised Teresa.

"I liked the Malay people I met. The climate was terrible though. Almost 100% humidity, no air-conditioning, heat that made me see through a red haze. And the storms. The rainy seasons washed away the roads and made travelling impossible. But we still had to march on."

"You've still got the scars, haven't you," I added.

"Yes, look at these." And he rolled up his linen trousers to show where his legs had fed the leeches, and he'd tried to burn them off with lighted cigarettes.

"No mangrove swamps for you, then," said Marcus.

Mags started to look worried. "I hope our trip into Malaysia isn't going to upset you, Dad."

"It's about time I faced up to it. It could be just what I need to get rid of the nightmares I still have sometimes."

"Go back to the scene of the crime," said Kevin. "That can change your perspective."

"And it was a crime, there certainly were crimes on both sides," said Oliver. "But this is supposed to be one long celebration." And he raised his glass,

"A toast to Margaret and Kevin, the happy couple."
"To Margaret and Kevin," we all replied.

Chapter 31

Two days later, we drove up to the Cameron Highlands.

"Anywhere you recognise, Oliver?" I asked.

"Rubber plantations all look pretty much the same, but, yes, this village seems familiar, and that name over there, yes. But where are all the kampongs? It seems to be high rise flats and terraced houses now, not little villages surrounded by banana palm trees."

"What lovely shapes they are, just like the ones outside Raffles Hotel."

"I hadn't realised bananas come in all shapes and sizes," replied Marcus. "Some are really tiny, and sweet. The ones we eat in the UK are the big ones, like pisang rajahs here."

Oliver recognised some of the places from his time fighting face to face with insurgents more acclimatised to jungle warfare. He said very little on the journey, but I knew from the way he shook his head and occasionally a moan came from his lips. I held his hand and he sighed deeply. The memories must have been overwhelming.

However, the mood lightened as we spotted a brightly coloured Red Junglefowl battling with the domestic cockerels around a rare kampong and the occasional sightings of the Orang Asli, shadowy figures who darted amongst the thick vegetation, away from the main roads, possibly collecting the butterflies that we saw in display cases in the markets we stopped at en route.

Our journey was made more pleasant by the change in temperature as we climbed into the Cameron Highlands. On our first evening we were all sitting in rattan chairs overlooking the Boh Tea Plantation from our Guest House patio. Marcus was reading from a guide book about the different types of tea harvested there. Where had I heard that name Boh before? It was lodged in the dark recesses of my memory.

However, when we were enjoying the contrasting coolness of the air in the Cameron Highlands my first love came into my mind. I consciously pushed away memories of tea at Fortnum's and focussed on luxuriating in the company of my extended family, and finding out more about my two sons in law who were instrumental in drawing out Oliver's memories of his time in the Malayan Emergency.

"Better out than in," Marcus had confided in me.

"I don't want him upset, it was obviously a terrible time for him," I pleaded.

"But he's such a good story-teller; I'm sure it will help him." Teresa backed up her husband, and gradually Marcus and Kevin teased out various tales of his experiences.

By the time I'd returned from fetching a shawl from our bedroom they were in the middle of one of Oliver's reminiscences.

"I'd crept through the rubber plantation keeping a look-out for the guerrilla fighters." We'd been told they were going to attack the British owner and his family. I was looking at the diagonal cuts in the bark and the latex collecting pots tied to the trees and was listening to the sounds, myna birds, insects, the occasional chatter of monkeys, as I moved round the perimeter as quietly as I could. Suddenly I felt hands grab me round my throat. I thrust my elbow back and struck his neck with my forearm. His grip loosened. He went down. I pointed my rifle at him and shot him right through the head. I was horrified at what I'd done.

"But he would have killed you, Dad," said Mags.

"It doesn't make it any easier, thinking that. Anyway, I was so stunned at what I'd done that my legs didn't seem to work. I just stood there. The next thing I knew I'd been thrown to the ground and almost smothered by foliage and branches. A young voice whispered, 'sh, sh.' I lay very still. I could feel the vibration of feet running past me. A little snake crawled round my foot, but I lay rigid, terrified it would go up my trouser leg."

"So that's why you don't like snakes."

"Perhaps. Luckily, it just slithered away. After what seemed like hours later, but was probably no more than half an hour, a girl's brown face appeared. She was clearing the leaves and branches out of the ditch she'd thrown me into."

"She'd saved you."

"Yes. She was only about 14. Her family lived in a nearby kampong and took me in. They cleaned me up and put me in a sarong and shirt; gave me a bowl of rice with a few pieces of curried vegetable on it, and tended to my scratches. One of the sons retrieved my gun and gave it to me ceremonially. All I could say was 'Terimah kasih, terimah kasih'."

"Was that where you learned Malay, Dad?"

"I already knew some. We had to learn a bit before we went out, and I always carried two phrase books with me: one Malay, the other Chinese, which wasn't much help as the terrorists spoke different dialects, and my book only had Mandarin phrases. Anyway, I didn't intend to get near enough to them to have a conversation."

"Where did this happen?" I asked.

"Down south. Johore State. Where we drove today. The rubber was collected in the morning. It was dusk when the terrorists used to start their attacks. The workers had returned home, so the owners were pretty defenceless."

"Were those owners killed?" asked Kevin.

"I didn't find out till later. I was only 19. But yes. Can you imagine what killing that man did to me?"

"It made you the person you are today. You should be thankful to him in a strange way," I commented. "That's what must have given you the dedication to bringing about peace; like in your CND days."

"Maybe."

"Carry on Oliver," said Marcus. "I've never heard you talk about those times before."

"I didn't want to bring on my terrifying nightmares. You can't imagine how frightened we were of the CTs, the terrorists, mainly because we didn't know who or where they were. Most Chinese were respectable business people, with shop houses and companies, like this tea plantation. But the British and Malay police put lots of them into camps, and guarded them."

"What, just any Chinese?" Marcus asked.

"Yes, there was no way of knowing if they were terrorists or not. They had cause to be. They weren't allowed to vote, they weren't allowed to own land, go to local universities, and there were lots of other restrictions on them. I gather there are still many, now that the Bumiputerahs are in charge. They, the indigenous Malays, still have preference over much employment and university places."

"So the Malay Chinese are immigrants?" asked Mags.

"Well, very ancient ones. The Straits Chinese are descended from the early Chinese settlers, traders who came to Malaya in, oh, as early as the 15th century, many people say. There's a story that a beautiful Chinese Princess, Hang Li Poh, was presented to the Sultan of Malacca. She brought a huge entourage with her, and of course, they intermarried with the local Malays. This new breed was called Peranakan, Straits Born Chinese. A lot of people are proud of their mixed heritage. That curry we had the other night in Singapore was a Nonya dish. The Peranakan men were called Babas, the women, Nonya."

At that point we were called inside for dinner. The guest house deal included a cook who was determined to give us a vast selection of local dishes. This evening it was a Chinese meal: some cold meats first, with some pickles, then a wonton soup, followed by steamed garoupa fish flavoured with garlic, ginger and spring onions. I could have stopped there, but then we were offered stir fried vegetables then shredded lamb wrapped in lettuce leaves, noodles and fried rice. It would have been churlish to refuse such delicious food. After that we had a selection of fruits starting with wild durian, which looked like a dried armadillo turned into a medieval weapon. Although it had an over-powering smell, the taste was like parsnip custard.

"Once tasted, never forgotten," said Marcus.

"Brings back memories," said Oliver. "In our quarters we had notices saying 'No durians allowed.'"

"There was one on the back of our hotel door," I said.

"A durian or a notice," asked Teresa. We laughed, but the smell was truly overpowering, like an open drain.

"These are more delicate," said Oliver as he helped us to slices of mango, papaya, star fruit and oranges. A banquet. All accompanied by oolong tea or beer. We were offered brandy afterwards, which we all accepted apart from Margaret and Kevin, who decided to have an early night. Oliver had gone quiet, his only brief conversation concerning the food.

The following day, he came on to the balcony wearing his old army shorts.

Mags almost had a seizure she was laughing so much.

"No, no, no, Daddy, absolutely not."

"Can't believe you can still get into them," I said.

"Well, I did trim up especially for the wedding, just about got into my suit. These are a bit tight though."

"Fancy keeping them all this time."

"You'd laugh if you saw what else is at home!"

"Such as?"

"Gas masks, my kit bag. Old copies of 'Peace News' 'Times Lit. Sup'. 'New Left Review' from way back in the 1960s, old envelopes from…."

"No! When we get back I'll sort that out."

"Oh no you don't."

"Dad, don't be silly. You can't keep them for ever." Both my daughters agreed with me.

"You don't understand," said Oliver, "They're as valuable to me as my books; some of the early copies could be worth something too." He sounded quite adamant.

"OK love, let's enjoy our holiday; no need to worry about that now." I was curious as to why it was becoming an issue.

Fortunately the atmosphere was lightened by a young man arriving to take us on a jungle walk. Oliver changed back into long trousers and we made sure our arms and legs were covered in case we got bitten by any of the insects that might decide we were tasty specimens.

"I'd rather stay here," Mags said. "You go with them, Kevin. I want to read for a while." So the five of us followed Zainal, our guide, into what turned out to be a long trek past a waterfall that drowned out our speaking voices, through dense vegetation where we spotted what Zainal called some 'Mata Hari' birds, which we later checked were colourful Mountain Minivets, and Drongos, like shimmering crows with long tail feathers . We slid along slippery tracks until we came to a group of trees with orchids cascading from them.

"Get your camera out, Kevin," Oliver shouted. "Margaret will be really annoyed if she missed these."

"Some of them are so tiny I don't think I'll get them."

"Kecil, terkecil," said Zainal.

"Small, smallest," nodded Oliver.

"Yes, small, smallest. You speak Bahasa Melayu?"

"A few words. From the Emergency."
"British soldier."
"Yes."
"Terima kasih, thank you." And Zainal bowed slightly.
"Sama sama."

Oliver and Zainal spent the rest of the trek in conversation. By the time we returned to the Guest House they had exchanged addresses and mobile numbers. Zainal returned the day we were leaving and spoke quietly to Oliver as the rest of us were packing our cases into the mini-bus.

"What was all that about?" I asked.

"I told him about the girl who rescued me, and he's helping me to find out if she's still alive. She lived in a kampong near Tebrau, Johor Bahru. Apparently it's full of high rise apartments, really built up now. I'd like to go there."

Marcus brought out Teresa's case. "We can easily go back that way. It's on one of the main roads to Singapore."

"Would you mind? I don't want to inconvenience everyone."
"No problem."
"Thanks. I think it's important to me."
"Don't be upset if you can't find her."
"I doubt if I'll be able to, but I'd like to try."

So we altered our schedule to take in Oliver's quest.

When we left the Cameron Highlands, we checked into a hotel in Kuala Lumpur.

Mags came into our room.

"Anyone seen Kevin? D'you know where Kevin's got to?" she asked.

So Mags and I went down in the lift and after a few moments found him coming out of the shopping arcade beside reception.

"Pressie time, Maggie," he said, handing over a bag with a well-known logo on the side.

"Oh! That's lovely; so soft," she remarked, as she discovered a navy suede handbag with a gold coloured clasp and the same logo as on the carrier bag.

"Glad you like it. Don't you think it's time," he whispered as she kissed him.

"Time for what," I said.
"Let's go upstairs, Mum."

We returned to our room. Oliver was on the phone.

"I phoned the mosque in Tebrau. Zainal gave me their number."

"Any luck?"

"They'll ask around. I only know her as Mina Siti, but no other name. But I'm 65 now, and I was 19 then; she must be 60 or 61. One of her brothers was called Ahmed. That's all I could tell the Imam's secretary."

"Ask Teresa to come in, Kevin," said Mags. Out he went, returning with Teresa and Marcus.

"We've got some news for you," Mags said, holding Kevin's hand tightly.

"We're expecting a baby."

"How wonderful; what great news. When?" we all clamoured.

"Five and a half months to go. Didn't say anything before 'cos I wasn't sure it would survive the flight and all this travelling, but I feel OK about it now."

"Great news," said Oliver, and started crying.

"Don't be upset, Dad."

"I'm so happy. Tears of happiness."

"So that's why you decided to get married so suddenly."

"Well, one of the reasons, yes."

I was particularly happy; I was to be a grandmother!

***

Marcus's driving seemed to be even more careful than usual, or perhaps it was because we were aware of the new life in the minibus with us. When we arrived at our hotel in Malacca there was a note for Oliver at Reception. Although our journey from Kuala Lumpur had been under 100 miles, it had taken its toll as we had to drive through a horrendous tropical rainstorm. Marcus was driving blind. "Can't see a bloody thing," he exclaimed. "Have to stop." We had several of these hold ups so it had taken us several hours to reach the hotel on the beach.

Oliver read the note.

"Anything interesting, or just the usual 'Welcome to our Hotel, Mr and Mrs Mooney'?"

"The Imam's Secretary has traced two people called Mina, both around 60. One works in a supermarket, Cold Storage, I think it was called. Can you believe it? The other is a school secretary."

Marcus overheard us talking.

"I'll go with you, if you like. Or drive you there at least."

"I'll phone and find out when it might be convenient," said Oliver. "But I can't imagine either of them would be my Mina. Her family worked on the land."

He made arrangements and after we had all explored Malacca and bought some presents for our friends back home we lazed by the pool. Marcus and Oliver planned their excursion which meant dropping us in the centre of Johor and meeting up with the Iman's Secretary.

Our two and a half hour journey took us from Malacca through more rubber plantations. We stopped occasionally when Oliver thought he recognised a village. He asked some roadside stall holders about Mina, but either they couldn't understand his Malay or they didn't know. I wondered if he was placing too much faith in the Imam's Secretary and that he would be bitterly disappointed.

In Johor Teresa and Margaret went off to explore the shopping centres and markets, Kevin went to visit the Istana Besar which had only been opened to the public as a museum for a few years, and I sought refuge from the heat in an air-conditioned tea house. While Oliver and Marcus were on their mission I started to reminisce about the other man in my life who had been involved in the Emergency: Finchie. What had seemed for Finchie to be an intellectual exercise, for Oliver it had been a terrifying physical ordeal.

'I was ordered to do things I shouldn't have done. I would never have been capable of doing them had I not been brutalised by the Call Up system,' he had said. But who had ordered those things in Malaya? Was Finchie somehow to blame for Oliver's trauma? I found myself becoming angry with Finchie. Yes, I had every right to be because he had kept his marriage from me, but these thoughts were speculative and unfocussed. I didn't actually know what he'd been involved in during the Emergency. He must have behaved bravely to win a Military Cross. That implied some physical action, not just an officer who sat in the Head Quarters analysing information then.

By the time the girls had returned I had calmed myself enough to admire their purchases, some traditional, such as lengths of sarong, others modern knick-knacks such as a tea caddy shaped like Johor's Grand Palace, and postcards depicting old and new aspects of Johor.

We all met up in a restaurant that evening. Oliver was in good spirits.

"It wasn't her, the school secretary, but the one who worked in Cold Storage thought she might know my Mina."

"How amazing!" I said. "Did she give you her phone number?"

"Better than that. She took us to a market stall where there were four women working. One of them reminded me a little of Mina. Then I noticed an older, shorter woman weighing out bananas. Mina."

"My goodness! Did she recognise you?"

"Not at first, but the Imam's Secretary and Cold Storage Mina explained who I was. Her mouth fell wide open. I kissed her hands. They translated for me: she had got married soon after she'd saved my life, and had six children. Two of her daughters were working with her on the stall. Her elder brother had taken over the banana plantation and two of her sons worked for him. The other son was studying hotel management in Kuala Lumpur. Another son had died in a fight when he was a teenager."

"Will you keep in touch?" asked Teresa.

"If my Malay is up to it. Her husband has two other wives now so I don't think he's in a position to complain if a man writes to his first wife."

"What did the Imam's Secretary think?"

"He thinks that, as she saved my life I have a duty to help her if she needs it."

"And does she?" I asked worried that our meagre resources might not stretch to taking on a long term obligation.

"She doesn't need help now. I might leave her something in my will. I did give the Imam's Secretary a donation to the Mosque in gratitude for helping me find her."

"And what about Cold Storage Mina?"

"She didn't want anything. Just pleased to help. Her English was quite good."

We chatted on about how satisfying it must have been for Oliver. He looked exhausted by the emotion of his meeting, but managed to eat some satay. However, the spicy curry made him cough for several hours after, including during the hour long journey back to Singapore. We later realised that this holiday was when his debilitating illness took hold.

Chapter 32

I had felt dislocated from what had happened to Oliver in Malaysia, partly because our trip had brought back memories of my relationship with Finchie, and increased my curiosity about the son I had given away, and partly because I was helping Margaret prepare for her baby, my first grandchild's birth. Oliver also seemed to have separated from me, become more introverted at home, spending long hours pottering about in the garden, or catching up with former CND mates. Then, a few months before the baby's due date, we were sitting finishing our, till then silent, dinner, when he told me that he'd been referred to a consultant as he was dropping weight, and feeling so breathless he had to stop on the half landing before attempting the next flight. He had cancer; squamous cell carcinoma, cancer in one of his lungs. Although the consultant had reassured him that there was every reason that an operation to remove part of his lung would prevent it spreading Oliver had made himself believe it was incurable. When he told me I understood why he had withdrawn into himself.

"I wish you'd shared this with me."

"You had so much on your plate with Margaret. I didn't want to worry you."

"What can I do to help now," I asked through my tears as I hugged his bony body.

"Just be with me. Oh, and make sure my will is up-to-date with something for Mina, as I promised."

"Oh, Ollie," I cried.

"That's what comes of marrying an older man," he joked. "I have to go and leave you with all this to deal with." He indicated the unusually untidy pile of papers on his desk, and the bulging box files containing his accounts and personal correspondence.

"Shall we tell the girls?"

"I don't want to worry them, particularly Margaret."

"She knows you've lost weight. She only remarked on it last week when I took her for a check-up."

"Well, tell her I'm ill. Don't mention the incurable bit."

"I wish you'd take heart from what the consultant said."

"It was probably all those years of smoking; but we never thought of the consequences when we were young and were going to live forever."

"And let's face it, many older people still thought it cleared the lungs; they followed the advice they were given in the 20s and 30s."

"But I'm supposed to be an intelligent person; I tried to stop a few times, but it went hand in hand with me writing, and the odd times I gave up I didn't seem to be able to write as fluently."

So I focussed on Oliver, trying to make what he thought would be his last months as comfortable as possible.

The distraction of Margaret giving birth to a baby boy, and the memories it triggered for me were tempered by exhaustion from Oliver's anxiety and the many hospital visits for scans and consultations. He had an operation to remove part of his lung and then chemotherapy, during which he lost the sparse remainder of his hair.

"I don't think they make wigs for men," he said.

"I'm sure they do, but actually I rather like the skinhead you've turned into."

"And you thought I was some sort of weirdo when you met me, with my longish hair and beret, trying to look arty and bohemian, always with a Gauloise in my hand."

"It seems a rather dramatic way to stop smoking though, when you've smoked since your teens."

Cradling Margaret's baby provided us with well-needed distraction. It brought forth tears of joy and wonder that our little girl could have produced such a gift to us. But these emotions were confused with the pain of recognition that I had never seen my baby boy's attempts at walking, talking and writing, or helped him with his reading. Surely he could do all those by now! I forced myself to focus on the here and now.

Oliver joked that they shouldn't call him Oliver, as Kevin had suggested, as he would always be asking for more. Eventually they called him Jacob Oliver Evans.

I had phoned Teresa to keep her up-to-date with Oliver's progress. She arrived the week after her nephew was born, planning to stay for ten days including Easter.

"I wasn't prepared to see Dad so wasted away," she said after she'd been up to his bedroom shortly after touching down at Heathrow courtesy of Singapore Airlines.

"He'd lost weight when we were in Malaysia, but I hadn't connected it with an illness," I commented as I made us all cups of tea.

"Remember that bout of coughing? We should have spotted something was wrong."

"Don't you think I've gone over it time and again. Could I have got him to the doctor earlier? Why didn't I notice he was ill?"

"It's no use blaming yourself. He's never liked being ill, always laughed it off, or gone into his shell for a few days without saying why."

"Just what he seemed to do with this."

"How's Mags taken it? I can't wait to see baby Jacob."

"Well, she's very emotional, of course, after the birth, but she's pleased he arrived to give Oliver something else to think about."

"And who was it you met at the hospital? An old friend?"

"Well, someone who was in the mother and baby home I went to before I got married. A girl called Fatima. The other girls called her Fatty."

"Poor thing! I'm so glad you told us about that baby. It explains why you smothered me."

"No, I didn't, surely?"

"Well, I felt a bit overwhelmed by you at times. But that's something you can talk to her about perhaps. She must feel the same about giving a baby away."

"No. She lost her baby. It was stillborn. And she was very ill afterwards."

"Oh, that's terrible." Teresa's hands went up to her mouth as she gasped and sat down heavily on a kitchen chair. I looked at her anxiously, but she waved me away.

"Just tired after the journey."

"You do look all in."

"Just the time difference probably. But carry on."

"Well, you'll never guess what she does now?"

"What?"

"She's an obstetrician. She was looking after Margaret at the birth. I couldn't believe it. I spotted her in the corridor and wanted to ask if everything was going well with the labour. We looked at each other, and gradually it dawned on me that I'd known her before. I looked at her name tag and yes, Fatima, Dr Fatima Shah. She told me she'd got married to a fellow doctor, had two sons and was working in the hospital part-time. We'll meet up for lunch one day."

"So you've had lots of memories come rushing back. Has it been alright?"

"Yes, but my focus was on your dad and, taking Margaret to and from the hospital. You know she had a false start and Kevin was working. Then being there all night during her labour."

"Not during the birth."

"No, Kevin was with her, and it didn't last too long. Thank God for epidurals, she coped with the pain."

"Don't talk to me about the pain. I'm going to experience it myself soon. Well early October."

"Oh, my goodness. How wonderful. Let's go and tell Oliver."

So over a cup of tea Teresa told him the exciting news.

Chapter 33

"At last I feel like a human being again," said Oliver as we returned from one of his hospital sessions.

He still looked thin and walked hesitantly as though he didn't expect his one and a half lungs to ensure enough breath to propel him towards the car.

"Just a few more visits and scans and…" I started.

"Not quite back to normal, but at least I can get writing again." At last he seemed to realise that he would still have more years ahead of him.

"The consultant said take it easy; don't go gadding about the countryside researching your next book."

"But I promised Springwell I'd do their history."

"Look, I probably know as much about the place as you. I could caretake the project until you're fit enough."

"You deserve a rest too. All the anxiety and daily visits when I was in there."

"Well, you'd arranged to stay there for a few weeks to do the research. If they've got room I could stay. It would certainly be a change."

We continued our journey from Fulham Palace Road to Mortlake. I concentrated on navigating the dense traffic and Oliver's head sank onto his chest.

Margaret was just lifting the baby seat out of her car as we arrived home. Oliver brushed me away from supporting him as he made tentative steps to the front door. He fumbled with the house keys and Margaret rushed to help him over the threshold, leaving me to carry baby Jacob and all his paraphernalia.

He settled into the sofa in the front room and started to snore. Margaret and I went into the kitchen to make cups of tea. It struck me that the kitchen seemed to be where we always felt comfortable and able to talk out any problems. It certainly was the heart of our home.

"Great idea, Mum. You go to Springwell and I'll sort Dad out. I'm on maternity leave so I've got the time, and Jacob just feeds and sleeps at the moment."

"But I could be away for a while getting the book sorted. Your dad had planned on a six week stay there for the research, local history and finding pictures. I know it worries him, that Springwell wants the book ready for their new shop. Opens in September."

"Anyway it would entertain Dad seeing little Jacob. We could even stay overnight sometimes if necessary. Kevin won't mind: he might even come too."

"I'll put it to Pru the Matron at Springwell. I know Oliver discussed an outline with her."

And so it was that I moved into a room above the old stables and started the project that Oliver had suggested on one of our visits before Grandad Preece died.

Chapter 34

"Come on in," said Pru stepping out into the sunshine as I approached the shadow of the pillared portico.

"I hope you're not too disappointed that Oliver can't do the research."

"As long as it gets done. That's my main concern, getting it printed and in the new shop by the autumn."

"That's quite a tight schedule. Oliver said he'd help me with it once I've done what I can. And he's getting stronger by the week."

"I was sorry to hear about his illness. Pleased he's making a good recovery."

Pru guided me round the far side of the mansion to the stable block and carried my case up the stairs into a bedroom furnished modestly with a desk and table lamp, two chairs, the fabric of one of which was rather worn, but it looked comfortable. The single bed was against one of the walls. I sat on it briefly and it felt firm, so I anticipated some restful nights. A narrow wardrobe was fitted into an alcove and beside the window was a four-shelf book case housing various magazines and newspapers.

She drew back the curtains revealing a passageway and then the brickwork of the side of the mansion.

"Sorry there's not much of a view, but hopefully you'll be out and about. At least it's got a bathroom. Those things on the shelves have articles and reports about Springwell. You might find them useful."

"I feel I'm turning into a detective."

"You're certainly welcome to do as much sleuthing as you like. Feel free to go anywhere. The only difficulty would be the cellars. There's quite a bit of stuff left over from when this was used by the military. I've arranged for someone from the MOD to come and check it out."

I was getting excited.

"I'll let you settle in and then give you a chance to wander round. You've really only seen the public areas, and of course, Mr Preece's room."

And so my exploration began. I was seeing the place with fresh eyes. First, Springwell's accommodation: 18 bedrooms, all en suite according to a chart in the office and 6 living rooms allocated to various functions. My favourite room in the Nash-designed house became the erstwhile ballroom approached through double mahogany doors. The lintel was carved with horizontal scrolls, shining dark brown, with a few chipped areas where stray bits of glass from Second World War bombing blasts had made indentations detected only by climbing up and feeling the otherwise smooth surfaces. I stood recklessly on a chair one afternoon and my fingertips had explored these when everyone else had seemed to be asleep or engrossed in work. I felt as though I'd made a secret discovery; like being at school, a mischief, evading the prefects and teachers. I'd even jumped down when I heard the tap, tap scraping of a Zimmer frame approaching the doors. I opened one just enough to see an elderly resident making his way towards the front entrance. My fast-beating heart quickly restored its natural rhythm; I replaced the chair and looked round me. The ballroom was separated into two sections, each retaining its Adam fireplace in the brothers' Neoclassical style as well as remnants of its ornate ceiling. One section was used as a sitting room with large French windows leading onto the terrace. The other, accessed through heavy folding partitions, was a dining room, again with its windows overlooking the terrace and beyond that the lawns and shrubberies and distant views of the Downs. It occurred to me that before the partition was erected, this must have been where Toby, John and I sneaked up to when Grandad came to talk about his work in the First World War. According to Pru the original owners could look out from the terrace and content themselves that everything they surveyed belonged to them. However, the intervening years, together with death duties, had shrunk the estate to its more manageable current acreage.

Pru suggested that I share an office with Janet. Janet was a divorcee with a background in 'public service', whatever that might have been. Rumour had it that she had worked for an MP who had lost his seat during the 1992 election. An alternative view was that she had become involved with the MP and had jeopardised both his marriage and his anticipated bright future. She certainly had strongly held political views and always dressed as though expecting to be photographed carrying a minister's papers. She dealt with the residents' accounts and the complexities of maintaining such an ancient pile that had benefitted (or not) from the various uses to which it had been put since the last heir of the original owner had died. From what I'd discovered from the papers in my stable block room it became a boarding school until the late 1930s when it was requisitioned as a hospital for injured servicemen in the Second World War; the dormitories served as wards and these remained pretty much intact when it continued its military service as a training facility for National Servicemen who had been identified as possible candidates for Military Intelligence. From 1963 it had metamorphosed into a retirement home for the elderly, many of whom were connected with the Military, which was how Grandad had become a resident. The major alterations to the building reflected its changing use. The most recent was The Old Stables where I lodged, adapted from their wartime use for "the walking wounded". The straw lofts where generations of grooms and stable boys had lived benefitting from the heat of the animals below had recently been turned into en suite bedrooms with radiators connected to a large boiler next to the original tack room on the ground floor. The tack room itself had become a laundry room with washing machines and tumble dryers but with memorabilia of its former use displayed on the walls, more suited to a country pub than a laundry room, the residents' often observed. The stables themselves had been converted into a tea room where members of the public could recuperate on the bi-annual Open Days, having explored the 30 or so acres, and contribute to the financing of the upkeep of such an expensive estate. The residents' families made use of this room too as the en suite bedrooms above were the smallest in the retirement home and not suitable for permanent lodgings or for housing personal pieces of furniture and reminders of residents' more independent lives.

An earlier, necessary, and some felt inappropriate addition, was the lift in the main house. When Grandad had first arrived

Oliver had pulled the spring-loaded metal gates apart making a resounding clanging noise which embarrassed the silence of the entrance hall. We had loaded the lift with boxes of the favourite possessions he'd brought from Eastbourne, and accompanied him up to his room. He later used it reluctantly to come down for meals when he found the stairs impossible to navigate. Instead of admiring the elegant sweep of a curved staircase as visitors entered through the front door, their first view was the sight of this cage tucked to the right of the staircase, under the first floor balcony, drawing the eye and ear to it as both the residents and the staff whirred it into use. There was also a service lift behind, invisible from the entrance hall. This was capable of taking residents' large pieces of furniture to their rooms on the first and second floors when they arrived. It was also where they descended when they 'moved on', their furniture following to make way for the next resident. There were the statutory number of fire escapes marring the external western and eastern walls of the house, but as far as I knew they had only been used by the clandestine smokers, not for any other sort of fire.

I discovered from Janet that there were three different types of accommodation: the single bedrooms above the Old Stables, the suites on the first floor of the main building, each of which had a bedroom with bathroom attached and a sitting room with views over the gardens or surrounding countryside, and the double or single rooms with private bathroom on the second floor, one of which Grandad Preece had occupied. I remembered the stunning view and how much he enjoyed it particularly in the later months when he could no longer move from his room. There were a few attic rooms with a shared bathroom where relatives could stay for emergencies. The two most expensive rooms were on the first floor: dual aspect sitting rooms and larger bedrooms. However, I had never visited these rooms as they were both occupied by infirm residents who had regular nursing support. The only residents I encountered were in the dining room at meal times and those who wandered about in the main hall or sat in the large sitting room dozing.

A further facility was in the process of development: a nursing wing. Pru, being Matron, organised medical matters, such as visits to the nearby GP surgery and local hospital, and had pressed for this for years. Currently nurses or carers were brought in from an agency to look after the increasingly bed-ridden elderly or confused residents in their own rooms or suites. A set of secure, but beautifully appointed rooms around an internal courtyard, had been designed for nursing those residents needing additional medical care or suffering from the increasing challenges of dementia. This was separate from the main house, but still with restorative views over the sloping lawns, and near the working farm which provided Springwell with eggs, occasional irritation from the cockerels, and the connection with nature which many of the older residents enjoyed. Jeremy was "Clerk of Works" and had a separate office in a portacabin next to the site of the new wing. Jeremy was, as Janet remarked once, "a bit of a flirt", but efficient at his job although working what we considered to be excessively long hours, perhaps as a substitute for his lack of home life. There were several groundsmen who had an outhouse nearby where they kept their tools and the motorised sit-on grass cutter used for manicuring the main lawn to the south of the mansion. They looked after the vast acreage and the small lake to the west of the grounds, which seemed vaguely familiar when I first walked round its shady perimeter. The groundsmen occasionally helped with minor repairs to the interior, but were an almost secret society, keeping themselves to themselves, so immersed in the mysteries of their calling they even took their meal breaks in their potting shed or out in the grounds rather than in the dining room with the rest of us.

The office I shared with Janet during the day was to the right of the entrance hall so I occasionally opened the door to visitors. It seemed difficult to keep track of which residents had gone out. They were supposed to come and let the office know if they were going off the estate and she had commissioned a beautiful In/Out board from an oak tree slaughtered by the Great Storm, to hang in the hall to help them. However, most of them didn't bother, so we were often leaping up from our seats when we heard the heavy front door close to see who had escaped the simple system, required by the Fire Regulations.

I enjoyed the research, and phoned Oliver regularly to update him on my discoveries and to make him feel as involved as possible. I was also checking that Margaret and Kevin had time to visit, make him meals and generally keep an eye on him in spite of having the distractions of a new baby. In any case I went home most weekends although I felt that I was living at Springwell. It had become a second home.

Chapter 35

For several days now Jeremy seemed to be hovering around inside Springwell Manor rather than focussing all his attention on the building work.

"Come on, Christine, come and have coffee over at the extension; you'll be impressed with how it's getting on."

"OK, that'll be nice. It seems to be much colder inside than out today." And turning to Janet I said, "You don't mind, do you? You don't need me for anything?"

"No, I'll open the door, if needs be. When you get back, I might go out myself for a bit. I haven't been down to the lake for ages. I hear the swan's eggs have hatched."

"I might make a detour then."

When Jeremy had gone my colleague Janet said, "Watch him. He's a bit smitten with you."

"No, surely not. Thanks for the tip."

Sure enough, over coffee on a bench outside the developing Nursing Wing, Jeremy made a tentative attempt at asking me out that evening.

"I've been watching you. You seem lonely. You don't have anyone visiting you here."

"Well, I'm here to do a job. The history, you know. I'm trying to be focussed, interview a few of the ones who were here in the war, gather information about the previous owners and all that."

"What about your family?"

"I see them at weekends, most weekends, anyway. Two homes, you could say. One a stable, the other a house."

"Really!"

"No boyfriend then."

"A husband, yes."

"He won't stop you coming out for dinner with me, tonight."

"That would make a change. I've heard about your reputation. Friendship, yes; sex, no."

"My goodness, you're outspoken. It's only dinner."

"Just wanted to make sure there was no misunderstanding."

"Alright. Dinner with a friend. No hanky panky."

"You sound like my Auntie Vi. That's the sort of expression she would have used."

"Is she someone you see at weekends?"

"No, she lives in Spain. Oh, she must be approaching 80 now, or even more. Look, I can't leave my work for too long. I'll just walk down to the lake and then go back. What time tonight?"

"Seven OK for you?"

"Fine. See you at the front gate at seven."

"I could collect you from the Stable Block."

"No, really. The gate is fine, especially as it's such good weather."

We went to a local gastropub, dining on a verandah for the first course, but retreating inside as the evening grew chilly.

After some random comments about the pub, the progress of the Nursing Wing, and whether the menu catered for our taste in food, Jeremy asked me

"How did you come to live here at Springwell? You're not old enough to be retired, are you?"

"Certainly not. You know I'm doing on the spot research for the history of the place."

"But to live here? And why here?"

"It's because of my grandfather really. He lived in Eastbourne until he came here. And I'm only here till I've finished researching the history. It's for the new shop. 'A History of Springwell'."

"That should go down well. People are always asking about the place, but no-one's had time to get all the information together. Come and see the shop; it's nearly built, just needs the fitters."

"Yes, another day. Grandad would have liked a shop; too far to the village. He was gradually becoming more and more frail, and unable to care for himself. Not that he was very good at that anyway, but it was becoming dangerous for him to stay where he was. He left the gas on, he would trip over the rugs on the floor. His sight wasn't good, so he'd get confused with change at the shops, and sometimes buy the wrong things, because he recognised the colours on the packaging, and then find out he'd bought dog food instead of tinned spaghetti, for example."

"Dementia?"

"Not really. In some ways he was bright as a button, particularly an army one."

"Ah, so he came here, did he?"

"Yes, he'd visited an old army friend here once. In fact I brought him, and he said, 'I wouldn't mind coming here.' So when the time came, and we had to wait a while before a vacancy came up, he decided to move in."

"So at least he had a friend. Very important that, to help the new resident settle in."

"Yes, and his friend, Old Johnny, I think he called him, lasted a couple of years."

"Probably because he had a mate. Kept him alive."

"Could be. The only issue was, that having lived by the sea, Grandad was worried he'd miss that, and his walk along the prom. But Pru told him about the regular trips to the coast. 'You can sign up for those' I remember her telling him. 'About 6 residents in the minibus, plenty of time for a stroll, fish and chips and perhaps a cream tea later, and then back for dinner.' So he was satisfied."

"She was here then?"

"It was only a few years ago."

"Well, I've been on site for the last 10 months. I don't suppose I'd have met him, your grandad."

"No, he spent 4 years here. He was 99 when he died, only 2 months off 100!"

Jeremy started talking about his business and how he'd won the contract for the nursing wing, but I was only half-listening as thoughts of Grandad Preece had taken over.

I remembered collecting him and some of his belongings including his favourite chair and a couple of side tables and him waving goodbye to the sea, like a child at the end of a holiday. I'd kept his lease going for another 3 months just in case. But, of course, he was happy at Springwell in a room opposite his old army buddy, and Oliver and I used his flat as a bolt hole. It gave us a change of scenery and fresh sea air and helped us acclimatise to the girls' emergence into adulthood.

"What do you think of Pru and Janet?" Jeremy asked jolting me back to the meal, just as our main courses arrived.

"It was Pru's idea that Oliver should research the history of Springwell. He's been ill so I took over. He'll probably do the finishing off. He's a writer."

Jeremy didn't ask about what he'd written or Oliver's illness. I got the impression that he was quite self-centred, which was confirmed when he carried on talking.

"I went out with Pru for a while, last year, when my divorce came through. We'd been working together on the plans, her input was medical, of course."

"Ah, yes, as Matron, it would be. But I bet she had lots of ideas to make people feel at home too."

"Yes. We fell out a bit over the safety issues though."

"What do you mean?"

"Well, the original plans had all the rooms facing outwards, but she, now I understand, quite rightly, was concerned that some of the more advanced residents would use the French windows as a way of escaping."

"So that's why you have the internal courtyard feature. A secluded, safe garden area that keeps them confined, but in a pleasant way."

"Yes, they won't be able to get far out of there."

"But they'll still have a feeling of freedom?"

"Should they be aware of it."

"So you're not involved with Pru now."

"No. Amicable separation."

He went on for a bit about various unsatisfactory relationships he'd had, but I had started to feel the effects of our bottle of wine, and was getting too tired to pay much attention, or too lost in my recollections of the previous few years.

We left the pub soon after 11.00 and he took my arm as he escorted me back to Springwell. That was as far as I wanted any physical contact to go.

When I returned to my room, I found myself weeping. Perhaps it was memories of Grandad, or missing Oliver, or even thoughts of my Kitten-boy which seemed to emerge unbidden recently. Perhaps I was just tired and had drunk too much of the 14% Merlot with my meal.

The following weekend I went back home. Oliver had filled out quite a bit with Margaret's cooking. He was curious to know how the research was progressing.

"I'm quite jealous. That's the bit I enjoy most, the research. The rest can seem quite a chore."

"Not done enough research yet. There are piles of disorganised files, some of them 'Classified' in rusty filing cabinets and boxes in the cellar."

"How come?"

"From when it was a military training place. I've got someone coming next week to sift through them, and hopefully, give me permission to use some of them. I've pretty much finished researching the time when it was a school, and I've found a few plans from when it was built in the 18th century, so the military bit is a missing link."

"Have to sign the Official Secrets Act?"

"I doubt if they'll let me use much of it, so I shouldn't think so."

"Perhaps part of Springwell's history will remain a mystery."

"I hope not. I'm sure I can negotiate some access."

We spent the weekend admiring little Jacob's progress and making plans for when Teresa and her husband would return and we would meet our new grandchild.

When I returned to Springwell that Monday a retired Colonel arrived to look through the papers in a disused section of the cellar. I went down with him. The cellar was just how I'd imagined a wine cellar to be: vaulted ceilings, lightbulbs hanging low from old corded flexes, pillars with old posters curling off them, a smell that was musty and only damp in places. Sadly no wine bottles or casks, although there was some staining on the uneven flagstones where wine might have spilled. We navigated some dusty upturned chairs and desks stored haphazardly in our path, cleared away some sticky cobwebs that impeded our path and arrived at a bank of large filing cabinets standing to attention against the far stone wall. The Colonel took out a key from his khaki shoulder bag and, after squirting some WD40 into the lock, managed to pull out one of the drawers.

"Stand back while I check these."

"Not dangerous, are they?"

"Might be, if the information gets into the wrong hands."
"We're not at war now though, are we?"
"Always at war somewhere."

Although he was dressed in civvies, his bearing and authority gave away his occupation and rank. He methodically and scrupulously examined each paper file.

He sorted them into two piles on a metal table beside one of the filing cabinets. Yes and No. 'Yes' gave me permission to quote from them or to use information as background, and he promised to photocopy those for me. The 'No' pile, which of course was much larger, went into crates and another retired soldier took them away. I couldn't even sneak a peek at them. However, he did give me a verbal summary.

"Cyphers and how to break them; lists of officers names; where they were to be deployed, often overseas during the war, and then in various hot spots in the 1950s."

"Like Malaysia," I wondered aloud.

"Yes, Malaya, the Emergency, amongst other places."

"My husband served there."

"Oh, what regiment?"

"I forget. He was only doing National Service."

"Lots of bright lads came here. Did more than was expected, some of them. Even called back a few of the best after their eighteen months."

And I told him, Colonel Thomas, Retired, about our trip to Malaysia and Oliver's experiences there.

"He wouldn't have been trained here. All officers. Bad show. Glad he found the girl again. Lucky that."

The whole process took a week. I stayed with the Colonel for a few hours most days. I was left with a small beige 'Yes' folder containing some plans of the house when the MOD had occupied it, a few letters thanking named staff for making their training so stimulating. "We won't let you down," was a repeated comment. One of the documents was a list of the previous owners and what improvements they had made to the mansion. The list included some accounts and drawings dating from the end of the 18th century to the 20th. There was a ragged loose-leaf folder entitled 'A Brief History of Springwell' with a few notes and sketches of architectural features compiled by someone with the initials AJTE or was it F. The damp had distorted the lettering. Back in my room I set about adjusting my plan for the book to accommodate this new information.

I already had some copies of school magazines from when Springwell had been a boarding school, together with newspaper articles discussing the change of use when it was requisitioned by the MOD early in the war. The magazines showed groups of boys aged from 13 to 18 in various guises: some dressed up for Empire Day celebrations, some looking triumphant after beating better-known public schools at cricket, some wearing the uniforms of the Combined Cadet Force, some just recording their membership of a particular year group. All the teachers were male and wore gowns and mortar boards, many of them wore half glasses making them look extremely fierce. Academic achievements were set out in each year's magazine: several 6th formers went on to universities, Oxford, Cambridge and London mainly. A couple went to music conservatoires, so there must have been considerable talent on display at school concerts. No-one went to art school, although one boy became a potter and held an exhibition in Cornwall which was reported proudly. I didn't see one podgy or fat boy in the photos and wondered if the regime of cold showers and lots of sport had created a healthy generation who could cope with the rigours of the Cadet Forces that inculcated them with a desire to join one of the armed forces. The only women were Matron and a couple of kitchen staff. There was one picture which illustrated the class differences that were more obvious in those days: a boys versus groundsmen cricket match. Judging by their clothing, the groundsmen could have come straight from the fields and were still wearing their working clothes. The boys, of course, were neatly turned out in their whites. From what I read about the parents many of the fathers had careers as officers in places like India, some were in the diplomatic service, and others had just wanted to fulfil the expectation that their son would board, while they worked in the City. There was no information on the mothers, although there were a few pictures of them attending school functions, such as an early 1930s Garden Party welcoming a new headmaster. The mothers' clothes reflected the changing silhouette of the time, more bosom than in the androgynous '20s, mid-calf skirt lengths and mainly slinky cloth cut on the bias. The men's clothes didn't seem to have changed much from what I remembered in the

1950s. Together with the sparse information about the military occupation, and the information passed on to me by Grandad Preece, I felt ready to start writing a few chapters. However, I had got no further than writing the blurb, a sketchy outline and the introduction when my attention was drawn away from my project.

Chapter 36

It was late May. I walked savouring the warmth of the afternoon, my cardigan thrown casually over my shoulders. I looked around at the lush foliage and the dappled sunlight it filtered onto the gravel. I had returned from the Post Office where I'd posted my latest research to Oliver in preparation for our analysis at the weekend. The winding drive to the mansion was bordered by rhododendron bushes, their dark waxy leaves illuminated by the abundant pinky-mauve multiple trumpets hanging from the branches. I remembered telling Teresa and Margaret that, as a child, I took the speckled interiors of the blossoms as evidence that fairies wiped their feet before entering. This was further confirmed, I thought, by the footprint marks at the entrance to foxglove flowers. Fairies undoubtedly existed and I was captivated by them as a child. I saw them on cobwebs in the hedgerows on my way to school. Sometimes they appeared in the classroom, peeping out from behind the black board, or I glimpsed them under my writing slate when I was practising writing the letters of the alphabet in my early days at school. I wondered whether our grandchildren would be interested in fairies, or whether my interest had been prompted by the Arthur Rackham illustrations in Grandma Aldrich's *English Fairy Tales* and Cicely Mary Barker's Flower Fairy books. I certainly remembered receiving Flower Fairy pictures on birthday cards and calendars. With these whimsical thoughts in mind I approached the entrance. I saw the Car Park was filling up. Most of our visitors came in the afternoons or early evenings.

Amongst the neatly parked cars I noticed one with a 'P' for Poland on the Number Plate: a relative come to see a very elderly airman, who had decided to stay on in the country he had defended in the war, and there was a car next to it which I hadn't seen before. Its country of origin stated 'F' for France. I nipped into the loo and then went into the office. As I was hanging my cardigan over the back of my chair, and was just about to sit down, the door-bell rang.

"Do you mind getting that, as you're up," said Janet.

"Sure," I said and went into the entrance hall and pulled the heavy door open.

A man stood with his back to me calling to a little boy of about 4.

"Allons nous en. Viens vite!"

A woman, who looked in her twenties, smiled at me as she stood cradling a baby in a papoose and holding a spray of pink lilies edged with white. They had long stamens heavy with orange pollen and a scent to match.

"Veux-tu venir avec nous?" The little boy obeyed at last with a reluctant, "Oui, Papa." The man took his hand and turned towards me. My heart stopped. I seemed to have forgotten to breathe. Was I seeing a ghost: Andrew? Tall, distinguished bearing, good looking, darker hair, but greying slightly. After what to me seemed ages, but didn't seem to have registered with them, I collected myself.

"You are?"

"I'm Christophe. To see Mr Turnbull-Finch, my father."

I walked backwards indicating that they should come in.

"Please wait here a moment."

"Merci," said the woman.

I went into the office.

"You've gone quite white," said Janet. "Had a shock?"

"Something like that. They've come to see a Mr Turnbull-Finch."

"Yes, in the suite on the first floor. Do you want me to show them up?"

"Would you mind, Janet. I want to check something."

She went into the hall to meet them. As she closed the door I rushed to the filing cabinet. I looked under F. Farrow, Fletcher, Frost. No Finch.

Then I pulled out the drawer marked S-Z. "Turnbull-Finch, Andrew James. Admission date…" a Paris address, a Hampshire address and a London apartment. There were some brief biographical details, which I skimmed through: Married since 1959 to Francine Renard, deceased. Military connections:

trained with Military Intelligence at Springwell, MC for services in Malaya; later joined International PR Company, partner, based London and Paris.

Interests: Opera, ballet, architecture, art, World War 2, books on Malaysian Emergency.

Financial Status: Self-funding via monthly Standing Order in advance.

Other information: slight confusion, hearing loss, emphysema, not very mobile. Prefers eating in room. Rarely has visitors apart from relatives and some former army colleagues. Next of kin: son, Christophe Henri Turnbull-Finch. These notes were typed. At the bottom of the page, handwritten: "Contact son, urgent. Signed P. Armitage. 25th May 2004". So Pru had sent for Finchie's son.

How could I have been unaware of Finchie's presence? Had he taken my baby, our baby? Why? How could I confront his son, my son with the fact that I am his mother? I was walking round and round the office, overwhelmed.

When Janet entered, I hurriedly returned the file to the cabinet.

"I didn't know Mr Turnbull-Finch was a resident?"

"Keeps himself to himself. Lives in the past. No trouble at all. Someone you know?"

"Knew, a long long time ago."

"You should go and see him, then, although he's very frail and his memory's not so good."

"I'll wait."

"Don't wait too long, he's fading away. Pru sent for his family. That's why they're here now."

Well, I went through the motions of working for the rest of the afternoon and only became aware of where I was again when there was a knock on the door, and Christophe told us he was going.

"How was your father," Janet asked.

"Hardly with us. He held the baby and cried, but apart from that, he didn't really respond. Not even when Thierry ran a car over his foot."

"The carer said he calls for someone occasionally and looks around."

"Probably for my mother, she died, oh it must be 6 years ago now."

"I'll let you out," I said.

"Severine's changing the baby, she won't be long."

"How old?"

"Five months."

"So sweet."

"Her brother doesn't think so. He was madly jealous: the king dethroned."

"He'll change, become protective."

"Yes. Ah here she is!"

I accompanied him into the hall.

"Where are you staying? You know you could stay here."

"Difficult with the little ones," Christophe replied.

"A, how do you say, country house, B & B," said his wife with a strong French accent as she caught up with our conversation.

"We'll be back tomorrow. Here's my English mobile number."

He handed me a card: "Christophe Turnbull-Finch, CEO, Finch and Renard, PR Consultants, London, Paris, Milan" and a website and email information.

I turned the card over. His mobile number was printed in a very French style.

I didn't think I should declare my hand at this stage. But my heart was racing, seeing in Christophe a young version of my beloved Finchie. My eyes followed them to their car. I watched as they struggled to get the boy and the baby into their respective safety seats. I waved as they reversed out of the parking space and drove away, veering slightly too far to the right in their left-hand drive Citroen.

How does one tell a man you've just met that you're his mother? Should I go and see Finchie or would I erase the cherished memories by seeing him as a frail old man?

I phoned Oliver.

"Yes, you're right to tell him; he might already know, of course, but his name gives a hint, Christophe. It might help him get over the loss of his father when he dies. But what an amazing coincidence."

"I'm so worried that he'll reject me, think I was callous giving him away."

"You had no choice in those days."

"I had no idea Finchie was here."

"I hope it won't upset you seeing him as he is, rather than the idealised version you might have had in your mind."

"Hardly idealised. I was so angry with him for deserting me. I felt it bubbling up when I read his file."

"Shall I leave you to tell the girls?"

"I hope it won't upset them."

"They will be delighted you've found him. Of course, if he does decide to meet us…"

"I hadn't thought of that."

"It will change the dynamics of our family in a wonderful way when we welcome him into it. That's if you want us to meet him."

"And if he wants to."

I suddenly felt anxious about how I was going to broach the subject. My palms became sweaty and the phone almost slipped from my hands.

"How can I tell him?"

"You'll manage somehow. It might come perfectly naturally. You're good at dealing with unusual circumstances."

I laughed, but my heart was fluttering. Granny Aldrich would have said I'd come over all unnecessary.

I went to my room above the stables and sat and sat, reliving those times of so long ago.

The following day Christophe appeared on his own. He came into the office and asked if he could check that all the finances were up-to-date, and whether it covered the extra money for the two carers who took it in shifts to be with him.

Janet checked the accounts.

"We might need to increase the Standing Order next month to cover them. But, how can I put this…"

"I know, he hasn't got long."

"Yes, the doctor thinks it could be very soon, not even days, let alone months."

"Shall we leave the Standing Order then, and I'll settle up after…"

I had heard part of this conversation as I was helping a very slow resident walk to the front door.

I came into the office.

"Hello, again," I said. "No children today?"

"No, they've gone to visit some of their cousins. Severine's taken the car."

"Are you going to visit your father?"

"Yes, I must. He hasn't got very long." The phone rang. Janet answered it.

"Christine will take you up," she whispered, "You might have to wait. The Nurse is with him."

As we walked up the curved stone staircase, I summoned up my courage to find out more about 'my son's' upbringing.

"Tell me about your family? You mentioned your mother died recently."

"Well, six years ago."

"Was she English?"

"No, French. They met when he was on a visit when he was a teenager, 17, I think. One of those school exchanges. He was supposed to make friends with my uncle, Jerome, but his sister was the one that captivated him."

"Francine?"

"How did you know?"

"I think I knew your father when I was very young."

"No! And now he's here with you. He chose Springwell because he'd spent his time here training, for Military Intelligence. He liked remembering how stimulating he found it, better than university, he said, and the beautiful grounds, he loved them. He must have been delighted to know an old friend was here. A few of his army colleagues were here, but they've all died now. He's the only one left."

"I didn't know he was here till you came. I only knew him as Andrew Finch, Finchie."

"That's him all over. He went out of his way to be ordinary. He felt uncomfortable about his privileged upbringing. A wealthy family in the tea trade for centuries. But Turnbull-Finch was his real surname. I don't know why I'm telling you all this. But as you knew him…"

We had to wait in Finchie's sitting room overlooking the garden. One of his carers was attending to him. His Nurse went out saying, "I'll be back shortly. Sherie will call you in when she's finished washing him. I've changed his oxygen, but it's not helping much now."

Christophe poked his head round the bedroom door.

"They'll obviously be a while."

We sat across a small coffee table. My breathing became shallower, and I felt anxious.

"Did he ever mention someone called Kitty?" I asked bravely even though I could guess the answer.

"That's what his carer says he calls out sometimes."

"I think that's me."

"No! And you didn't know he was here?"

"Until you arrived. Oh, Finchie," I cried.

"Don't say any more." His eyes had widened and he gasped for breath. All of a sudden he started to gabble and leant further across the table.

"I know, I know I was adopted. My mother couldn't have children. She had a rare blood group, incompatible with my father's. Her family felt it was a disgrace she hadn't had a child in the first two years. He'd gone back to England and then off to Malaya, not a marriage separation, but an obligation. He was recalled to the army. She worked in banking and came to London sometimes, so they stayed together at my English grandparents' place. After she died, my father told me everything. He'd had an affair, a cinq a sept, he called it. She'd got pregnant. An accident. He told Maman; it was like a gift from heaven for her, and Papa fixed the adoption so he could take the baby himself."

"Oh, Finchie, Finchie." Tears were running down my cheeks. Christophe took my hands.

"They returned with me. The Renard grandparents assumed she'd given birth in England – they must have been told a story about the pregnancy, I assume. They never knew I was adopted. I did, and my T-F grandparents knew too."

"Oh, Finchie, I hoped you'd taken the baby."

"The Renards were so delighted they bought us a Maison de Maitre near the coast, Cagne sur Mer, and…" he stopped. "I was named after you, Christine."

"He called me Kitty. I'm adopted too," I said.

"So it runs in the family." We both stood up and hugged each other. We had tears running down our cheeks when the carer, called Sherie came for us.

"I think he's fading. Come in quickly."

We went in. There was a smell of lilies from the flowers Christophe and Severine had brought on their previous visit. It almost masked the medicinal odour. We sat by his side. We each held one of his hands. The other carer came in with the doctor. Gradually Finchie's breathing changed. He'd gone.

Over the weeks and months since my lover died, this is how I told my story to my long lost son.